UNMASKED

Ysobel cursed under her b
secretly leaving Karystos was an advantage, but it was an advantage that she would waste if she could not confirm his destination.

She stared at the ship, willing it to reveal its secrets. As she watched, a monk scrambled awkwardly down the gangplank. He wore the cowl of his robe over his head, despite the summer heat.

Abruptly, she straightened. "That's him," she said.

She could not say how she had recognized the emperor—there was something about his gait and how he held himself. That and the fact that he kept tugging the cowl so that it shielded his face, despite the melting heat.

She and Burrell followed as the apparent monk reached his destination—a small, aged cargo ship. She must have been mistaken. But then the monk turned for one last look at the harbor and a gust of wind slid the cowl from his face. There was no mistaking those features.

Lucius, emperor of Ikaria. Standing on the deck of a common freighter, wearing the robes of a monk instead of imperial silks. It was impossible. And yet there it was before her eyes.

"It looks like him," Burrell said. "But what's he up to?"

"I don't know," she said. "But I'm going to find out...."

Also by Patricia Bray
Published by Bantam Spectra Books

THE SWORD OF CHANGE TRILOGY
BOOK 1: DEVLIN'S LUCK
BOOK 2: DEVLIN'S HONOR
BOOK 3: DEVLIN'S JUSTICE

THE SEA CHANGE
THE FIRST BETRAYAL

THE FINAL SACRIFICE

Patricia Bray

BANTAM BOOKS

THE FINAL SACRIFICE
A Bantam Spectra Book / July 2008

Published by
Bantam Dell
A Division of Random House, Inc.
New York, New York

This is a work of fiction. Names, characters, places, and
incidents either are the product of the author's imagination or
are used fictitiously. Any resemblance to actual persons, living
or dead, events, or locales is entirely coincidental.

All rights reserved
Copyright © 2008 by Patricia Bray
Cover art by Steve Stone
Cover design by Jamie S. Warren Youll

Bantam Books and the rooster colophon are registered trademarks
and Spectra and the portrayal of a boxed "s" are trademarks of
Random House, Inc.

ISBN 978-0-553-58878-1

Printed in the United States of America
Published simultaneously in Canada

www.bantamdell.com

OPM   10 9 8 7 6 5 4 3 2 1

Acknowledgments

Being a writer is about making sacrifices, and I'd like to thank all those whose generous support helped me complete this book. My friends, who understood when my writing meant I couldn't spend time with them. My family, who have learned to accept that even when on vacation, I still have to work. And my writers' group, who understood my absences, and were always happy to see me on the rare occasions that I could join them.

Thanks, guys. This one's for you.

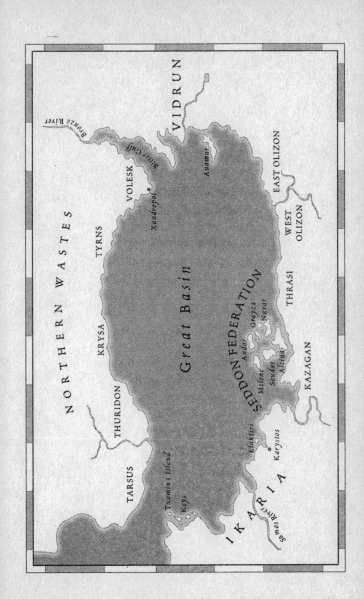

Chapter 1

Lady Ysobel slowly waved her fan, but there was no relief from the stifling heat of the crowded theater. Around her the other patrons fluttered their own fans, filling the theater with a low rustling, as if a flock of birds had taken up residence. Certainly they were as colorful as any bird, though birds, at least, did not have to worry about sweating through costly silks.

Ysobel had chosen to wear a split robe of embroidered dark green linen over a high-necked cotton tunic—a fashion popular in her homeland, and far more conservative than the revealing, tightly fitted silks favored by the women of the Ikarian court. Her escort, Captain Burrell, wore his dress uniform—an unsubtle reminder that he was as much bodyguard as companion. The two stood out among the other patrons, as she had intended.

"Proconsul Zuberi's not here," Burrell murmured, gesturing as if to draw her attention to the action on the stage.

She smiled as if he had said something particularly witty. "Unwell? Or secure enough in the emperor's favor that he need not dance attendance upon him?"

"Or perhaps he is the only sensible one among them and has retired to enjoy the cooler breezes of the countryside."

It was possible, but not likely. Not as long as the emperor remained in the capital.

She glanced over at the imperial box, where Emperor Lucius sat in splendid isolation, flanked only by his servants and bodyguards. There had been much gossip in the court over whom Lucius would choose to share his box this evening, but no one had expected him to attend alone.

Then again, the emperor had repeatedly shown himself to be unpredictable. Which made him all the more dangerous.

It was Ysobel's job to understand him. To anticipate his next move and be ready to counter it. The truce she had negotiated with Lucius on behalf of her country was merely that—a temporary cessation of hostilities, while both countries retired to lick their wounds.

But if she could not guess whom Lucius would take to the theater, then how could she predict when he would cast off the chains of peace and once more attack the Seddonian Federation?

Years ago, under the reign of Empress Nerissa, Ysobel had woven a network of spies that spanned the imperial city, from the dockyards to within the very walls of the imperial palace. But most of her contacts had been killed after the aborted rebellion, and those who remained were unwilling to risk their lives—no matter what threats or inducements she offered.

She attended each session of court, and a bevy of social occasions, gathering what gossip she could. But it was not enough.

Lucius was impossible to predict. One day he was a virtuous emperor, listening to endless petitions from his subjects. On another he would hide himself within his chambers, canceling all his official appointments. Sometimes, rumor placed him in the great library at the collegium of the Learned Brethren, while others swore that he traveled incognito to the hippodrome outside the city walls, taking part in mock races observed only by the grooms.

A year ago, he had ascended to the imperial throne under an extraordinary set of circumstances. The first of the old blood to sit on the throne in over one hundred years, many had expected that he would swiftly move to restore his followers to power. But instead he had followed Nerissa's policies as slavishly as if he were her own son.

The worship of the twin gods remained the official religion of the empire, rather than the triune gods favored by his ancestors. Nerissa's former ministers remained in power—all except her advisor, Brother Nikos, who had either left on a scholarly pilgrimage or fled ahead of the imperial guards, depending on whom you believed.

The newcomers retained all of their former power, while the old nobility grumbled—quietly—about Lucius's failure to favor his own people.

The only sign that one of Constantin's line sat on the throne was the lizard crown that he wore on state occasions—and the lizards themselves, which flourished throughout the capital after years of being exterminated.

Ysobel shifted in her seat, envying Burrell's ability to remain motionless. He detested the theater as much as she did, but they were not there for pleasure. The unwritten rules of the Ikarian court demanded that she show an interest in whatever amusements captured the attention of the emperor. Indeed, she'd had to pay hefty bribes to secure a private balcony on the most desirable tier, so that her presence could be duly noted.

She winced as the singers hit a particularly unfortunate high note. Tonight's performance appeared to be about a shepherd courting the daughter of a wealthy merchant. Ysobel had caught only one phrase in ten, but she was certain that before the final act, it would be revealed that the shepherd was actually the son of a nobleman.

The names had changed, as had the setting, but the plot was nearly identical to every other recent offering from this theater. There were frequent interludes where the central characters paused to allow barely clad dancers to take the stage. These interludes had grown longer as it was observed that the dancers were the only parts of a play guaranteed to bring the emperor's full attention to the stage.

As the young swain proclaimed his love, Emperor Lucius turned to survey the crowded theater. He nodded to Ysobel as he caught her gaze—a rare show of respect. She saw several others try to attract his attention, but his gaze swept over them. He gestured sharply at a servant, who fetched him a cup of wine.

The young lady ran from the stage, followed by her suitor. The music rose, loud enough to drown out the rustling fans, as the dancers replaced them.

The emperor turned to face the stage, but Ysobel's attention remained on him as he raised his cup to his lips. It appeared that he was frowning, perhaps displeased by the wine, or perhaps even he had finally had his fill of insipid drama.

Then Lucius twitched, and his wine cup flew out of his hand, hitting one of his servants in the chest.

She blinked. "Did you see that?"

Captain Burrell shook his head.

The servants in the imperial box stood frozen, unwilling to attract the emperor's wrath. Could it be as simple as a fit of temper? Or had the wine been poisoned?

Lucius started to rise, then fell back into his chair. His servants hastened forward, but he waved them away. Grasping the arms of his chair, he pushed himself to his feet.

He was immediately surrounded by his guards, hidden from view. The music slowly halted, the dancers forgotten, as the emperor and his escort swept out of the imperial box.

It had happened so suddenly that it was only as the emperor left his box that the other patrons realized something was wrong. All around the theater, heads turned toward the imperial box, and raised voices drowned out the sounds from the stage.

"Quickly, go after them and discover what you can," Ysobel said.

Burrell hesitated, clearly unwilling to leave her alone. "Go," she urged. "I would do it myself if I could."

Burrell's uniform would make him stand out, but not as much as she would. Ikarian society had very rigid views on the roles of women. If she tried to force her way through the crowd, she would be looked at in suspicion, but Burrell could move freely.

Instead she remained in her seat, watching as the patrons put their heads together, trying to determine what had happened. Was it an assassination attempt? Was the emperor merely indisposed?

She had been looking directly at the emperor, and even she did not know precisely what had happened.

The silk curtains rustled as Panya, the wife of Senator Columba, entered the balcony.

"A shame that the emperor was overcome," Panya said. A plump, matronly woman, she paused to flutter her ivory fan meaningfully before continuing, "I confess that I myself was feeling quite faint from the heat."

Senator Columba had rented a large box on the lower tier—the best he could hope for as the representative of a minor province. He and his wife would not have been able to see what had transpired, and thus Panya was seeking out gossip, while her husband no doubt did the same. Panya must have reasoned that of all those who were privileged to sit on the same tier as the emperor, Lady Ysobel, as a foreigner, would be the most likely to receive her.

"It is quite warm," Ysobel agreed.

"I heard someone say that one of the emperor's guards

was covered in blood," Panya said, letting her voice trail off.

"Wine, actually," Ysobel said. "Apparently the vintage was not to his taste."

Panya's eyebrows rose in confusion; then, after a moment, her face cleared, as she reached the obvious conclusion.

"How...distressing," Panya said.

Ysobel had chosen her words carefully. If it was an assassination attempt, then Panya would remember that Lady Ysobel had implied as much. But if the spilled wine was merely a fit of pique, well, then in hindsight Ysobel's words would be seen as the simple truth. In either case, she would have enhanced her reputation as someone who knew the intimate workings of Lucius's court.

And the more people thought you knew, the more likely they were to try to impress you by sharing their own secrets in return.

Burrell peered around the curtain, and as he caught her eye, he nodded sharply.

Ysobel rose to her feet, shaking out the folds of her robe. "And if you will forgive me, my escort is here. Kindly convey my respects to your husband."

"Of course," Panya said. And she brushed hastily past Burrell, clearly eager to share what she had learned.

Lucius shook, as if in the grip of a fever, but he kept moving. He could not collapse. Not here, where he would be seen by all. Ahead of him, a functionary rushed to open the door to the private staircase that led from his box directly to the plaza below, where his carriage would be waiting. As he reached the stairs, which would shield him from curious eyes, he gave a sigh of relief.

But it was too soon, for his left leg gave way beneath him. He would have tumbled down the stairs were it not for the guard behind him, who grabbed his arm, wrenching it in his haste.

Then another was on his right side, and between them, they hauled Lucius upright.

Later he would feel the humiliation of this moment, but for now there was only the bitter taste of fear, as he struggled to regain his balance.

"Gently," the functionary known as One admonished. "The emperor is unwell."

Lucius could not feel the left side of his body. His arm hung limp in the guard's grasp, while his leg trembled with spasms that he could not feel.

"I will fetch a litter," One said.

"No," Lucius said. "I will walk."

He looked at the guard who held his left arm, his eyes carefully downcast, as if this somehow made it acceptable to have laid hands upon the emperor.

"I will walk," he repeated. With his right leg, he took a step down. His helpers, after a frantic glance back toward the chief functionary, supported him between them as he continued down the stairs.

It was not walking, precisely. If it were not for the guards bearing most of his weight, Lucius would surely have fallen. But it was less humiliating than being carried, as if he were a fainting woman.

In his mind, he called out to the monk. *Wake. I need you.*

But there was no response. The monk's consciousness must be slumbering—something had not happened for several months.

Finally, he reached the safety of his carriage and was helped inside.

"I have sent a runner, and the healers will be waiting in your chambers," One said, as he climbed into the carriage and took the seat opposite Lucius.

As the chief functionary, and most trusted of the emperor's personal servants, One held a position of responsibility over all the other servants in the emperor's employ. And, at times, it seemed he would command the emperor himself—for his own good, of course.

"There is no need for a healer," Lucius said.

He could heal others. He had even healed himself, recovering from injuries that would have killed a lesser man. But whatever was happening now, it was no mere illness. Neither Lucius's own powers nor the skills of the imperial healer would be of any aid.

At least the trembling had subsided once he was in the carriage, though he still had no sensation on his left side. He could only hope it returned before he had to be carried through his own palace.

Josan, he called in his mind. There was still no response. He shivered again, struck by a new fear, then turned his head so he would not have to meet One's gaze.

Strange. He had long chafed against the spell that had bound two souls in one body—wishing to be freed from the monk's persistent presence. Yet now that he was alone, he was afraid. What was happening to him? This was not the first time his body had betrayed him, but each attack was more severe than the previous one.

Josan was the only one who understood, the only one with whom he could share his fears. Yet, at the moment Lucius most needed the monk's wisdom, he was gone.

There was nothing a healer could do for him. He could not confess the source of his affliction. No one must know that the emperor was the victim of sorcery—the victim of a spell meant to transform Prince Lucius into a willing puppet under the control of the Learned Brethren.

The spell had both succeeded and failed. The soul of a dying monk had been transplanted into the body of a prince, but the prince's own soul remained. Rather than a willing puppet, Brother Nikos had created an implacable enemy, as the souls of both men found common ground in their hatred of what had been done to them.

And now it seemed the spell had other, unintended consequences, as the gradual failing of their shared body would attest.

Lucius knew the rumors that swirled around the capital. The kindest said that the emperor was fatigued from the events of the past year, when he had simultaneously quelled a rebellion against him and personally led his fleet to victory over the ships of the Federation of Seddon.

Others were less kind, hinting at a fatal illness, or that he had been poisoned.

But more and more he heard the words *God-touched*, whispered when they thought he could not hear them. His attacks were seen as the consequences of the gods' favor—the price of the magic that he had inherited from his ancestors.

His left arm began to tingle, as if he had lain upon it. Slowly he flexed the fingers of his hand, welcoming the prickling pain.

Lucius, the monk's mind voice called. *Prince!*

Where have you been? Lucius demanded.

I was here, but you disappeared, the monk responded. *It was as if you had retired, but I could feel only part of our body. And I could not take control.*

He could feel the echoes of his own panic in the monk's thoughts. Normally, when Lucius could no longer maintain his grasp on consciousness—or when he was overwhelmed by tedium—he retreated into a kind of slumber while the monk took control of their shared body. They had become accustomed to switching in this fashion, until it could be done within a heartbeat, while those around him remained completely unaware.

Yet this time something had gone wrong.

I could not feel my left side, Lucius said. *Nor could I hear you.*

And I could feel only the left.

There was silence between them. Then, finally, Lucius voiced what they must both be thinking. *The spell is failing, isn't it?*

He felt his shoulders shrug. *I cannot say for certain,* the monk thought.

Of course not. The monk never committed himself, instead choosing to study one useless scroll after another. Gathering knowledge, he would say. Collecting facts with which to build a hypothesis, as if their shared fate was a merely scholarly preoccupation.

"Do you require assistance?" One asked.

Lucius was startled to realize that they had already reached the palace. He'd been so lost in his internal struggles that he hadn't paid any attention to his surroundings.

He wondered what he looked like when he and Josan were conversing. Did he appear as a man deep in thought? Or as a madman, his expressions changing in response to a voice only he could hear?

"I am recovered," Lucius said. The carriage door swung open, and One descended, then turned to offer his arm.

Lucius accepted the courtesy, as was his habit, but as soon as both feet touched the marble stones of his courtyard, he shook free of One's grasp. He headed toward his private chambers at a brisk pace, his servants scurrying behind him.

His body was under his command, but his relief was tempered by the knowledge that this was a momentary respite. At any moment, he could be struck down, again.

He could not live like this. He could not rule an empire in this condition—a weak emperor was too inviting a target.

There was no more time for the monk's leisurely scholarship. Lucius had to find a cure before they were both destroyed.

Chapter 2

They were not the only ones trying to leave the theater, and it took all of Burrell's considerable muscle to force a path through the crowds. As Ysobel followed, she paid close attention to the fragments of conversation that she overheard. There was curiosity, but no signs of panic. If it had been an assassination attempt, the patrons would have been far more nervous—and with good reason.

In the last decade, the ranks of the Ikarian court had been dramatically thinned, as Empress Nerissa eliminated all those suspected of disloyalty. Lucius had not yet committed his own purges, but the possibility was ever-present, and it would not be the first time that the innocent had been swept up along with the guilty.

Outside the theater, patrons milled aimlessly in the square; the shortened performance meant that their carriages and litter bearers would not arrive for hours.

"It will be faster to walk than to try and find a litter for hire," Ysobel said, as they fought their way out of the plaza and turned west toward the Seddonian embassy. Burrell fell into step beside her, his right hand resting on the hilt of his sword.

It was a clear summer's night, the cool air refreshing after the heat of the theater, though her flimsy sandals were not intended for walking. The hour was still early enough that many were only now venturing out to attend the evening's entertainments. A few stared at the sight of a well-dressed woman walking the streets of Karystos after dark, but they reached the embassy without incident.

Only when they were inside did she breathe a sigh of relief. Dismissing the servants, she led Burrell to her private sitting room, where they would not be disturbed.

"What did you learn?" she asked, as she seated herself on the couch closest to the door. Drawing her swollen feet up beside her, she untied her sandals, wincing at the bruises.

Burrell unfastened his sword, leaning it up against the wall before he took his own seat opposite her. In public he played the part of her aide, but in private he was a friend, and the only person in Ikaria in whom she could place her wholehearted trust.

She knew that her servants thought that she and Burrell were lovers, and had they met under different circumstances she would have enjoyed taking him to her bed. But such was not possible, not while he was her subordinate. Such personal indulgence would be a foolish distraction at a time when both were surrounded by their enemies.

No matter how much she might wish otherwise.

"I knew I could not reach the imperial box, so I used the servants' staircase to descend to the plaza, and managed to arrive before the emperor. He was clearly unwell, leaning on guards as he walked. They had to lift him into his carriage."

"Unwell," she repeated. "Fatigued, perhaps? Or something more serious?"

Burrell shrugged, unwilling to venture a guess. "What did you see?"

She cast her mind back. "A servant handed him a cup of wine. Lucius took a sip, then a moment later he threw the goblet, which struck one of his guards. If he suspected his wine was poisoned—"

"He would have said something, and his guards would have arrested the servants, and all those in the theater who had access to the imperial box," Burrell pointed out. "The functionaries with him were not looking for an enemy, they were merely concerned with the emperor."

"And we've heard rumors before that the emperor is unwell. An illness, or a slow-acting poison."

She'd discounted those rumors as the efforts of Lucius's enemies to sow doubt and weaken the emperor. He'd been unpredictable, true, but this was the first evidence she'd seen of poor health.

"Some have said that the gods speak to him, and this gives him fits," Burrell said.

Ysobel shook her head. "Credulous fools. They would also have us believe that Lucius can cure fatal illnesses and call up storms to strike down his enemies."

Lucius had a few small magics—evidence that he was indeed descended from the old imperial line. She had witnessed him calling fire to his palm, a trick that impressed the gullible; but she would not credit him with greater powers, not without proof. Those who claimed the gods spoke to him were merely trying to build loyalty to the new emperor, for what man would be so bold as to rebel against one directly favored by the gods?

"He has an audience tomorrow, does he not?" Ysobel asked.

Burrell nodded.

"Send a runner to say that we will attend," she said. "And we need to find some reason why I must speak privately with the emperor."

In a general audience, even the petitioners drew no closer than several paces away, but the emperor usually granted a few private audiences as well, which allowed for true conversation.

If Lucius was indeed in failing health, then her mission—not to mention her own life—was in jeopardy. Should Lucius die or be removed from power, his replacement would almost certainly be Proconsul Zuberi. Zuberi had made no secret of his hatred for both Ysobel and the Seddonian Federation, and his first act as emperor could well be to break the truce.

"We have not received a response to our proposal to turn the disputed colony at Seneka into a free port," Burrell said.

There was no chance that Lucius would agree to the absurd proposal, which was the product of wishful thinking from those in the federation who continued to underestimate the new emperor's resolve. Still, she was duty-bound to request a formal response so she could report back to

THE FINAL SACRIFICE   17

her people, and it would serve as a reason for her request to meet with him.

"Do so," she said. She needed to judge Lucius's health for herself. Only then would she know what she must do—for herself, and for her country.

It had happened again. This time, the episode had lasted an entire morning. One moment Josan had been strolling in the garden, and the next he'd fallen to the ground, his limbs twitching under conflicting commands.

He'd been carried back to his private chambers, and the healer had been summoned. Of course the healer had found nothing wrong, instead proclaiming that the emperor was suffering from the summer heat. He'd recommended that the emperor retire to his estate at Sarna, where the cool mountain air would refresh him, though he'd refused to look Josan in the eyes as he offered this advice. Even he did not believe the words that he had uttered.

Josan had lain in bed, periodically searching for any trace of Prince Lucius, but it was nearly noon before the prince made his presence felt. And with the return of full sensation in his limbs came the prince's anger.

He could feel Prince Lucius trying to take control of their shared body, but though Josan yielded, Prince Lucius's presence could not rise to the fore. Instead, there was a dizzying moment when neither ruled—his limbs slackened, and he stopped breathing. Panicked, Josan once again surged to the forefront.

What happened? Lucius demanded.

I don't know. This had never happened before. In the past, there had been times when Lucius was strong enough to seize control, despite Josan's best efforts. These days they managed an uneasy truce, and Josan— conscious of his status as an interloper—would yield whenever the prince wished to take charge. But this was the first time Lucius had been strong enough to communicate with Josan, yet too weak to take control when it was offered to him.

You are worthless, Lucius declared. *You know nothing. You do nothing.*

The words stung, for all he knew them to be unfair. Were it not for Josan, they would both be dead. He had kept them both alive—not only that, but it was his discoveries that had led to victory over the Seddonians and secured Lucius's place on the throne.

Josan had spent much of the past months scouring the great library of the Learned Brethren, seeking out the smallest scrap of knowledge about the forbidden magics. The records of the spell had been destroyed, as had all of the private journals of Brother Giles, who had performed it. But there were other writings, ones not obviously associated with the forbidden magics, and he had used these to try and piece together what had been done to him. To them both.

The only reference he'd found to soul magic was a ballad that told of a man who placed his soul in a piece of amber so that he could guide his descendants after death. Josan had been inclined to dismiss it as a mere fable, meant to explain why amber luck stones were passed down from one generation to the next. But then he'd remembered that Brother Giles had studied rare minerals as well as plants, and so he'd searched for any other reference to soul-bearing gems, with no success.

If he'd been a mere scholar, he could have made better progress. But he was also an emperor, and there was a limit to how much time he could spend away from his other duties without explaining to anyone else why this research was so important.

Your books will not save us, Lucius said. *Or is it that you do not wish to be saved? Perhaps you have already found the cure, but resist, since you know it means your own death.*

And there was the crux of the matter. The souls of two men, but only one body between them. Josan's own body had been destroyed by fever, his lifeless corpse dumped in the harbor to be torn apart by the scavengers that fed off scraps from the docks. He should have perished with his body, but instead he wore another man's flesh, cheating fate. It was not until Prince Lucius's spirit returned that he'd realized that he'd unwittingly benefited from an abomination.

He did not want to die. But neither could they continue as they had been. So he searched for a spell to undo what had been done, hoping that when the time came, he would have the courage to act.

Though there was no guarantee that it would be his soul that was banished. This might be Lucius's body, but Josan had a far firmer grasp upon it. Josan could remain in control for days, while Lucius struggled whenever he was in control for more than a few hours.

In private, he'd wondered if it was possible to live the

rest of their lives in this state—if the two of them could move past grudging cooperation, to tolerance, and, perhaps even friendship.

He hadn't realized that things could get worse. But this second attack frightened him just as much as it did Lucius, though Josan was too disciplined to lash out.

We have an audience this afternoon, and must be present, to counteract any rumors, Josan thought. *But tomorrow morning I can return to the library—*

And do what? Lucius demanded. *Is there a book within their walls that you have not read?*

Of course. It would take a lifetime to master all of the knowledge contained within the collegium.

Are there any that are likely to prove useful?

Josan paused. He'd searched every work that could be relevant, tracked down every reference he could find. There was nothing left but enlisting others in his search— or begin reading books at random.

Just because I cannot find it, doesn't mean the knowledge doesn't exist, Josan argued. *Brother Giles did not invent the spell; he found it.*

And Brother Nikos destroyed all traces of his work, lest he be accused of treason, Lucius reminded him.

Brother Nikos might know enough to undo what had been done. Brother Giles might have mouthed the spell, but it had been Nikos who schemed to put a puppet emperor on the throne. He would have been present when the spell was cast, unwilling to leave this to another.

Lucius had wanted to try Brother Nikos for treason, but Nikos's crimes could not be exposed without also revealing the truth of Lucius's condition. In the end, all he'd told his advisors was that Brother Nikos had sheltered Prince Lucius after the first disastrous rebellion, in direct defiance of Empress Nerissa's orders. And if it had been simply his word against Nikos's, it was unclear whom they would have chosen to believe. But in the end, it had been the knowledge that Josan had looted from the libraries of the Learned Brethren—knowledge that had turned the tide of battle with the Federation—that had convinced Proconsul Zuberi and the rest of his councilors that Nikos was not to be trusted.

Without proof of treason, Proconsul Zuberi had suggested exile, and Lucius had been forced to agree. The former head of the collegium of the Learned Brethren had been allowed to take passage for Xandropol, where his order had their headquarters. But spies reported that Nikos had not arrived in Xandropol, and his whereabouts were unknown.

Pity. If he'd gone to Xandropol, Josan would have been tempted to seek him out. No matter that the journey would take weeks; the risk would be worth it.

I'm a fool, he thought. *A fool,* he repeated, so that Lucius could share this knowledge. *We must go to Xandropol.*

But Nikos is not there, Lucius objected, showing that he'd been able to follow at least that much of Josan's internal musings.

We do not need Nikos. The library here in Karystos has but a fraction of the knowledge that the brethren hold in Xandropol. And there the study of magic is not forbidden. The very spell that Giles used may well have come from Xandropol.

Emperor Lucius would not be welcomed, but Josan the

scholar had once visited Xandropol and been allowed to pursue his studies undisturbed. He could do so again.

You want me to abandon my empire. My throne.

What will Zuberi do when he sees our weakness? Would you rather wait for him to destroy you?

Either way, we risk everything. And there is no guarantee that your books will save us.

It is our only chance. If we are to find a cure, it must be now. Every day we delay is another day that we grow weaker.

He could feel Lucius's indecision. Lucius longed to be free of him, but even his freedom meant less than the prospect of losing his position as emperor. An emperor simply did not leave his country for months—not when he could not explain where he was going, nor why.

Stay or go, we must decide today. If we wait, we may be too weak to make the journey, Josan thought.

As it was, it might already be too late.

Chapter 3

The emperor was unwell; Lady Ysobel could see that at a glance. His guards kept anyone from approaching close enough to determine whether the color in his face was natural or the result of carefully applied paints and powders, but their very efforts revealed their concern. She watched as Lucius sat erect upon his throne, smiling or frowning sternly depending on the verdict pronounced for each petitioner. His voice was firm as he pronounced his judgments, but he was unnaturally still.

Those in attendance spoke softly among themselves, their eyes flickering toward the emperor, then back again, lest they be perceived as staring.

She wondered why he had not canceled this audience. He could easily have pled ill health, and after last night's incident at the theater, no one would have been surprised. Of course, the cancellation would have sparked its own rumors, but mere rumors could not be as damaging as the evident truth.

Ysobel circulated among the courtiers present, pausing to exchange greetings with those she knew. The lesser members of the court were warily polite—as a special envoy from the federation she nominally outranked them, but despite the long years of being ruled by an empress, the Ikarian court did not know how to deal with a woman who held power in her own right. The women of the Ikarian court were meant to be decorative, and while they might advise their husbands in private, they were not welcome at official functions such as this one.

Ysobel was despised not only for her sex but also for her involvement in the rebellion against Lucius's predecessor. Never mind that her efforts had been upon Lucius's behalf. He was apparently forgiven for his role in conspiring against Nerissa, but she was not.

Still, while Lucius's advisors were forced to deal with her, they took every opportunity to make their displeasure known. Thus she was not surprised that Proconsul Zuberi turned his back when he saw her approach. Admiral Septimus, who'd once profited greatly from mutual business ventures, unbent only enough to give a frosty nod, while Senator Demetrios offered even less.

She stifled a sigh as Aeaneas sidled up beside her. Descended from the old nobility, his family had maintained their traditional holdings in part because they were so completely undistinguished that they had never been invited to join any of the factions, and thus avoided offending anyone. A lesson that seemed lost upon Aeaneas, who assumed that everyone would welcome his presence.

Especially her.

Aeaneas's gaze swept her from head to toe, as if she wore a revealing dancer's costume rather than the sober garb of the court.

"Lady Ysobel, your beauty brightens this solemn affair. Indeed the tedium of government would be wholly relieved were more beautiful women allowed to take part."

Ysobel smiled. "Then perhaps you should recommend that your wife take a seat in the senate, when her father retires."

Aeaneas rocked back on his heels, then laughed. "Wit and beauty. Would that you would see fit to grace one of my private dinners, so that my friends could have the pleasure of your company."

He patted her arm until her glare forced him to hastily remove his hand.

In her earlier visit to Ikaria she'd deliberately cultivated a reputation for licentiousness, hoping that the Ikarians would underestimate her. It had worked all too well, for men like Aeaneas still presumed that her favors would be freely given.

Ordinarily the presence of Captain Burrell was enough to discourage unwanted intimacies, but armed bodyguards were not welcome at an imperial audience.

"I am flattered by your interest," she said. Even a slug like Aeaneas had his uses, and she would not cut off any source of information. "But my time is not my own, and there are many demands for my attention. Perhaps someday in the future . . ."

She let her voice trail off suggestively.

The last of the petitioners was repeatedly bowing to the

emperor, while proclaiming his thanks so that all could hear.

"Do you recognize him?" she asked Aeaneas.

He turned his head toward the throne, where one of the guards was encouraging the petitioner to retreat.

"Tobias the Younger," he said scornfully. "His father was convicted of bribery but committed suicide before his sentence could be carried out. From the sound of it, the emperor must have spared the son from having to take his father's place."

"The emperor shows great mercy." Though any who had observed Lucius should not have been surprised by the pardon. Empress Nerissa had executed hundreds during her reign, but so far Lucius had shown no inclination to follow in her footsteps. Most death sentences were commuted to exile or outright pardon.

Though the mystery was not the son's pardon, but his father's conviction. Bribery was common at all levels of Ikarian government. His father must have been unusually clumsy to have been caught—or made powerful enemies.

The chief functionary took his place at the foot of the dais, and at this signal those assembled turned toward the emperor, ready to perform one last obeisance before the emperor left.

Lucius rose to his feet, showing no sign of fatigue, then nodded to his chief functionary, who proclaimed the audience at an end.

Ysobel and the others in attendance bowed deeply as the emperor was surrounded by his servants, then escorted from the audience hall.

As she straightened up, a functionary appeared at her side.

"Lady Ysobel, the emperor is pleased to grant you a few minutes of his time," he said. His heavily tattooed features made it impossible for her to tell if she had encountered him before. She could recognize Greeter, but the rest were a mystery to her. It bothered her that she could not identify them as individuals. Mere men might be open to bribes, but a faceless mass was impervious to most forms of persuasion.

The functionary led her to the emperor's private receiving room, which was adjacent to the audience chamber. Lucius had removed the lizard crown, but this was not an informal occasion, so she bowed deeply and waited to be acknowledged.

"Lady Ysobel," Lucius said.

"Emperor Lucius, I thank you for seeing me."

Earlier she had declared him ill, but at this distance she was forced to revise her opinion. He looked not so much ill as tired, with carefully applied paint masking the dark circles under his eyes. There were several chairs in the reception room, including a smaller version of the imperial throne, but Lucius stood, so perforce she stood as well.

A servant brought him a goblet of pale yellow liquid— wine perhaps, or fruit juice. He tossed back the contents with a grimace, then handed it back to his attendant.

He did not offer her any refreshment, so she came quickly to the supposed point of this meeting.

"Have you reached a decision regarding our petition for a free port at Seneka?" she asked.

"The request is absurd, as you know," Lucius said,

turning slightly away from her as he began to pace. "My ministers have not brought it to me for consideration, but when they do, we will reject it."

"The people of Seneka have long sought independence—"

"Strange that their desires meant nothing to you when you seized the port for your own gain," Lucius interrupted. "You had ample opportunity to grant them the status of a free port, but instead declared them a federation colony and installed your own governor."

Lucius spoke the simple truth, but it was not her role to agree with him. Diplomats did not deal in truths but rather used high-minded words to disguise low intents.

"The federation presence at Seneka was never intended as a permanent occupying force, but rather as a temporary measure until they could provide their own defense and governance."

Seneka was a small port located between Kazagan and Thrasi, owing allegiance to neither country. During Empress Nerissa's reign it had been seized by the Ikarians in preparation for their invasion of Kazagan. But there had been no invasion—the rulers of Kazagan had yielded to the inevitable, preferring to rule as clients of the Ikarian Empire rather than risk a ruinous defeat. For the past decade the Ikarians had maintained a token presence at Seneka, but the port was too small and poor to be given much attention.

The federation had seized Seneka during last year's strife, not out of any sense of economic or strategic value but merely because they could. And now the Ikarians wanted Seneka back. For her part, Ysobel would gladly hand the silt-choked harbor and rotting docks over to them, but her strategy was to yield nothing without challenge—she might not win this argument, but her persistence was gradually wearing down the Ikarian negotiators.

"You know better than to waste our time in this fashion," Lucius said. "If that was all you wished to speak to us about—"

Strange that he kept using the imperial *we* to refer to himself. She had noticed that on some days he referred to himself as *I*, but on others as *we*. There was no pattern that she could see, and he was as likely to use the formal address on an informal occasion as he was to do the opposite.

"I came to consult with you about Seneka, yes, but mostly to assure myself that the rumors of your ill health were unfounded," she said.

Her plain speaking startled him, for he raised both eyebrows.

"You are the first of our court to question our health," he said.

"In your presence, perhaps. But I am not the only one concerned. The summer fevers are taking a heavy toll in the waterfront districts."

She did not mention the rumors of poison, nor that he was afflicted by the gods' touch. He would have heard those as well.

Lucius shrugged. "Today was the final audience for the summer," he said. "Tomorrow I will announce that I am retiring inland to my villa in Sarna, and urge my courtiers to follow my example."

Sarna. Interesting. The villa in the hills at Sarna was

reputed to be quite large, with adjoining estates for members of the imperial family, but it was a private retreat. If he'd gone to the summer palace on the island of Eluktiri, his ministers and chief courtiers would have followed, while at Sarna the emperor would be expected to do nothing but rest and amuse himself with the diversions offered by the countryside.

Perhaps the strain of the past year was beginning to tell on him. Or perhaps it was only now that Lucius felt safe enough to leave the day-to-day governance of his realm in the hands of his ministers.

"I wish you a safe journey and hope that you find delight in the pleasures of the countryside," Ysobel said.

After a few more pleasantries she took her leave. As she made her way back to the embassy, she pondered what she'd discovered.

The emperor would not leave for his country retreat if he thought his empire in danger. If he'd been planning on breaking the truce between their countries, he would want to stay in Karystos, so he could oversee the preparations for war.

On the other hand, the news was not entirely in her favor. Once Lucius and his ministers left the city, she would be left to negotiate with midlevel bureaucrats, with any agreement she reached subject to change once the court returned in the autumn. Still, she had learned what she needed to. From all signs Lucius was suffering from nothing more than fatigue—and still firmly in control of his empire. At least for the present.

*   *   *

"And a copy of Tarik's *Map of the Celestial Bodies*. The full version, with separate drawings for each of the principal seasons," Josan said.

Brother Mensah nodded swiftly. "Tarik's map," he repeated. Overwhelmed at being in the presence of his emperor, he kept his eyes on the deck, not daring to look Josan in the face.

Nor did he dare point out that the hour for sailing was fast approaching. If Mensah did not leave soon, he would miss his own ship.

"You should be able to find a copy for sale in the bookstalls around the great library. If not, use the purse that Brother Thanatos has provided to have scribes make a copy," Josan added.

Josan put one hand out to steady himself as the ship rolled with the waves. He had chosen Captain Chenzira's personal vessel for this voyage, as it was less conspicuous than the imperial yacht. It was also considerably smaller, and even tied up to the dock, the ship was in constant motion, bobbing with the swells that came with the freshening tide.

At least Josan's stomach was cooperating. For the present. He had not forgotten the misery of his last sea voyage—nor, would he wager, had his attendants. In his own body he'd been a seasoned traveler, undisturbed by even the strongest storms. But Lucius was a poor sailor, and this body became violently ill at sea—regardless of whether it was Josan or Lucius in control.

Brother Mensah fiddled with the straps of the journey bag slung over his shoulders. He must be wondering why the emperor had specifically requested him for this errand, then insisted on meeting him before he sailed.

His fellow monks would be wondering as well. Emperor Lucius had demonstrated an uncanny knowledge of the secret teachings of the Learned Brethren, much to the monks' distress. While the monks mouthed their loyalty to the emperor, Josan knew that they had spent months trying to find the traitor within their midst. Their efforts would be futile, of course, since as far as they knew, Brother Josan had died nearly ten years before.

Still, it was within the emperor's purview to request a favor from the monks—in this case sending one of their order to fetch rare manuscripts from Xandropol. But specifically requesting Mensah, implied a personal acquaintance between a junior monk and the emperor.

Once it would not have occurred to Josan to use an innocent in this way, but expediency had forced him to reconsider his principles. The taint of suspicion that Mensah would bear was a small burden when compared to the fate that awaited Josan.

It was Mensah's misfortune that he was nearly the same height and build as the emperor.

Mensah shuffled his feet against the floor, then dared to look up at the emperor. "And what should I do if I meet Brother Nikos?"

"What were Brother Thanatos's instructions?"

"That Nikos was no longer part of our order. If I see him, I should not acknowledge him, but rather send word back at once, so the brethren will know that he has been found." Mensah's words came out in a rush.

Nikos had been head of the Learned Brethren in Karystos for most of Mensah's life. No matter that Nikos had been disgraced, it would be difficult for the young monk to ignore someone who had played such a major role in his life. Mensah was naïve enough to believe that Brother Nikos had kept his word and accepted his exile to Xandropol, but Josan knew better. After months of searching, yesterday his spies had reported that Nikos had been seen in Vidrun. It worried him that Nikos had sought safety in a land long known for its enmity toward Ikaria, but whatever mischief Nikos might one day wreak paled beside Josan's more immediate concerns.

"Brother Thanatos has given you wise counsel," Josan said. "And now, a toast to a successful journey."

He went to the sideboard, where a chilled jug held tipia, and poured equal measures into two carefully prepared goblets. Josan handed Mensah the goblet from the right side of the tray, while he kept the other for himself.

"To a safe journey and swift return," Josan said, lifting the goblet to his lips. He took a swallow of the sweet mixture of wine and fruit juices, hoping his stomach would not object.

Mensah was overwhelmed at such condescension on the part of his emperor, and the goblet shook in his hands. Under Josan's watchful gaze, he gulped the contents in hasty swallows.

It took mere seconds for the drug to act. Mensah swayed, and Josan leaned forward to catch the goblet before it fell to the floor.

"Why?" Mensah asked, as Josan grasped him by the shoulders. "What have I done?"

"Nothing," Josan said. He could not explain. Would not explain. Even now, Mensah was so cowed that he did not think to call for help. Why would he? Who would dare gainsay anything that Emperor Lucius might do?

Swiftly, Josan unfastened the journey bag and placed it on the table, then positioned Mensah so the monk was propped up against the wall. Hastily, he tugged the monk's robe up, pulling it over Mensah's head. Mensah's arms briefly became entangled in the sleeves, and by the time Josan had tugged them free, Mensah's head lolled on his slack neck muscles, his eyes closed in drugged sleep.

It was hard work to drag him over to the bed—harder still because Josan must be silent. He must give the guard standing outside his cabin no reason to investigate. If he'd been aboard the royal yacht, this plan would never have worked. The yacht's large cabins meant that the emperor was always attended by servants. But Chenzira's ship was a military vessel, and even the captain's private quarters, which Josan occupied, were so small that it was impractical to expect the servants to pass the journey in such close proximity to their emperor.

Finally, Mensah was in the bed, and Josan hastily stripped off his purple tunic and donned the monk's robe. He picked up the journey bag, ready to leave, then looked down at his feet, cursing as he realized that he still wore dyed-leather sandals fit for an emperor. Returning to the bed, he took precious moments to untie Mensah's sandals and relace them on his own feet.

He checked himself one last time, patting his side to confirm that his purse was fastened to his undertunic. He'd left two sealed notes carefully weighted down on his dressing table—one addressed to Captain Chenzira, and the other to Proconsul Zuberi. As for Mensah's journey bag, he'd have to assume that the monk had known how to pack for a long journey at sea. There was no time to waste, the evening tide was about to turn.

Josan pulled the cowl of his hood up over his head, then exited the cabin, shutting the door behind him.

"The emperor has requested that he not be disturbed for any reason," Josan told the guard, pitching his voice low. "His stomach is troubled, and he desires to sleep."

The guard nodded. Josan had given similar orders to his attendants earlier when he had boarded *Green Dragon,* but it was only prudent to reconfirm them.

The ship would sail for Eluktiri on the evening tide and arrive with the dawn. And by the time his ruse was discovered, Josan should be far away.

Leaving the guard behind, he made his way to the deck, hesitating as he approached the gangway that led down to the docks. His body froze for a moment, paralyzed by indecision. *Once we do this, we may never be able to return,* he heard Prince Lucius say.

We leave now, or we die, Josan reminded him. *You were the one that urged us to act.*

Lucius did not respond, but he no longer fought for control, and Josan was able to resume making his way off the imperial dock, then through the bustling crowds and over to the eastern edge of the anchorage, where neutral trading vessels were anchored. He inquired of *Tylenda* from several dockworkers. A few cursed him for wasting their time, but at last one took pity on the lost monk and pointed it out.

Tylenda was a two-masted coastal trader, similar to others Josan had sailed in his youth. Poorer passengers wandered on the deck, making space for themselves among stacked crates of cargo that would not fit in the hold, while sailors cursed them for being underfoot. Eventually these passengers would learn which sections of the deck were safe for sleeping, and how to scurry out of the way when the sails needed tending.

One of the crew stood at the top of the gangplank, greeting each passenger as they came aboard, and checking their names off a list scratched on a slate.

"Brother Mensah," Josan said, when it came his turn to be acknowledged.

The sailor did not even look up. "You're on the second deck, in the port cabin," he said. "Cargo deck and crew quarters are off-limits at all times, understood? Any passenger who fails to follow the rules or endangers the ship will be put off at once, regardless of how far we are from land."

"Understood," Josan said. The deck was crowded with those who wished one last glimpse of Karystos, but he took himself belowdecks, and found the cabin that he would share with the other male travelers who could afford a berth out of the weather. Stooping as he entered, he saw that it was unoccupied, and so he claimed a prime spot on a pallet near one of the portholes. A faint breeze stirred the air, bringing with it the dockyard smells of salt air and rotting fish, which did little to alleviate the stench of humanity that clung to the very walls of the cabin.

With a shrug he settled himself down on the pallet, leaning his back against the curved side of the ship as he prepared to wait. He would not count himself safe until the ship had sailed, and there was no sign of pursuit.

It took a moment for Lady Ysobel to recognize that the scruffy sailor leaning carelessly against the dock railing was indeed Captain Burrell. He had a leather flask in one hand and a canvas sack at his feet. Laborers cursed at him as they shouldered by, bearing sacks of supplies for the navy ship anchored at the end of the pier. There was nothing unusual about the sight of a ship being supplied for a voyage, though the frenzied pace of the dockworkers and loud shouts of the deck officers seemed evidence of a hasty departure.

She was glad that she'd paused to change into leggings and an unbleached canvas smock before hastening down to the dock in response to Burrell's message. Lady Ysobel would stand out, but dressed as she was, Ysobel could pass for a federation sailor idling away her hours in a foreign port.

It was a disguise that worked equally well for Burrell, who had built a network of informants who believed him to be gathering intelligence for rival traders, while in truth he watched for signs that the Ikarian navy was preparing to break the truce.

Burrell grunted as she came up beside him, and handed her his flask. She took a sip, not surprised to discover it was merely water.

"Recognize the ship? That's *Green Dragon*, commanded by the emperor's favorite."

"Captain Chenzira." The man who had taught the rest

of the imperial captains how to calculate the position of a ship at sea, when no landmarks could be seen. Some said that he had invented the technique himself, while others claimed that the knowledge had been a gift from the gods to the Emperor Lucius.

As for what she believed, well, several federation captains had gone missing during the Ikarians' campaigns against those they deemed pirates. One of them might have betrayed the secret teachings under torture—or bargained with them to save his life.

"The emperor boarded her two hours ago," Burrell said. "He came aboard with a small entourage, and a short time ago, a monk from the Learned Brethren came on board as well."

"Are you certain?" There was no reason for the emperor to be here, not when he was supposed to be preparing to journey to Sarna, located in the foothills west of the city.

"I would not have sent for you otherwise," he said. He leaned over the railing and spit into the water below.

An ensign left the ship, and Ysobel held her tongue as he brushed by. She watched as he turned and started climbing the stairs that led to the harbormaster's office.

"So it is not Sarna after all," she murmured.

"Eluktiri, I would wager," Burrell said. "There are no signs of his ministers, yet . . ."

"But they can follow without being remarked upon," she finished for him.

She noticed one of the deck officers staring at them, so she laughed, then poked Burrell in his side, as if inviting him to share the joke. There was nothing that an idling sailor enjoyed more than seeing his unfortunate fellows hard at their labors.

Burrell grinned, but only she was close enough to see the serious expression in his eyes.

Ysobel thought furiously. It was possible that the emperor was traveling in secret because of fears for his safety, choosing the anonymity of a naval ship over the comfort of the imperial yacht. But after a public announcement that he was retiring to Sarna, it seemed odd that he would secretly sail to his summer palace on Eluktiri. Were his ministers aware of his true destination? There would be much grumbling if only his favorites had been informed, so that they could constitute the summer court.

Or was this trip more sinister in nature? Was Ikaria intending to break the truce and attack the federation? What if Lucius sailed not for his summer palace but once again personally to take charge of his navy, as he had done the year before?

"Did you hear their destination?" The federation could not afford to be the first to break the truce, but neither could they risk being caught unprepared. If Lucius sailed to war, her people must be warned.

"The sailors were grumbling about having to load a month's worth of supplies for an overnight voyage," Burrell said. "Eluktiri seems a reasonable bet."

"But orders can change at sea," she pointed out. The extra supplies could be prudence on the part of a captain carrying an emperor, or a sign that the ship had another destination in mind.

"Do we have a ship that can follow him?"

"None of ours are in harbor. *Sprite* sailed this morning."

The tide would turn in less than an hour, and when it did *Green Dragon* would sail. She could have commandeered a federation vessel in that time, but it was not time enough to hire any other craft for her purposes.

Ysobel cursed under her breath. With one hand the Sea Witch gave and with the other she took away. Discovering the emperor secretly leaving Karystos was an advantage, but it was an advantage that she would waste if she could not confirm his destination.

She stared at the ship, willing it to reveal its secrets. As she watched, a monk scrambled awkwardly down the gangplank. He wore the cowl of his robe over his head, despite the summer heat.

She watched as the monk reached the end of the pier. If he turned west, toward the city, his path would take him by where she stood. But instead he turned toward the east.

Abruptly she straightened. "That's him," she said, and began to follow.

Burrell grabbed his sack and hastened after her.

"Who?" he asked.

Ysobel nodded toward the monk. "Our friend who is not going to Sarna," she said, conscious of the crowds that surrounded them.

Burrell raised one eyebrow but did not protest. She could not say how she had recognized the emperor— there was something about his gait and how he held himself. That and the fact that he kept tugging the cowl so that it shielded his face, despite the melting heat.

Curious, that there was not a single guard following him. She began to doubt her instincts as the monk stopped one laborer, then another, apparently asking for directions. Surely an emperor would not expose himself to danger in this way? Perhaps she was mistaken?

Her steps slowed as the apparent monk reached his destination—a small, aged cargo ship. The figurehead was unrecognizable, but fading letters proclaimed it as *Tylenda*. The monk stood with the others, waiting his turn to be acknowledged by the purser.

She shook her head, realizing that she must have been mistaken. She opened her mouth to say as much, but then the monk turned for one last look at the harbor. A gust of wind slid the cowl from his face, and there was no mistaking those features.

Lucius, emperor of Ikaria. Standing on the deck of a common freighter, wearing the robes of a monk instead of imperial silks.

It was impossible. And yet there it was before her eyes. She wondered that no one else could see what she did, but there were no cries of amazement, no protestations of loyalty. Instead the so-called monk simply disappeared into the mass of humanity that crowded the deck.

"It looks like him," Burrell said. "But what's he up to?"

"I don't know," she said. "But I'm going to find out."

Chapter 4

Burrell held a double-copper piece just out of the boy's reach. "Repeat the message," he ordered.

The boy, a scrawny lad of nine or ten summers, made one last try for the coin, then grimaced. "I'm to go to the Federation embassy and tell them that the captain from the house of Flordelis had to sail unexpectedly and will send word from the next port," he said.

Burrell dropped the coin in the boy's outstretched hand. "Off with you. When you've delivered your message, they'll give you another of these for your time."

The boy scampered off, and Burrell hoped that he intended to earn his keep. Given even a quarter of an hour more, he could have found paper and parchment and contrived to send a coded message. But there was no time. Even as he was thinking this, he had already turned and begun racing the short distance to where *Tylenda* was anchored.

He cursed as he saw the last of the ropes that anchored her to the dock being cast off. The gangplank had already been withdrawn, but there was a stack of crates waiting to be loaded on the adjoining vessel. Burrell raced down the pier, jumped on top of the crates, then leapt across the widening gap.

He landed on *Tylenda*'s deck, twisting as he fell to avoid landing on a wooden coop filled with ducks, who squawked indignantly at his arrival. Scrambling to his feet, he was swiftly surrounded by curious passengers, and one irate officer.

"Here now, there's no free passage, nor room for those fleeing the law," the officer said, eyeing Burrell disapprovingly.

"It's not the law I'm afraid of, but a woman," he said, glancing over his shoulder toward the wharves as if he'd been pursued. "As for passage, I have enough coins to pay for the next port."

He made a show of pulling out a flat purse from inside his tunic, and rooting through it until he found a half-silver.

"That will get you space on deck," the purser said. "But if the harbormaster sends a patrol boat after you, I'll take it out of your hide before I toss you to them."

Burrell shrugged with the air of a man who had nothing to hide. "Fair enough. It's unlikely my wife wants me badly enough to row out after me, but if she does, I'll help you raise the sails."

The men surrounding him chuckled, and as the crowd dispersed, Burrell made his way to Lady Ysobel's side.

From the expression on her face, he knew she was furious.

"I told you to take word to the ambassador," she said.

"And what could I tell him? That you had sailed? I sent a runner instead."

The ship heeled on her side as it slipped away from the dock, and the sailors ran to the masts, shoving novice passengers out of their way. Well used to the chaos of shipboard life, Ysobel unerringly picked her way around them, moving to the vacant portside railing, where they could speak undisturbed. The sailors were busy with their duties, and the passengers on deck were on the starboard side, waving to friends left behind.

Burrell scanned the passengers but saw no sign of the monk, though he noted that Lady Ysobel's gaze kept returning to the hatch that led belowdecks, where presumably her quarry could be found. When she finally stopped, he was not surprised that she had chosen a spot directly opposite the hatch.

"I asked you to inform the ambassador that the emperor had left Karystos in secret, for an unknown destination," Ysobel whispered.

"And you are certain that it is he?" he asked.

He trusted Lady Ysobel—he had fought at her side, and risked death based on nothing more than her word. But his loyalty warred with his intellect and his own instincts. He could think of no reason for the emperor to have come aboard such a modest craft. The one tantalizing glimpse they'd had was intriguing—but hardly proof.

"He disguised himself as a monk once before, in his

time of exile," she said. "Surely I must have told you that."

If she had, he had forgotten it. But that was not the point. "Why now? Why flee his own capital? Where are his servants, his guards? If he must travel, why not take Chenzira's ship?"

Ysobel shook her head, frustrated—with Lucius, himself, or perhaps both. "I don't know," she said through clenched teeth. "But I know I cannot leave this ship, not while he is on it."

The triangular foresail caught the wind as *Tylenda* began picking up speed. In a few moments she would pass by the moles and out into the open sea.

"We don't even know where this ship is going," Burrell objected.

"North along the coast, all the way to the Northern Keys, if he stays with her," Ysobel said.

The time for a decision was passing. If Ysobel had made a mistake, they would have to disembark—without assistance from the crew. It would be a long, hard swim, but it would not be the first time he and Ysobel had swum for their lives.

Or they could stay aboard, at least until the next port. Which could be equally perilous.

"Look," he said, pointing to where *Green Dragon* was anchored. He could see the bright sails of the imperial navy being raised. "If the emperor is still aboard her . . ."

He let his voice trail off.

"Then I have made a grave mistake," Ysobel said. "But I am not wrong. Trust me."

Burrell shivered, wishing he could claim it was merely the

freshening sea breeze. He trusted Ysobel with his own life—but if she were wrong, it was not just he who would pay the price. All of the federation would be imperiled if Lucius sailed on *Green Dragon,* ready to lead an attack, while he and Ysobel were elsewhere, unable to give warning.

He hesitated, and as he did so, the ship slipped into the open sea. He turned and watched as the sun began to set over Karystos.

"He's belowdecks, right?"

The tightness eased from Ysobel's features as she nodded. "There are two cabins on the second deck—one for men, the other for women and children," she said. "The monk paid for sheltered passage."

Burrell nodded "Then I'd best find someone who wishes to trade his space for a few coins," he said.

They had nothing. No provisions, not even a change of clothes. He had a long knife tucked in his belt, in keeping with his disguise as a laborer, but Ysobel did not even have that much.

They were in for an uncomfortable few days, at the very least. The secret purse that he kept for emergencies would only stretch so far.

"I have coins enough for supplies," Ysobel said, proving that their minds ran along similar channels. "And we can draw upon my credit at the first port we pass."

He straightened. What was done was done, and it was up to him to make the best of it. First to secure a spot belowdecks, then a chance to observe this monk for himself. If Lady Ysobel was correct in her suspicions, then it was essential that Burrell not let the emperor out of his sight.

And if she was wrong...Well the sooner he proved that she was mistaken, the better it would be. Ysobel would forgive him for doubting her, but if her actions endangered the federation, then it was unlikely that she would ever forgive herself.

Tylenda cleared the harbor and turned north. Some of the passengers watched Karystos shrink in the distance behind them, while their more practical brethren began claiming spots on deck.

Burrell observed those who were not claiming spaces, knowing that they would be the ones sleeping below. He circulated among them, until he heard a man comforting his obviously pregnant wife. The man's voice had a sharper accent than that commonly heard on the streets of Karystos, and it did not take long to realize that they were returning to the country to join his family. Likely he'd come to the capital hoping to make his fortune, but instead had found a different kind of treasure to bring back.

The man had paid good silver to buy his family space below, but was willing to give up his own berth for twice what he'd paid—money that would ease the rest of his journey. Haggling with one of the sailors eventually yielded a small seabag, including a set of nearly clean clothes left behind by a passenger who hadn't survived a previous journey, along with a blanket for sleeping.

When Burrell finally made his way below to the second deck he found the door to the men's cabin propped open, though he had to bend down to enter. Once inside, he realized that the low ceiling meant it was impossible for him to stand erect.

Two smoking lanterns swung on hooks, providing dim illumination. There was space for about twenty pallets laid on the floor for landsmen, rather than the hammocks that sailors would have used. Most of the pallets were claimed, except for a pair on the right-hand wall, which were the least desirable as they were farthest from both the portholes and the door.

A group of men were cheerfully gossiping in the left corner, while one of them tossed a set of dice in his hands. The rest seemed to be traveling alone—some already lying down, trying to sleep, while others sat with their backs against the walls, lost in their own thoughts.

The monk was sitting opposite the door, underneath one of the portholes. The pallets adjacent to him were already occupied, but that could be remedied. The man to the monk's left was an older man, dressed in clean clothes but his hands were stained. A weaver, he surmised, come to Karystos to purchase dyes he could not find at home. The man to the monk's right wore the garb of a laborer, and had the crooked nose and battered ears of one who had seen his share of brawls.

Burrell nudged the weaver with his foot. "You're in my place," he said.

The weaver shook his head. "I was here first," he said.

"And I am here now," Burrell said. He disliked having to intimidate the other man, but he needed to be near the supposed monk. He scratched his jaw, then let his hand fall as if by accident onto the hilt of his knife. "I always sleep under the porthole while I'm on a ship. Otherwise I get ... tetchy."

He waited, but the man did not move. Burrell bared his teeth in a grimace. "I'd hate to have anything disturb your sleep," he advised. "The pallets over there will be more peaceful for a man of your age."

With a jerk of his head he indicated the far wall.

"There is no need for you to move," the monk said. "The sailors said we were free to choose our own berths ..."

But the weaver was already getting to his feet, recognizing a threat when he heard one. The crew of *Tylenda* would not interfere in the affairs of the passengers—not until they endangered the safety of the ship or blood was spilled.

"Thank you," Burrell said, as the weaver brushed by him.

He dropped unceremoniously to the deck.

In the dim light the monk's features had been obscured, but at this distance he could see the fear in his eyes. The monk was afraid—but was it fear of being recognized? Or merely the fear felt by an unarmed man when faced with a potentially violent companion?

"I'm Burrell," he said.

The resemblance that he'd seen from a distance was even more pronounced in person. But in this dim light, a resemblance was all he was willing to swear to.

"I am Brother Josan," the monk said. "And the man that you chased off was Tomasso of Umber, a cloth maker by trade."

A cloth maker, not a weaver. He'd been close.

He stared at the man who called himself Brother Josan, but the man returned his gaze calmly, apparently recovered from his earlier fright. If he were indeed Emperor Lucius, then wouldn't he be worried over the possibility that he'd been followed by whatever enemies had caused him to flee his city in the first place? But if this man was worried, he hid it well.

The monk's robe was clean but obviously not new, and the sandals on his feet showed similar signs of wear. His hair was close-cropped, shorter than would be worn by an emperor or noble, but hair could easily be altered. It was hardly telling evidence.

Burrell sighed at his own foolishness. Had he expected the man to be wearing the imperial crown? Or to introduce himself by his given name? The emperor would not be likely to give himself away so easily.

"Flattered as I am by your interest, my vows prevent me from lying with one who is not of my order," the monk said.

Burrell could feel his cheeks heat as he realized that the intensity of his scrutiny had been misinterpreted. Hastily he shook his head. "It's not that . . ." he said, then his voice trailed off.

The monk raised one eyebrow, as if daring him to continue.

And why not? He had nothing to lose. "You remind me of someone," Burrell said.

He watched carefully, but the monk did not twitch. Either he was superb at dissembling, or this was indeed not the emperor.

"Has anyone ever mentioned that you resemble the emperor? Like enough to be his brother."

"All monks are born fatherless. It is unseemly to speculate upon their connections," the monk said primly, as if Burrell had uttered a vile obscenity.

The monk made a point of moving the bag that held his possessions from the left side of his pallet to the right, where it would be out of Burrell's reach. Then he lay down, using his bundled cloak for a pillow.

Burrell had been dismissed. He settled himself in for the night, though he doubted that he would be able to sleep. He knew Lady Ysobel would want answers, but he had none to give. Hopefully by the time morning came, he would have come up with a plan.

Tylenda dropped anchor shortly after dark. The frugal captain had not wanted to pay another day's harbor fees, but he appeared equally reluctant to brave the strait of Eluktiri in full dark. Whatever navigation secrets the Ikarian navy had mastered, they had not shared this information with their merchants. Despite his unease, the rocking of the ship at anchor eased Burrell into a restless sleep. He woke only when he felt the ship begin to move, as the sails were once again unfurled at the first signs of light.

With a start he rolled over, wondering if his quarry had slipped from his grasp, but the monk was still there. He slept peacefully, unarmed in a room full of strangers, as if he had not an enemy in the world.

It made no more sense than it had the day before.

Burrell sat up, rubbing sleep from his eyes as he considered his next move. If he could catch the monk alone, he might be able to threaten him to get at the truth. But there were few places on such a small ship that would offer any degree of privacy—and even if he could find such a spot, he could hardly expect that the monk would tamely follow him there.

As Burrell pondered, others began to stir. The cloth maker Tomasso rose to his feet and left the cabin, presumably to relieve himself.

Burrell heard voices in the corridor, and then a moment later a sailor appeared in the doorway. "You want food go up on deck now, or wait till sunset," he said, evidently not caring that his voice was too soft to wake the sleepers.

Those who were awake got to their feet, while the gambler from the previous night woke his comrades. Burrell leaned over and shook the monk's shoulder.

The monk jerked back from his touch.

"Breakfast," Burrell said.

The monk nodded, but did not offer his thanks.

Burrell got to his feet and left the cabin, pretending indifference to whether or not the monk followed him. They were at sea, so it was not as if there was any danger of losing his quarry. Like the others, Burrell carried his possessions with him—the newly acquired seabag was too valuable to risk losing.

Near the deckhouse two sailors were dispensing soup and torn pieces of flat bread. There were no orderly lines. Instead the three dozen or so passengers on deck simply milled around, shoving until they reached the table, then holding out their bowls to be filled.

Burrell was fortunate that the dead passenger's possessions had included a bowl—his public purse was nearly flat, and he had no wish to flash gold in this company.

Elbowing his way to the front, he accepted his ration, then wandered over to join Lady Ysobel.

She wore a cloak that she'd not possessed when they boarded, and held a wooden bowl between both hands, blowing softly on the contents to cool it. She must have acquired her own supplies last night, after they'd parted.

"Burrell," he said, conscious that they were being watched. Yesterday all eyes had been focused on the rapidly diminishing shoreline, but now the passengers had nothing better to do than observe their fellows. "Lately of Ikaria, but I've been on traders all along the southern rim. You have the look of someone I once knew—three years ago, sailing to Kazagan with Captain Rupert?"

"Four years ago," she said. "And from your arrival yesterday, I see you have not changed."

Burrell shrugged, in keeping with the role he had adopted. He took a sip of his soup, which was, perhaps, an improvement upon whatever sloshed in *Tylenda*'s bilges. Or perhaps not.

But food was not to be wasted. They both finished their rations, then went over to the water butt, where they were allowed to drink their fill. At least there was no shortage of drinking water, though he was not looking forward to his next meal.

"Strange to see you as passenger instead of crew," he said.

"I missed my ship," she said. "With luck I can catch her in Skalla. The captain is a cousin of mine, and may be in the mood to let me rejoin."

"If you can put in a word for me . . ."

Ysobel made a show of eyeing him up and down. "You have until Skalla to convince me that you are worth it," she said.

Ysobel nudged him as the monk made his way to the serving table. He'd declined to push his way through the crowds, and thus was one of the last to be served, receiving whatever dregs were left.

"Is it him?" she asked.

Burrell shook his head. "I don't know."

Ysobel drained her cup in one long draught. "Then it is time we found out."

Half a fish head stared up at him from amidst a watery broth. Josan poked it with his finger, to see if there was anything else in the bowl worth eating before giving up in disgust. He tossed the remnants of his soup over the railing, wiping his bowl with a rag, then returned it to his leather pack. After gnawing on the stale bread for a while, he made his way over to the water butt for a drink to relieve his dry mouth.

His stomach was uneasy—so far it had not minded being at sea, but breakfast had been a rude shock to a body grown used to the delicacies served up by the imperial chefs.

I am not an emperor, he reminded himself. I am Josan, a humble scholar. Logic said that a single year as emperor should not outweigh the half dozen years he had spent living as a peasant, when he was in exile on Txomin's island. Not to mention the two decades before, though that had been when he wore his own body.

But logic had little to do with how this body felt. He would have to rediscover how to live as a monk. Quickly. Before anyone became suspicious.

That traveler, Burrell, he knows you are not who you say you are, Lucius said. *He recognized us.*

If he intended us ill, he would not have announced his suspicions, Josan argued, though privately he shared Lucius's fears. There was something familiar about Burrell, something that warned him of danger, but he had pushed that feeling from his conscious mind, not wanting Lucius to panic. It was difficult enough to master his own emotions— when Lucius's were added to the mix, it was easy for him to be overwhelmed and lose all sense of reason.

If Burrell had been hoping to provoke him by mentioning his resemblance to the emperor, he must have been gravely disappointed. Josan had remained utterly still, seemingly indifferent to the accusation. Though it was not courage, but rather simple paralysis as his two selves warred for control of his body. With neither Lucius nor Josan in ascendance, there was no guilty start, no inadvertent twitch. The battle had lasted only the space of a few heartbeats, but it had been enough. Hopefully he had deflected the man's curiosity. He could not count on being so fortunate again.

Josan began to wander the deck, picking his way between the cargo and his fellow passengers. He cast his mind back to the first time he had left Karystos, when he had been sent to study at the great library in Xandropol. The young monk that he had been had been endlessly fascinated by every detail of sea life, and by his fellow travelers.

If Brother Mensah were here, no doubt he would be taking full advantage of this opportunity to learn. But Josan was wary—and with good cause he realized, as he came around the deckhouse and found himself face-to-face with Lady Ysobel.

His heart froze. He knew her at once, for all that she was dressed as a common sailor. There was no disguising her features, nor the flash of recognition in her eyes. Of all the dangers he had feared, all of the people who might be sent after him, it had never occurred to him that she would be the one to find him.

"Lucius," Lady Ysobel said.

Josan fought down his instinctive terror. How had she found him? Who else knew of his presence?

Was she certain that it was he? Or could he hope to convince her that he was merely a monk?

Hard at her heels was Burrell, the man who had confronted him last night. As Ysobel halted, Burrell moved to her side, his hand resting on the knife he wore at his belt. It was the practiced move of one who had guarded her before, and it was by this act that Josan finally recognized him as Lady Ysobel's ever-watchful aide.

Last night he hadn't even guessed that his interrogator was from the federation. Mongrels, all of them, the only distinctive feature of their race was that they had no distinction. Josan could perhaps be forgiven for not having recognized Burrell, who'd never once spoken in the emperor's presence. But as surely as he recognized them, they must have recognized him in turn. He doubted they would believe the noble bastard story that he had spun for Burrell, but he had no choice but to continue the pretense.

He let his eyes widen in confusion. "I have met your companion, but I do not believe that I know you. I am Brother Josan, of the collegium in Karystos."

"What game do you play?" Lady Ysobel asked.

"Game?" he repeated.

Lady Ysobel reached for him, but he took a hasty step backwards, blushing furiously. One of the brethren was not meant to be touched by a woman, not even casually.

Josan turned toward Burrell. "Pray tell your companion that there is no cause for rudeness. Nor do I welcome her favors."

From the corner of his eye he could see that Lady Ysobel was taken aback by his remark, and the tightness in his chest began to ease. If they'd intended murder, he could have easily been killed last night in his sleep. Either they intended something else, or they were not sure of his identity. It might still be possible to convince them that he was indeed a mere monk.

He tried to imagine how Brother Mensah would have reacted had he been accosted by a strange woman. From there it was a simple matter to nod civilly to Burrell, then brush by them, gathering his robe close around him as if he feared Ysobel's mere touch would contaminate him.

He reached the dubious safety of the men's cabin, entering only when he saw that there were a handful of others already inside. Surely Burrell would not harm him in front of witnesses. And what else could he do? Proclaim to the others that Emperor Lucius was in their presence? Burrell would be mocked as a madman.

And he had other worries. Lucius's presence had disappeared the moment that he had seen Lady Ysobel. Josan searched, but could find no trace of Lucius, though there was a lingering numbness in his limbs that he had begun to associate with those times when Lucius's consciousness was severed from his.

He tasted despair. Lady Ysobel's presence complicated a journey that was already perilous. He might have sown the seed of doubt in her mind, but all doubts would be eliminated if he were to fall into a fit where she or her accomplice could witness it. A monk who resembled the emperor could be a coincidence, but if the same monk shared the emperor's malady? Even a lackwit would realize that they were one and the same.

But fretting accomplished nothing. He opened Mensah's journey bag and withdrew a slender volume contained within. A book of poetry, written in Taresian, the language of Tarsus. Perhaps Mensah thought himself a poet, or perhaps he merely wished to improve his grasp of the language. In any case, it would serve as a diversion for his wayward thoughts.

Josan opened the book. It had been some years since he had read or spoken Taresian, but this, at least, was a challenge that he understood. In moments he was wholly absorbed in puzzling out the nuances of the first poem.

* * *

It was him. Lucius. She *knew* it. He had even introduced himself to Burrell as Brother Josan, the name under which she had first met him, when Lucius was in his exile.

Yet she could not wholly cast Burrell's doubts from her mind. Why would Lucius abandon his empire and everything that he had fought so hard for? What possible threat could have driven him from Karystos and his supporters?

Had Proconsul Zuberi finally moved against the emperor? But surely Lucius would have fled to his supporters rather than taking passage on a common ship.

And if this was Lucius, he should have been terrified at being discovered. Ysobel the envoy had reason to deal carefully with Emperor Lucius, but if he were indeed fleeing, powerless, then Ysobel of Alcina might choose this moment to settle old scores. Or simply take him hostage and sell him to whichever of his enemies offered the fattest purse.

But by all appearances he was not afraid. He avoided her efforts at conversation, but he avoided all women on the ship equally, careful never to address them nor to get within arm's reach.

Ysobel was puzzled, and it was small comfort that Burrell found himself equally confused.

They sailed for four days, passing through the straits of Eluktiri, then following the coast to the Bay of Samos. Ysobel hated every hour of the journey. Idleness did not suit her, and she made a poor passenger on someone else's ship. She could not help noticing that *Tylenda* listed slightly to port, nor that her sailors idled whenever they could, working diligently only when under the supervision of an officer. She made a list of things that she would have fixed if this were one of her own craft—from the fraying patches on the mainsail to the rotted planks in the common lavatory.

It was not that *Tylenda* was a bad ship—she was no better or worse than most that plied their trade in these coastal waters. But Ysobel's standards were high, for herself and those who sailed for her. If one of Ysobel's captains had let his ship fall into such a condition, he would have found himself set ashore on the first land she came across with nothing more than the clothes on his back.

The captain had promised that they'd reach Samos Harbor today, but the winds had proven fickle, forcing the ship to tack from one side to the other, and back again. It was dusk when they dropped anchor, the lights of Samos Harbor flickering in the distance.

Ysobel stood at the prow, her gaze focused on the distant lights. Come morning, she would have to make a decision.

"It's the usual," Burrell said.

She started, not having heard him approach. She turned as he held out a bowl of savory beans, topped with an ungenerous slice of cured pork.

"Thank you," she said as she accepted the bowl and the husk of bread that came with it. Dropping down to sit cross-legged on the deck, Burrell joined her a moment later. They ate the pork first, then used the bread to scoop the beans into their mouths.

"What shall we do?" Burrell asked, when he had finished.

"I don't know," she replied. Burrell's doubts had proven infectious. When she had followed him aboard she had sworn that the monk was actually the emperor in disguise, and yet . . .

In a way it would have been better if she had not come aboard and let Burrell be the one to follow him. Lucius might have let his guard down around a stranger, but once he knew she was aboard, he would know that his life depended upon convincing them that he was indeed a monk.

"What if we're both right?" Burrell asked.

"What do you mean?"

"How often have you told me that the emperor's moods change from day to day? One day he was jovial, the next aloof? A wastrel at times, then at other times a politician who spent his days closeted with his advisors?"

She nodded.

"What if there were two men playing the part of emperor?" Burrell asked.

"A double?"

"Precisely. The true emperor is unwell—poisoned perhaps, or suffering from a wasting disease. On his good days he is seen in public, but when he cannot be seen—"

"The monk plays his part," she finished.

It fit. And it was far more logical than the idea that the emperor of Ikaria had taken passage aboard a common trading vessel. It even explained the monk's hasty flight from Ikaria. Once his usefulness had come to an end, he would be banished or killed to preserve his secret.

Burrell, whose frame had been stiff with tension, relaxed. "You recognize him because you have seen this man act the part of emperor. But this is not Lucius."

Perhaps it was sheer stubbornness that kept her from

agreeing. Or perhaps it was the instincts honed from all of the time she had spent bargaining with those who sought to cheat her. Whatever the reason, even as her mind told her that Burrell's answer was the logical one, she still hesitated.

"I will think on what you have said," she finally responded.

"That's all I ask," Burrell said. If he was disappointed by her answer, he gave no sign.

"Watch over our monk," she said. "And meet me here at dawn tomorrow, and I will tell you what I have decided."

Chapter 5

In the absence of the emperor—and, some said, even in his presence—Proconsul Zuberi was the most powerful man in Karystos. Nobles and senators alike vied for his attention. At least a dozen invitations arrived every day, offering everything from lavish spectacles to select gatherings of the elite. His numerous clients were also eager to offer their hospitality, as a sign of their loyalty. Should he choose to host his own party, any guests would be flattered by his invitation. But instead he chose to dine alone, in the suite set aside for his use at the imperial palace.

He was not a solitary man by nature, but tonight his thoughts were too private to be shared with another. He had allies, of course, but no one with whom he could speak candidly.

Not when he was contemplating treason.

Even as the word crossed his mind, he shook his head, shying away from it. It was not treason. He had put

Lucius on the throne, and if he had the right to order a man crowned, surely he had the same right to strip him of that crown.

He would never have a better opportunity.

Once Lucius had announced his intentions to retire to the countryside, the courtiers had begun making their own preparations to visit their long-neglected estates. Even Lady Ysobel had left the city, if his spies in the Seddonian embassy were to be believed.

Lucius would have to die, of course, but that could easily be arranged. It would be easy for Zuberi to seize the reins of power, and with Karystos in his grasp, the rest of the empire would fall in line.

The legions preferred order. They would back whoever held Karystos as long as he did not jeopardize their privileges. Admiral Septimus, who commanded the imperial navy, was a trickier matter. He was of the old blood, and had reason to be loyal to Lucius. But he was also a pragmatic man and could be bargained with.

As for the rest—Zuberi already controlled the ministries. The senate was split into factions—some looked to him for leadership, others looked to his fellow councilor Senator Demetrios. Once the council had been made up of four men, but Simon had been murdered, and Brother Nikos had fled ahead of the emperor's justice. Paradoxically, reducing the council to just two men had made it more difficult, not less, to reach agreement.

And Demetrios had his own ambitions. His elder brother Prokopios had been the victim of a mysterious attack last year, and after lingering for several months, he had recently succumbed to his wounds.

Or poison. It was impossible to know for certain.

Demetrios had professed himself grief-stricken; but even if his grief were genuine, he must have realized that his brother's death now made him a candidate for the imperial throne.

Zuberi chuckled mirthlessly. Last year there had been too few candidates for the throne. Now there were too many.

It had been desperation that led them to choose Prince Lucius to fill the role of emperor. Lucius had proven himself surprisingly competent—far exceeding the role that Zuberi had intended for him. And while Zuberi did not like him, even he had to admit that it was Lucius's arcane knowledge that had put an end to Seddonian predations, inspiring their enemies to sue for peace.

But that did not mean that Lucius deserved to be emperor. Any man could read books. It took skill to lead an empire. Without Zuberi's guidance, Lucius was nothing.

Zuberi could have been emperor himself. Should have been the one to carry on Nerissa's legacy. But at the time he'd been dying of a tumor in his bowels. And with only months to live, he'd known that if he took the throne, he'd merely be condemning his son Bakari to death. A boy emperor would never be tolerated.

Ironically it was Lucius's magic that had cured Zuberi, though the memory of that day still caused him to shudder. His stomach clenched in remembrance of that violation. He'd been as repulsed by Lucius's magic as he'd been by the bloody tumor that had been literally pulled from his bowels.

Even now he felt unclean, though the physicians assured him he was cured.

The emperor had healed him not out of kindness, but to convince Zuberi to spare his life. And Zuberi had done so—but surely Lucius had known that any such alliance would only be fleeting.

It was time for Zuberi to make a choice. He could take the throne that should have been his all along, or he could allow Lucius to continue to rule. But for how long? Was he prepared to see Lucius married, and to one day pass the crown on to his son? A man who would bear the same taint of magic in his blood as the emperor?

The longer Zuberi waited, the more time he gave Lucius to build alliances and secure his grasp upon the throne. In time, Lucius might be strong enough to challenge him.

Even if Zuberi did not claim the throne for himself, there was nothing to prevent another from launching his own bid. He wondered if Demetrios, too, was contemplating treason on this fine summer night.

Whatever choice he made was fraught with peril. He considered the problem from all angles but had reached no decision by the time he retired.

It seemed he had barely fallen asleep when he was rudely shaken awake.

"A thousand apologies," a voice said. "But he will not take no for an answer."

Zuberi opened his eyes and saw his servant Melfi standing next to his bed. The dim lamplight illuminated Melfi's features, revealing a man who looked as bleary-eyed as Zuberi felt.

"What is it?" Zuberi asked, pushing himself up into a seated position.

If the proconsul had been required, he would have been awoken by one of the palace functionaries. The fact that it was Melfi at his bedside indicated that this was not imperial business. And he knew Melfi would not disturb him lightly.

Terror gripped his heart.

"My son, my wife?"

Melfi shook his head frantically. "All well, at last report. But your nephew..."

"Needs to speak with you. Alone." Captain Chenzira loomed out of the darkness.

Zuberi stood up, absently accepting the robe that Melfi handed him. He waited as Melfi lit the lamps in his bedroom before bowing himself out of the chamber.

"I came here as swiftly as I could," Chenzira began, and his very appearance proved the truth of his words; his uniform was speckled with sea spray. He smelled of the salt ocean and the sour sweat of a day spent under the hot sun. "I tried your residence first, and they directed me here."

"The emperor, he is well?" Zuberi asked.

Chenzira glanced around, confirming that they were alone. "I do not know," he said.

"What? How?"

Chenzira reached inside his tunic and withdrew a scroll, which he handed to Zuberi.

"The emperor left word that he wished to pass his journey in sleep. When *Green Dragon* reached Eluktiri, I anchored in the bay and waited until the second hour after dawn before sending a servant to rouse him. The servant found a drugged man sleeping in the emperor's place, and two scrolls. The first scroll directed me to return and to give you this."

Zuberi's sleep-clumsy fingers could not undo the knotted ribbon. He tugged at it in frustration until Chenzira produced a knife and slit through it.

Zuberi, Proconsul of Ikaria, the missive began. Zuberi skipped through the formal salutations, noting not for the first time that the emperor's handwriting was as regular as any scribe's.

I would not lightly abandon my duties, but I am compelled to journey, traveling swiftly and in secret, Lucius had written. *I will return as soon as I may. I know I may safely leave the empire in your care. Do what you will to preserve her.*

"The thrice-damned fool," Zuberi raged, throwing the scroll on the floor.

Chenzira, greatly overstepping his place, picked up the scroll and read it, but there was nothing there for him to discover. The emperor's words made no sense.

If, indeed, the emperor had even written this.

"What did your letter say?" Zuberi asked.

"Merely that the monk should not be punished, and urged me to return to speak with you."

"The monk?" Did he see Brother Nikos's hand in this?

"I beg forgiveness, I thought I had told you already. Yesterday, or rather, two days ago, the emperor and his escort boarded my ship. He summoned a monk from the collegium and spoke with him at length. Shortly before sailing a man dressed as a monk left the ship, and I thought no more of it until I discovered that the emperor was missing, and the drugged man in his quarters called himself Brother Mensah."

Had Lucius suspected that Zuberi was plotting to seize the throne? Was that why he had fled? But if so, why send word of what he had done?

If Lucius had even written the letter at all. Whatever message he had intended could easily have been replaced.

Yet if there were another hand at work here, how had he persuaded the emperor to leave the safety of Chenzira's ship? If Lucius had felt threatened, surely he would have turned to Chenzira, who was far too close to the emperor for Zuberi's tastes.

Unless, of course, Chenzira was part of the scheme. Zuberi stared at him, searching for some sign of guilt, but Chenzira returned his gaze steadily.

Still, illegitimate nephew or not, he could not afford to spare Chenzira. He had only Chenzira's word that the emperor had boarded the ship, then apparently left it of his own volition.

"Your men will need to be questioned," Zuberi announced. "Discreetly, so we do not cause a panic."

Chenzira nodded. "I gave orders that no man leave the ship," he said. "I knew you would want to speak with them."

"Not me. Nizam," Zuberi said. It was too important to trust to anyone else. He could not afford to let his fondness for Chenzira blind him.

At the mention of the chief torturer, Chenzira swallowed hard. "And he will start with you," Zuberi added.

"I should have been told at once," Demetrios said. He rose to his feet and began to pace around the perimeter of the sunken bath.

Zuberi had chosen the private imperial baths as neutral territory for this meeting. With the emperor absent there was no risk that they would be disturbed, and the cascading fountains would make it difficult for any spies to overhear what was said.

But neither Zuberi's consideration nor the soothing elegance of their surroundings had served to mollify Demetrios.

"I thought it best to have the facts, first," Zuberi said. He remained lounging on a wicker couch, the casualness of his posture belying the seriousness of the situation.

"Time to decide how to twist this to your own advantage," Demetrios said, pausing in his circuit to turn to face Zuberi. "Be careful, you are not emperor. Yet."

Zuberi returned Demetrios's glare.

"As proconsul, I——"

"You oversee the ministries and implement the emperor's commands," Demetrios interjected. "But you are not the emperor, nor even his heir."

This was ridiculous. Demetrios raised points of precedence, ignoring the very real problems they faced.

Though it would have been easier if Lucius had named an heir. It had been tacitly assumed that Zuberi was that heir, but a formal confirmation would require the approval of the imperial senate—and that would require Demetrios to renounce his own ambitions. The balance between them had been too delicate for Zuberi to force the issue, but then he'd never expected this situation.

Still, all was not lost. Should Zuberi seize power, he could always *discover* that Lucius had left a private will, naming Zuberi as his heir.

If Lucius were dead, which was a distinct possibility. It was now three days since he had walked off *Green Dragon* and seemingly vanished. Dead, fled, taken prisoner—anything could have happened.

"I did not bring you here to quarrel," Zuberi said. "We need to decide what we will do."

Demetrios gave a short nod and made his way back to his chair. His face was flushed, from anger or perhaps merely the heat of the baths.

"Do you believe Chenzira?" he asked.

It was not an easy question. "I believe Captain Chenzira had told us the truth as he perceives it. But it is entirely possible that he himself was deceived."

"Though not by his crew. Nor the monk."

"No. Nizam made certain of that."

Nizam had questioned all those who had come in contact with both the monk and the emperor. If, indeed, it had been Lucius who had boarded the ship.

Perhaps the emperor had disappeared even earlier in the day, and the functionaries had been tricked by an actor playing his role. Though if so, the likeness had been good enough to fool even the palace functionary who had accompanied him.

"Why would he leave? What is this journey he spoke of? He mentioned nothing to me," Demetrios said.

"Nor to me," Zuberi said. Though, if Lucius had seen fit to confide in either of them, he would have picked Demetrios for his confidences. Demetrios had been the first on the council to support him, unlike Zuberi, who'd only been reluctantly persuaded that the emperor's suggestions occasionally had merit.

"He's been ill . . ." Demetrios's voice trailed off.

"Fatigued," Zuberi insisted. He'd heard the palace servants gossiping that the emperor was God-touched, but such superstitions were for the weak-minded. Lucius was merely fatigued, afflicted by nothing more than the relentless summer heat. Even the imperial physician had agreed that the emperor simply needed a restoring stay in the countryside.

"But if he did not write that letter, then who did? And why?"

"To draw us off the scent," Zuberi said. "As for who— Lady Ysobel left Karystos the very same day that the emperor disappeared."

According to his spies, she'd left in secret, not even informing the federation ambassador of her plans. At the time, he'd thought the deception meant to disguise her intent to follow the emperor to his estate in Sarna, in violation of the unwritten rules of the court. He'd amused himself by imagining her dismay when she realized that the emperor was on Eluktiri instead.

Now he wondered.

"He would not have gone with her willingly. But would

she be bold enough to kidnap him? In daylight, from amidst men sworn to defend him with their lives?"

"She was once bold enough to plot to overthrow Empress Nerissa," Zuberi argued. But privately he agreed that it was unlikely that she had kidnapped Lucius off *Green Dragon*. Still, she could have tricked him into leaving the ship, then taken him.

"What could she hope to accomplish?"

"His death gains her nothing," Zuberi said. Emperors could be replaced, and there was no guarantee that Lucius's successor would be any more favorably inclined toward the federation. "Alive, he can be brought to the federation in chains, to force us to agree to their terms."

And if they had kidnapped Empress Nerissa, Ikaria would have beggared itself to ransom her. But there were few who would shed a tear for Emperor Lucius, and fewer still who would risk their lives or treasure to recover him.

"Too risky to transport him so far," Demetrios said. "She may have taken him looking for the secrets of the Burning Terror, and will kill him once she learns what she needs to."

"A half dozen men know the same secrets, Captain Chenzira among them," Zuberi countered. "Far easier to take one of them than an emperor."

Though Chenzira and the others had sworn to take their own lives rather than risk giving such a deadly weapon to their enemies. So Ysobel might have rightly judged Lucius as a man more open to persuasion.

"Admiral Septimus has sent messages to his fleet, with the names and descriptions of all ships that sailed before we began searching them, and Petrelis's men are scouring the city," Zuberi said. "We will find him."

Hopefully before they had to make a public announcement that the emperor was missing. They could keep this quiet only so long. Eventually someone would talk.

"For now, we act as if nothing has changed. The emperor is resting on Eluktiri, and we are governing in his absence," Demetrios said.

"Agreed."

It was ironic. Mere days ago Zuberi had been contemplating treason and now he was fervently hoping for the emperor's safe return.

If Zuberi seized the throne and Lucius was later found to have been taken by the federation, everyone would believe that Zuberi had plotted with Lady Ysobel to bring about Lucius's demise. Even his own clients would distance themselves from a man they viewed as a traitor.

No, until he knew what had happened to Lucius, he could do nothing except play the role of the emperor's most loyal servant.

And Demetrios would do the same. Their alliance was preserved. For now.

Ysobel shivered in the chill dawn air, sipping the weak tea the crew had provided with breakfast. Passengers milled around her as those who were leaving the ship gathered up their possessions. Only a single set of sails had been raised as the ship maneuvered its way into the harbor. There was no dock space available, but the deck officer Maurizio had announced that lighters would ferry passengers to shore—for two coppers a head. Some grumbled, but most appeared to have expected this indignity.

Ysobel suspected a portion of those coppers would wind up in Maurizio's purse—a minor corruption that a good captain would have taken care to stamp out.

Any could disembark here if they chose, but those who were continuing on with *Tylenda* needed to return by midafternoon, or risk being left behind.

As the ship dropped anchor, a group of passengers surged to the port side of the ship, shoving to be first in line, though no lighters had yet arrived to bear them off. Guided by Maurizio's curses, the sailors began lowering *Tylenda*'s gig, in preparation for the captain's journey ashore.

She frowned as her eyes swept over the deck. There was still no sign of Burrell, who had not made an appearance for breakfast. Neither had the monk, which perhaps explained Burrell's absence. If anything untoward had happened, she surely would have heard. She'd found the sailors to be as free with their gossip as they were stingy with their provisions.

Still, she ought to see for herself and hope the confusion of coming into a new port meant that there would be no one belowdecks to witness her entering the forbidden male quarters.

She drained the last of her tea and tucked the empty cup into the bag she'd tied to her belt. Pushing away from the deck rail, she started to walk to the hatchway, only to pause as Burrell came into view.

Since they both followed the custom of carrying their

belongings with them, it would be simple for them to depart once the lighters began to arrive. There would be no need to jostle for a place in line. A few coins slipped into Maurizio's hand would ensure that she and Burrell left first.

"What kept you?" she asked. "I want to leave as soon as we are able."

It had taken her a long, sleepless night, but she'd made her decision. Burrell had convinced her; the man aboard *Tylenda* was not the emperor, merely someone who had the misfortune to bear an uncanny resemblance to the imperial family. Perhaps even a double, as Burrell had conjectured, fleeing once his usefulness was at an end.

Burrell shook his head. "Our friend was unwell," he said in a soft voice.

"Unwell?"

Burrell shrugged, his features revealing his confusion. "I do not know what else to call it. He woke last night in a fit. I tried to calm him, but I would swear he didn't know me, nor where he was."

"Was he drunk?"

"Not that I could tell. Nor feverish," he added, anticipating her next question.

"Is he still sick?"

Two sailors bearing a chest between them tried to shove past her, and after fixing them with a glare, Ysobel belatedly remembered her assumed role. She retreated back to the rail as Burrell followed. These sailors had no reason to pay her any deference; nor could she afford to rouse their suspicions.

"He was quiet for some time, after he calmed," Burrell said. "His eyes were closed, but I could tell he was not sleeping. When dawn came, he opened his eyes and asked if we were in Samos harbor. But he has not moved from his pallet. I don't know if he can."

The elderly were known to have such fits of confusion and paralysis, but the monk was still a young man. Nor had he asked for help, which meant that he, at least, knew what afflicted him.

"We know the emperor was suffering from fits . . ."

"If that was the emperor," Burrell added. "This may still be the same man—perhaps he's too ill to play the part of the emperor any longer, which is why they are getting rid of him."

"Or it could be Lucius himself," Ysobel countered. "Journeying in search of a cure."

Burrell threw up his hands in frustration. "What would you have us do?"

"You will stay here to keep watch over the monk. If he tries to leave the ship, then you will follow him. I'll go ashore and send word back to the ambassador, and to the federation. Let them know that Lucius is not resting in the countryside but rather sailed to an unknown destination, and we are following a man who may lead us to him."

"Let us hope the warning reaches them in time," Burrell said. "I still think Lucius sailed aboard *Green Dragon*."

He disagreed with her, but she did not mind. She appreciated his candor, as much as she valued his honesty. Once she'd announced her intention to leave this ship, he could easily have kept quiet about the monk's strange illness.

Instead he'd shared the news with her, knowing that she might see it as proof that her suspicions were right.

"Even if we sailed on the fastest of ships, we could not hope to catch *Green Dragon*," Ysobel said. "Not without knowing her destination."

It was a peace offering, of a sort. There was nothing they could do except send word and urge others to prepare.

"And if Lucius leads his fleet to war while we are ferrying ducks and peasants along the coast?"

"The mistake will be mine, as will the consequences," she said.

"I stand by you, whatever you decide," Burrell said, refusing to accept her generosity.

He would question her to her face, but resolutely defend her before all others. Such loyalty was rare, and she strove to be worthy of his trust.

If she was wrong—well, she would deserve whatever befell her. As for Burrell—if she thought with her heart, she'd be tempted to send him away so that he would not suffer for his loyalty. Which would have been foolish, since she needed him. Needed him to go to places where she could not, needed to know that if anything happened to her, there was someone who would carry on. Which only served to remind her of all the reasons why she had not taken him as a lover.

He trusted her judgment, and she needed to trust it as well. To know that she charted the course that had the best chance of success rather than giving in to her own desires. He was a friend, yes, and already that friendship had tempted her to put personal considerations first, ahead of her duty. Which was the surest path to a failure that would doom them both.

She must not forget that they were in enemy territory, where a single mistake could get them both killed.

Burrell would stay with her, as aide and confidant. And she would trust in her instincts to keep them both safe.

Chapter 6

Spray from the porthole above dampened Josan's cheek. He brushed it away, then wiped his hand on his robe before once again opening his book. Since recovering from his brief illness, he'd read the book of Taresian poetry twice and begun amusing himself by translating the verses in his head. They flowed easily enough into Ikarian, so he'd begun translating them into Decanese, the language of the Seddonian court, which was proving a greater challenge. Decanese held a wealth of terms to describe extended family relationships, and there were specific forms describing whether wealth was inherited, earned through the sea trade, or from other sources. But it had only two words for love—one for the affection felt for family and another for passion.

By contrast, Taresian not only had a word for a pure love that was the basis of true friendship, but such love was often the subject of their poems and dramas. *Herat* it was called, and there was no equivalent in Decanese. It held the flavor of affection, loyalty, and devotion, but it wasn't precisely equivalent to any of these.

He puzzled over the phrase,

> Bitter tears flowed, as Danya professed herat!
> But cold-handed Hadeon scorned his vow.

It was tempting to translate *herat* as love, but in context with the rest of the poem, friendship was likely closer to the poet's original intent. The poem was a tragedy in which Hadeon the magistrate is reunited with his old friend, only to have to condemn Danya to death, in accordance with the law.

The agony of being torn between honor and *herat* played out for over two hundred lines, until Danya was hanged, and Hadeon drank poison while contemplating his friend's corpse.

By Taresian standards it was a cheerful poem, in that the ending confirmed the overriding importance of *herat*. Josan did not quite understand the point of law under which Danya was condemned to death for merely witnessing a crime, but that did not matter. His translation was sound enough, as it was not a scholarly exercise but a mere diversion to while away the hours on a day when the weather was too foul to be up on deck.

Finishing the first poem, he began on the next, the tale of a magician who'd placed his heart in a crystal and thus thought to live forever. But his enemies destroyed the crystal and with that he perished. The point of the tale was to assure the audience that even the most powerful could not escape their destinies, but it was the mention of the crystal that intrigued Josan. Lost in thought, he was abruptly yanked from his musings when he found himself sprawled on the floor.

He blinked up at the hanging lantern, which swung wildly above him. Both he and his pallet had slid across the floor as the ship lurched to one side.

His back ached from where it had struck the deck, and his palms stung where he had scraped them in his awkward slide. Pushing himself back into a seated position, he took deep breaths as his stomach objected to the violent pitching.

The deck continued its tilt, so he did not bother standing but rather crawled back to his place, dragging his pallet with him.

"Here you are," Burrell said, handing him his book, which must have fallen from his grasp.

Unlike the others in the cabin, who grumbled as they recovered their possessions, Burrell had not been taken off guard. Then again, Seddonians were practically born at sea. To him, such a storm was likely nothing compared to those that had rocked him to sleep.

"Thank you," Josan said.

Burrell had continued to keep an eye on him, but after that first day there had been no further mention of his suspicions regarding Josan's true identity. Having shared sleeping quarters with the man for the past fortnight, he would wager that Burrell did indeed believe him to be nothing more than a monk.

Lady Ysobel, on the other hand, was apparently not convinced. Why else had she remained aboard this ship, if it were not to keep an eye on the man she believed to be Emperor Lucius?

Tylenda's journey along the coast had been slow, the ship pausing every two or three days to put into port. Gradually the number of passengers decreased. The men's cabin was less than half-full, and the space on deck that had been given over to the lowest class of passengers was now occupied by crates of cargo.

It seemed to Josan that the ship rode heavier than she had at the start and tended to wallow in the waves, but he was not enough of a sailor to be certain.

Either Lady Ysobel or Burrell visited each port that they called at, but they always returned to the ship. They had taken no actions against him, which gave him hope that in time they would give over their suspicions entirely. Failing that he might be able to lose them when he changed ships at Skalla.

"The storm is growing worse," Josan observed.

Burrell shook his head. "Feel the rolling of the ship? That's not the storm. We've changed course and are heading due west by my reckoning."

Burrell's voice was calm, but his mouth was tight, and Josan felt the first niggling of fear.

"Our next port is Skalla, to the north, isn't it? Why would we change course?"

Burrell shrugged. "Maybe the captain's seeking sheltered harbor, preparing to wait out the storm." Then he rose to his feet. "It's time to relieve myself."

"I will go with you." Josan had to brace himself against the curved planks of the hull but managed to struggle to his feet. Habit made him sling his journey bag over one shoulder before setting out after Burrell.

The common lavatory was down the corridor to their right—a small room at the back of the ship, where passengers and crew alike squatted over holes that voided their waste into the sea—or sprayed it upon the hull of the ship, depending. It was a foul place, and in fairer weather most simply relieved themselves over the rail, when no one was looking.

Burrell, despite his declaration, turned left, and Josan followed as Burrell climbed the ladder and pushed open the hatch cover that was closed in wet weather.

Josan climbed out after Burrell, the wooden cover falling open beside him. As the rain-slick deck tilted crazily beneath him, he paused on his hands and knees and cursed his foolishness.

Burrell dogged the hatch closed, then offered his hand to Josan, bracing him till he found his feet.

He could see Captain Aldo standing by the wheel, while amidships the deck officer clung to a line, cursing the sailors who scrambled in the rigging above him.

To Josan's eyes the scene was chaos, but Burrell took it in with a glance.

"See, the storm has eased," Burrell observed, his voice raised to carry above the sounds of flapping canvas and creaking timbers.

Josan blinked at the rain that pelted his face. It was true that the clouds were light gray rather than the ominous dark clouds that had greeted them at dawn, but it was still storming.

"Come," Burrell said.

Josan hung on to Burrell's sleeve as he made his way to the bow, where a familiar figure was standing.

Lady Ysobel. Of course. Josan hesitated, then squared his shoulders. As a monk, he was curious about all things, and it would not be in keeping with his character if he were to avoid her.

"She's running for shore," Burrell said.

Lady Ysobel glanced at Josan, and appeared to weigh her words before responding, "Indeed. And he picked a poor place for it."

"Was the ship damaged by the storm?" Josan asked. If the captain feared his ship was sinking, his only choice would be to head for shore as swiftly as possible and hope that he could beach her, or at least get close enough to make rescue possible.

"I thought I caught a glimpse of sails on the horizon," Burrell said.

Where? Josan turned in a full circle but saw nothing. The deck lurched again, and only Burrell's hasty grab kept Josan upright.

Embarrassed, he grasped the deck rail with both hands.

"A navy ship," Ysobel said. She and Burrell exchanged a speaking look.

"What is a federation ship doing here?" Josan asked.

"Your navy," Ysobel said, speaking slowly as if he were wit-damaged. "A three-master, based on the short glimpse I had. Captain Aldo won't be able to outrun her for long."

"But why would the captain flee?" He would pretend that by *your navy* she had meant that he was a citizen of

Ikaria rather than implying that as emperor any navy ship would be under his command.

"I suspect that has something to do with the cargo we took on board at the last port," Burrell said.

Smugglers? He was on a smuggler's ship? How had he not noticed?

But neither seemed concerned with his ignorance. As Josan looked behind them, searching for a glimpse of the navy vessel, he saw that Ysobel's and Burrell's gazes were focused firmly to the west, the direction in which they were traveling.

Though not without some difficulty, as the direction of the wind meant that the ship was heeling hard to starboard. Yet even as he watched, the sailors struggled to set even more sail in their frantic rush to escape their pursuers.

"See that? White caps, two points to the starboard," Burrell said.

"I see them." Ysobel's voice was grim. "And another set, ahead. If the captain doesn't turn—"

But even as the words left her mouth, the ship began turning, though far too slowly for Josan's taste.

Josan closed his eyes, frantically trying to remember the shape of the coastline. Skalla was the next port of call, but rather than hugging the coastline, the captain had charted a course that took them out of sight of land. He pictured the great map of the empire in his mind, and the approach to Skalla—

Which was marked with warnings of the shoals that guarded the approach to the Southern Keys. Only local fishermen in their shallow skiffs dared sail these waters, and even they were known to come to grief as the shoals shifted without warning.

Those very same dangers were responsible for his first meeting with Lady Ysobel, when her vessel had been shipwrecked, stranding her on Txomin's island, where a humble monk had once tended the imperial lighthouse.

There was good reason for them to fear these shoals.

"He's a madman," Burrell observed.

"And he won't listen to either of us," Lady Ysobel added.

"What should we do?" Josan asked. He shivered in the wind-driven rain, but had no intention of taking shelter belowdecks. If anything happened, those below would be trapped.

"Wait," Ysobel said. "And pray the captain knows what he is doing."

Still, there was no sense in standing without shelter. Clutching the rail with both hands, Josan made his way along the portside of the ship until he was opposite the deckhouse. The ship was tilted so steeply that at times when he glanced over the rail he saw the sea beneath him rather than the side of the ship. Another few degrees and the waves would begin lapping at the deck.

He wondered about the stability of the ship. How far could she heel over before she simply turned on her side? He'd wager Ysobel would know, but he was not inclined to be enlightened. Contrary to the brethren's teachings, he had learned that there were times when the comfort of ignorance was preferable to the grim certainties of truth.

The deckhouse was a steep climb above him. As the ship cut through the waves, he timed her motion. The next time the port side rose he was ready, and dashed up the deck, grasping one of the ropes that were tied to the side of the deckhouse.

The overhanging roof provided shelter from the rain, and this had been among the choicest spots for those travelers who had journeyed on deck. Looping his left arm through the rope, he braced his back against the deckhouse.

He was not surprised when a moment later he was joined first by Lady Ysobel, then Burrell. Either they recognized the wisdom of taking shelter, or they were determined not to let him out of their sight.

He would not have chosen either of them for companions, and yet, there was a part of him that was grateful for their company. It was cowardly of him, he knew, but he did not want to die alone.

What would happen to Ikaria if he perished? How long would Zuberi wait before taking the throne? Would his people accept a new emperor? Or would civil war break out over the succession, as it had nearly done a year ago?

And if both he and Lady Ysobel were to disappear, what would their two countries make of it? Would each side blame the other, leading to war?

He should never have left Ikaria, he realized. Leaving had been selfish, choosing his own life over the needs of the empire that he and Lucius had sworn to serve. Yes, staying would have been a death sentence, but it would have been his life alone that was at risk. Instead, in seeking a cure, he might have inadvertently embroiled two countries in a debilitating war.

He was thrown from his feet as the ship shuddered,

grinding to a halt. The rope cut savagely into his arm, but it saved him from being tossed overboard.

The ship was in chaos—a dozen voices raised at once. Some sailors clung to the rigging, while one had fallen to the deck nearby. Even as Josan watched, the sailor's body began to slide toward the gap in the side that was used for loading cargo. Josan looked around, but no one was paying any attention to the fallen sailor. He unhooked his arm from the rope, preparing to rescue him, but found himself firmly restrained in Burrell's grasp.

Josan struggled to break free, but was forced to watch as the hapless sailor was washed over the side.

"Why?" he demanded, when Burrell finally released him. He turned to glare at Ysobel, knowing that this was her doing. If she were a man, he would have struck her.

"He was already dead," Lady Ysobel said.

"You could not know that."

"Yes, I did," she countered.

He glared, but there was nothing to be done. As the ship groaned and shuddered, he was reminded that all of their lives were at risk.

"We've run aground," Josan said, wondering if this was a good thing or not.

"We scraped a shoal," Ysobel said, "but we're still sailing."

She was right, though their forward progress was slow. The ship continued listing to port, and the bow barely rose up after each wave.

"They've got to get the sails down," Burrell said. "The wind will tear her apart."

"She's too heavy at the bow. I'll wager she's holed

below, and there are more shoals ahead," Ysobel said. "She'll not survive another strike."

The two were as calm as if they were relating a story that had happened to someone else, not contemplating their own impending deaths.

"What can we do?" he asked.

"Hold on!" Ysobel ordered.

This time he heard the scrape as the ship slammed into the shoal, timbers screaming in protest. The nearest land was a mere smudge on the horizon, but they were as stuck as if they had run themselves onto a beach.

Canvas and wooden yardarms protested as the sails continued to flap in the wind, trying to drive a ship that could no longer move. One sail split from top to bottom with a rending sound, while from behind him he heard an ominous crack.

The sailors who were still alive were climbing down from the rigging and milling on the deck, in defiance of the captain's commands. At some point the hatch must have been opened, or been torn off, for passengers began to appear, their frightened cries mixing with those of the crew.

He heard no words spoken, but Burrell pushed himself away and began inching around the deckhouse. When Josan would have followed, Ysobel placed her hand on his arm. "Burrell's got the legs for this," she said.

Josan was paralyzed, able to do nothing but watch as waves began breaking over the bow. No one paid any attention to them. Officers yelled orders that were swallowed up by the wind, and the sailors obeyed or ignored them as they saw fit.

Burrell returned a few moments later. His face was grim.

"She's breaking up," he said. "And the navy vessel is standing off—looks like she's dropped anchor, rather than risk the shoals herself. They may drop boats to pick up survivors . . ."

"We should stay with the ship," Josan said. It was one bit of advice that he recalled from the journals of Kynon the Sailor—even part of a ship was better than none at all.

"The ship will roll and take us with it," Ysobel said. "Can you swim?"

Josan shook his head, not sure he'd heard her rightly. "Swim?"

"Can you swim?" she repeated.

He nodded, not trusting his voice.

"Come," she said. "Those crates by the bow will float if we empty them first."

He'd despised her for following him, but now he was ashamedly grateful to be included in her plans. Ysobel showed no concern for the other passengers and would have cheerfully abandoned Brother Josan to his fate. But an emperor was far too valuable to be left behind.

The rest of the ship's occupants were making their way aft, which was still out of the water, so they had to push their way through them to reach the bow. Most of the cargo on deck had already washed away, but there were two crates of ducks still lashed down. The ducks squawked their outrage as seawater streamed through their crates. Josan watched as Burrell unfastened their doors—the frightened ducks did not want to leave. He was pecked fiercely as he reached in and pulled them out.

Once the crates were empty, Burrell took his knife and began sawing at the ropes that held them to the deck.

So this was the plan. They would cling to crates that had formerly held waterfowl until they could be rescued by his navy. At which point he would have the unenviable task of convincing them that he was not a criminal but rather Emperor Lucius, and in desperate need of their aid.

"Wait," Ysobel called.

Burrell lifted his head and turned to look where she was pointing. Josan glimpsed the overturned hull of the ship's rowboat bobbing in the waves. Someone must have tried to launch her and failed.

Burrell left the crates and rejoined them. The boat was rapidly moving away from the ship. Burrell and Ysobel exchanged a glance, then both looked at Josan. Even so, he was unprepared for what happened next.

Burrell reached down, grabbed Josan's legs, and tipped him over the side of the ship. He fell headfirst into the sea.

The shock of impact stole the breath from his lungs. He gulped seawater, then flailed as he descended below the waves. Forcing panic from his mind, he folded his body until his legs were under him and began to kick. His arms frantically stroked, reaching for the gray light above him. Finally, he broke through, and sputtered as he tried to gulp air.

The sea churned around him. He turned in a circle, and saw that Burrell was a few yards to his right. There was no sign of Lady Ysobel.

"Come," Burrell shouted. "The boat is this way."

Josan did not trust him, but he had no choice. He began to swim toward Burrell, who watched him for a few strokes. Then, seemingly convinced that Josan would not drown, Burrell set off himself.

He caught only glimpses of the boat in between the waves, and a dark head that must be Lady Ysobel's as she cut through the water with smooth strokes. She reached the boat first, then Burrell joined her.

Josan's arms burned, and he continued to cough, trying to expel the seawater that had filled his lungs. As he drew near, he felt himself faltering, but forced himself to keep swimming. He reached for the boat, but an ill-timed wave swept him forward and he smashed his head into the side.

He was blinded and dizzy. Someone held the back of his robe, then placed his hand onto a wooden projection. The rail? He blinked away the blood that dripped down his forehead but could make no sense of what he saw.

Burrell and Ysobel spoke in low voices, and he could not hear what they said. The chill water stole the energy from his limbs, and he wondered if he would have the strength to scramble on top of the boat. It was a small thing—similar to those rowboats he had known on Txomin's island, capable of holding six men. The hull was steeply curved, which meant it would be difficult to balance upon.

Ysobel and Burrell had other plans, though. "Let go," Burrell said.

"What?"

"Let go," Burrell repeated.

"No." He was no fool. He could not survive in the

water without this boat, and he had no intention of relinquishing his grasp.

"Let go, and we'll pull you in," Burrell said. His expression was exasperated. "Come now, we won't have the strength for this later."

His words made no sense, but Josan doubted that Burrell was trying to kill him. Reluctantly he let go.

Burrell joined Lady Ysobel on the far side of the boat. They disappeared from sight and he wondered if they had been swept under it.

Then, as he watched, waves rocked the boat. Then rocked it again. And he realized that it was not the waves, but rather his companions, just as it rocked for a third time, then rolled over and righted itself.

It was only a few yards away, but it seemed to take an hour for Josan to swim back to it. Ysobel climbed in first, then Burrell.

Josan clung to the side, knowing that they dare not risk capsizing it again. Burrell took hold of his arms and Lady Ysobel moved to the opposite side of the boat to balance it.

The boat rocked as Josan heaved himself up. He hung, suspended on the side, then Burrell pulled him into the boat.

The bottom was covered in water, but he could get no wetter. Josan lay for a moment as the boat rocked crazily, then it settled into a motion with the waves.

Lady Ysobel took her place in the middle of the first bench facing them, and Burrell settled on the second. Josan gathered himself, then rose and clumsily sat next to

Burrell, who slid over to make room for him. He shivered in the cold, looking around.

In the distance he could see tree branches, then realized these must be *Tylenda*'s masts. They were nearly too far away to be seen.

"What's in your bag?" Ysobel asked.

Josan reached for his shoulder straps, surprised to find that he was still wearing it. No wonder it had been so hard to swim, as the weight of his possessions combined with the weight of his clothes to hinder him.

Neither Ysobel nor Burrell had burdened themselves with their seabags, though Burrell still had his knife, and Ysobel wore a ring on her finger that he had not seen before.

Shifting the bag from his shoulder, he undid it. "Papers, pen, and ink, which are no doubt ruined," he said. Pushing them aside, he encountered a change of small-clothes, which was not something he needed to announce. "And a bowl and cup," he added.

"Give them," Ysobel said.

He did, watching bemusedly as she and Burrell began to bail. It would take hours to empty the boat, but if they wanted to waste their time, he would not argue.

He craned his head, but could see no sign of the navy vessel that had pursued them. *Tylenda*'s masts were growing smaller—either she was sinking, or they were drifting away.

Or both.

He lifted his feet out of the water swirling around them, and propped them up on the opposite bench.

"They will not come after us," he said.

"No," Lady Ysobel answered. "Even if they saw someone reach the boat, which I doubt, they will stay with
Tylenda."

He was not unduly upset. The rowboat was uncomfortable, but better than clinging to a crate. And at least
this way he did not risk an embarrassing encounter with
his navy. Though it would be difficult to disentangle himself from Ysobel and Burrell, he was confident that he
could manage. Somehow.

"How long till we reach shore?"

"We won't," Ysobel said, reverting to the patronizing
tone she had used with him earlier. "The current is taking
us out to sea, away from the shoals, but also away from
land. And we have neither oars nor the makings of a sail."

He swallowed. Hard. "We could use my robe . . ."

"And lash it to what? Or do you propose to stand there,
holding it out in the wind?"

Her scorn hurt, for all it was undeserved. She was the
sailor, not he. She was the one who had gotten them into
this predicament. Left to his own devices, he would have
stayed with the ship.

"If the wind shifts, it may blow us back to land,"
Burrell said.

Ysobel nodded. "It's our only hope."

He did not like the look that she gave him.

"This is your fault," he said. "You and your man forced
me to come with you."

"We're alive," Burrell said.

"And we will stay that way," Ysobel added. "If you
help."

"What can I do?" Hadn't she just said that there was nothing that could be done?

"Brother Josan can do nothing," she said. "But an emperor who commands lightning from the sky can surely summon the wind to his bidding . . ."

Burrell gaped at her, openmouthed, and Josan shared his astonishment. Was she serious? Had she risked all their lives upon the conviction that he was Emperor Lucius, and that the emperor could indeed command the weather?

But there was no sign that she was jesting.

Even if he wanted to cooperate, he did not think that he could. To his knowledge, he had never changed the weather, though he admitted that Lucius had an uncanny knack for predicting the weather. But knowing when lightning would come was a far cry from making it happen.

She was mad. They were both mad, for Burrell merely sat there, rather than objecting to this insanity.

"I am Brother Josan," he insisted. He folded his arms across his chest and drew the hood of his sodden cloak over his head.

Ysobel shrugged. "Live or die, it is your choice."

He shook his head, but would not argue. He sat in silence as Ysobel and Burrell continued to bail. Gradually the rain eased, but the skies above remained gray.

The wind had dried his robe, but his flesh was chilled and he shivered. Ysobel's face was pinched and Burrell had moved to sit beside her, ostensibly to balance the boat, but Josan noticed that the two leaned upon one another, sharing what warmth they possessed.

Exhaustion sapped his strength and he slumped in his seat. The sun had set behind the clouds, and in the pitch-darkness he could see nothing—not his hands, nor his companions, nor even the shape of the boat around him.

It was as if he was alone, but he would not be the first to break the silence. He was cold, but he had endured far worse. Come morning, things would be different. As the storm passed, the wind would shift. They would make landfall, and Lady Ysobel would forget her ridiculous ideas.

He would not let her win.

Chapter 7

It was a long, cold night, warmed only by the pressure of Burrell against her side and the band of warmth where his arm encircled her shoulders. It was selfish of her, she knew, but she took comfort from his solid presence and the knowledge of his devotion. Whatever happened, she would not face it alone.

With no stars visible, there was no way to tell if they continued to drift farther from land, or if the waves had changed in their favor. She was unable to see, but every sound was magnified as she listened to the waves lapping against the boat and the sound of Burrell's slow, steady breaths.

Their companion was an unseen presence, the only proof that he was still with them an occasional snort as he roused himself from near sleep, or the sound of him shifting position.

She could not sleep, nor could anyone else. Yet by common accord they bided in silence.

Burrell had spoken briefly to her as they bailed, an effort that had taken hours, and sorely tried her wrists. But the most important questions remained unvoiced. Conscious of their witness, Burrell did not question her, not even in whispers, though she knew he longed to do so.

Burrell must think her mad, or, worse, that her arrogant certainty in her own judgment had condemned them all. She wished she could offer reassurances, but she dare not, not even in whispers. Not when Lucius might overhear.

Both men watched her, and for very different reasons she must not allow either of them to see her doubts.

She had not intended this. When she'd made the decision to try for the boat, she'd only been thinking that the boat was far more seaworthy than a crate. And she'd known that the prevailing currents in these parts would sweep any object toward the keys, where they could make landfall, or be rescued by one of the fishing vessels that ventured out from Skalla each day.

She hadn't counted on the effects of the storm, and the wind-driven waves that pushed them away from land, not toward it. Yet even if she had, she might still have made the leap. *Tylenda* had been doomed; she'd seen that at a glance. An undisciplined crew had doomed her, as much as the shoals. From the first, she'd thought Captain Aldo too lax with his crew, and in the end he had paid the price.

She wondered how many had survived, and if the captain was among them.

And she wondered what it said of her that this was the

third time a ship she'd sailed on had fallen into the Sea Witch's greedy grasp. The first had perished in a storm, along this very coast. The second had been set ablaze at her command. Now the *Tylenda* was a victim of a poor captain, and the ill timing that brought a naval vessel to these waters when the captain was carrying cargo he could not afford to have inspected.

Was it mere coincidence that the navy pursued them? Were they seeking smugglers? Or had they been searching for their lost emperor? And if so, why had Lucius fled rather than seek safety with his own people?

He had come with them—not willingly, perhaps, but in the end he had followed her orders. At least as far as this boat, though he was proving too stubborn to admit his identity. He still clung to the tattered illusion that he was a mere monk.

She did not truly expect that he could influence the weather; instead she'd hoped to provoke him into revealing who he was. But he'd refused, and she'd been made to look a fool.

Though he might change his mind when the reality of their situation finally sank in. Others had survived such voyages before, but it would take skill and a fair share of luck. What meager provisions they could harvest from rainwater and the sea would serve two better than three. And if he was no more than a monk, there was no reason for her to jeopardize her own and Burrell's survival for his sake.

Her bitter thoughts did little to warm her as the night slowly wore on. Stiff and cramped with cold, she half dozed while leaning against Burrell, trusting that he would watch over her.

The next time she opened her eyes, the dark seemed less impenetrable than before. Gradually, as she watched, the black lightened to pale gray. Clouds still covered the sky, but they were thin, and tinged with the pink of dawn in the east.

She nudged Burrell, who mumbled, then came fully awake.

"Dawn," she said.

Burrell rubbed his face with his hands, then looked around at the empty sea. Yesterday, they had seen land to the west, but there was nothing to be seen around them now except the endless waves.

Which were still bearing them east. The clouds disappeared, burned off by the sun, and she felt the first rays of what was bound to be a scorchingly hot day, and there wasn't the faintest breath of wind in the air.

She kicked Lucius's outstretched leg. He jerked, then his head rose from his chest. He blinked, bleary-eyed, but kept his silence.

"We drifted far out to sea last night," she said. "We've missed the northerly current, and are being taken deep into the Great Basin."

She felt Burrell stiffen beside her, but dared not glance over at him. He knew the truth as well as she—it was the emperor that she needed to convince of the perils of their situation.

"We have no provisions, no food, nor water, nor hope of gaining any." Her tone was pitiless. "What do you propose to do?"

"If I die, you die with me," Lucius said.

"It will take some time," she added. "Men have been known to go mad in the hot sun, but you might survive two days without water. Or even three."

It was not quite that hopeless. It was true that they were drifting away from both land and the usual shipping routes, but others had survived such ordeals. They could rig lines to catch fish, and at this time of year there was the hope that passing rain showers would refresh them. The emperor's leather journey bag would hold water, if any rain fell.

Their situation was desperate, but there was a chance they would survive, though she had no intention of telling him that. Not until he told her what she needed to know.

"If you are the monk you claim, we have no reason to keep you alive," she added. "Two can survive better than three. Once Burrell kills you, we'll feast on your flesh and drink your blood to slake our thirst."

"Give me the word," Burrell said, moving his hand to his knife.

It was a brilliant performance, for she knew that Burrell would not kill in cold blood. But the emperor did not know that.

Lucius's face was a mask of outrage, his lips curling in a sneer. "You loathsome bitch," he said. "And you are less than a cur for following her."

She waited, holding his gaze. At last, his eyes dropped. When he spoke, she had to lean forward to catch his whisper.

"What would you have of me?"

"Tell me who you are. Prove to me that you are Lucius," she said.

She had to know. Had to be sure that this was Lucius and that she hadn't risked everything on a fool's errand.

She waited for him to speak, to tell her something that only Lucius would know. But instead he closed his eyes, seeming to fold in on himself. Then, after a long moment, he drew himself erect. His head was tilted at a familiar angle, and the light of arrogance was once more in his eyes.

"Which way is Skalla?" he asked.

Burrell raised his left hand and pointed to the northwest. "That way, about a day's sail in a fast ship," he said.

Lucius shaded his eyes with one hand, as if his gaze could somehow pierce the miles that separated them from land. He took a deep breath, then another.

She grew impatient. Lucius had not spoken his name, nor confirmed her beliefs. She opened her mouth to protest, but Burrell nudged her.

"Wait," he whispered.

Lucius's hands grasped the bench on either side of him. He drew in a final breath, then exhaled it, in a long sigh that lasted for two dozen heartbeats.

Her hair fluttered in the breeze, and she brushed it away from her face.

Lucius smiled grimly.

The shifting breeze strengthened into a wind, blowing out of the southeast. White clouds appeared overheard, where there had been nothing only moments before.

The rowboat spun, propelled by the waves, and began moving northwest, in defiance of the current.

Toward Skalla.

This was not possible.

"By the Sea Witch's tits, I don't believe it," Burrell swore, the common sailor's oath sounding strange coming from his lips.

"As you commanded, Lady Ysobel. Is there anything else you require?"

Lucius's voice dripped honey, but the glare in his eyes revealed his true feelings. He hated her for having forced him to reveal himself.

"My thanks, emperor," she said. Her voice did not tremble but inside she was shocked.

She had sworn that this was Lucius, and convinced Burrell to follow her, but she realized that a small part of her had never truly believed it was he. She had never expected him to capitulate.

Nor that he could casually command the wind and waves to answer his bidding. He was a far more dangerous enemy than she had ever suspected.

Even as she watched, the arrogance faded from his features, and his face assumed a sickly greenish cast. He put one arm around his middle as he swallowed heavily. Then he lurched for the side of the ship.

The rowboat rocked, nearly overbalancing. Burrell threw himself to one side to right it, as she moved toward the emperor, who had begun to vomit over the side.

She reached for him—to keep him from falling over, or to offer comfort, she could not say. But he swatted away her hand.

"Do not touch me. Ever," he said. "You have no right."

She understood his anger, and withdrew her hand. Returning to her seat, she motioned for Burrell to move to the second bench, where he would be close enough to reach for Lucius if he overbalanced.

She needed Lucius. Needed this sorcerous wind for as long as he could hold it.

She would not antagonize him any further.

But when they reached shore, it would be a different matter.

"Drink," Burrell urged. With one hand he held the emperor's head up, while with the other he held a cup to his lips. Tipping the cup, he poured in half a mouthful.

The emperor closed his mouth and swallowed.

"More," Burrell urged, but the emperor shook his head.

"No more," he said. "Leave me be, brother."

Burrell hesitated. If the emperor had merely been suffering from the landsman's disease, then reaching dry land should have settled him. Instead Lucius remained feverish and dangerously dehydrated. But forcing water upon him would cause him to choke and vomit up what little he had already swallowed.

It had happened before.

With a sigh he lowered the emperor's head back to the pillow. He set the cup on the floor, next to the pitcher of water, then sat alongside them.

This room held a narrow cot and a pot for pissing. There were no other furnishings, no chairs, nor space for them. But the cheap lodging meant that no one would pay them any attention. And it had the advantage of being next to the docks, since they'd had to carry the emperor here, dragging him between them.

The emperor had become ill as soon as he did whatever he had done to change their course. Burrell felt queasy just thinking about it. No man should have power over the elements. It was an abomination.

One man might wish for fair weather to guide his journey, but what if every ship's captain could change the weather to suit his mood? To advance his own ship or hinder his competitors?

And if this power could be used as a weapon . . .

Though such efforts were apparently not without cost. While their course had remained northwest, the emperor had been gripped by debilitating spasms. He'd swiftly become dehydrated, his gut cramping even though there was nothing left but bloody bile. By the time a fishing ship had spotted them, he'd sunk into a fever and was unresponsive.

Ysobel had spun a tale of a simple journey between the islands gone awry when they'd been caught in a storm and lost their oars. Her eloquence, along with a double-silver, had inspired their rescuers to cut short their day of fishing and bring them to Skalla.

Once they'd settled into the rooms above the tavern, Ysobel had left, making it clear that Burrell was responsible for caring for the emperor.

He did not begrudge her. Someone had to stay here, and the emperor had made it clear that he would not tolerate her touch. Ysobel had promised to return as soon as she'd made contact with the local factor who handled her house's affairs and arranged a line of credit.

She'd said she would wait before sending any messages. She had not said why, but he knew as well as she.

It was one thing to have found the emperor. It would be another matter entirely if the emperor were to die while in their company.

At least no one seemed to recognize Lucius. If he died, they might be able to pass him off as the monk he had claimed to be, arranging for a quick burial in an unmarked grave.

Even having witnessed his powers, and heard the emperor respond to the name of Lucius, it was still hard for Burrell to believe that this man ruled over a vast empire. He couldn't reconcile the man who had humbly shared a cabin with two dozen other voyagers with the arrogant, self-confident princeling Lady Ysobel had oft described.

Perhaps Ysobel was correct in her belief that Lucius had spent the years of his exile living as one of the Learned Brethren. It would explain how he had learned to play the role so well. And why in the confusion of his illness he kept referring to Burrell as *brother,* and apologizing for causing so much trouble.

He placed a hand on the emperor's forehead, which seemed cooler than it had been. But Burrell had little experience in caring for the ill. He could offer water and keep the man from choking on his own vomit, but that was the extent of his skills. If the emperor was no better by the morning, he would send for a healer and damn the risk.

He decided to let the emperor sleep for an hour, then try again with the water. The tavern had offered fresh well water, and sent up ginger tea, though so far neither had been tolerated. Ysobel had promised to see if there was black root to be found in the markets—a cure that he remembered from his own childhood and the first time he'd set foot aboard a ship.

With nothing else to do, he picked up the emperor's journey bag and began to search through it. There were a handful of letters and a leather-bound book, both still dripping with water, and he spread them open on the floor beside him. The smallclothes he spread out on the windowsill—they could be washed later, or used as rags once they had dried.

The purse at the bottom of the sack was not unexpected, though its contents were surprisingly modest—mostly coppers, with a mere half dozen hexagonal silvers and an equal number of worn gold pieces. The gold coins were stamped with Empress Nerissa's profile on one side, and her father Emperor Aitor II's on the other.

It occurred to him that there were no coins with the new emperor's likeness—the imperial mint continued to use the old dies, even a year after he had assumed the throne.

Perhaps the emperor did not care whose face was on the coins. Or perhaps no one had expected him to live long enough to make it worth the trouble to change them.

He returned the purse to the journey bag. He would have expected an emperor to have an imperial purse, but the sum, while more than a monk might claim, was hardly riches.

The book was mostly ruined. What writing he could make out appeared to be Taresian—a book of stories or perhaps a history, since there were neither sums nor diagrams.

The two scrolls were illegible, the ink having washed away. Journey bags were intended to protect against rain, not meant to endure immersion in the salt sea. But one letter, folded into a square and coated with wax, had survived.

Burrell hesitated—the emperor was not a friend, but neither was he their enemy. The truce that existed between their countries could be said to extend between them as well. And yet, if there was any possibility that the letter would explain why the emperor had fled his capital—

He broke the seal with his knife and unfolded the letter. It was addressed to the master of the library at Xandropol, and bid him offer all due courtesies to Brother Mensah, a fellow scholar.

Mensah. Not Josan. A monk's journey bag, but perhaps both the journey and the bag belonged to another man? And the emperor had taken his place?

Or perhaps he'd intended to change his name yet again, from Lucius to Brother Josan, and finally to Brother Mensah, making it even more difficult for his pursuers to find him.

"He liked you."

Burrell turned, and saw that the emperor was awake—and watching him paw through his possessions. He could feel his face flushing.

"The monk liked you," the emperor repeated. "Thought you kind when you weren't following Lady Ysobel's commands. Well-favored, too. He wouldn't have minded bedding you, if he'd had a chance."

Burrell was stunned into silence. *Liked him?* Surely the emperor didn't mean to imply—

"Of course, I know differently," the emperor said. "You stink of treachery, as does your mistress."

"Lady Ysobel—"

"Is not here," the emperor said, pushing himself upright. "But I see she has found only the best for us. Tell me, as your prisoner, am I allowed food and water? Or must I beg for them?"

Hastily Burrell reached for the cup and filled it with fresh water. "Slowly," he said, as he handed it over.

Heedless of his warning, the emperor drained the cup, then held it out.

"More," he demanded.

It was as if this was a different man. The emperor drank three full cups with no ill effects, then repeated his demand for food.

Burrell was unwilling to leave him alone, but went to the top of the stairs and called down to one of the servants. Her ire at being summoned in such a fashion was soothed by the promise of a pair of coppers if she fetched soup.

The emperor disposed of the soup as quickly as he had the water. He still looked fatigued, but no longer did he appear at death's door.

"Where are we? And how did I come to be your prisoner?" the emperor asked, once his hunger was satisfied.

"We reached Skalla at midday," Burrell said. "It is two days since *Tylenda* sank."

He did not answer the second question. Emperor

Lucius was not precisely his prisoner, but neither could he let the emperor leave this room. Not until Lady Ysobel had returned.

He felt a wistful longing for his days of service in the marines, when his life had been orderly and predictable. True, he'd been frustrated at his inability to advance, and there had been no one whom he trusted in the way that he had come to rely upon Lady Ysobel. But at least back then he'd never been called upon to explain to a reigning emperor why he was being held in a squalid room above a low-class tavern for his own protection.

"Never mind," the emperor said as he settled himself back down on the cot. "I will not bandy words with a slave. I see I must wait for your mistress."

Burrell ignored the insult. He would not be provoked. Deprived of a target, the emperor closed his eyes and seemed to fall back asleep. It remained to be seen if he would be in a better mood when he awoke.

It was dusk when Ysobel returned to the tavern and climbed the stairs that led to the rooms above, which could be rented by the hour or day, depending on the needs and purses of the patrons.

It had taken her longer than expected to find the factor—Skalla was a minor port, so rather than a member of her house who would have known her by sight, Ysobel had to deal with a factor who handled the affairs of a number of trading houses. The woman was duly skeptical when Ysobel first presented herself. Ordinarily the signet ring of a master trader would have been proof of her identity—but not when such a ring was worn by a woman wearing the salt-stained garb of an Ikarian sailor.

Finally, when she'd proven her knowledge of both ciphers and the inner workings of her trading house, the woman's manner had changed. Suddenly she was eager to supply Ysobel with a full purse and a letter of credit that would be accepted anywhere in Skalla.

The woman had also shared the latest news from the capital—or rather the lack of news. Ikaria was calm, the emperor taking advantage of the peace to retreat to his estates to escape the summer heat, as was the custom of his predecessors. There was no word of uprisings or unrest.

Nor of a frantic search for their missing emperor. Though perhaps that news would come on the next ship. Unless Proconsul Zuberi had decided to keep this to himself.

It all depended on why Lucius had fled and what Zuberi knew of it.

She wondered if Lucius would be in any condition to tell them why he had left. The factor had sent her own clerk out to fetch black root, along with clean garb for all of them—simple tunics and leggings that would not be out of place in this part of the city.

The factor had also provided the name of a healer who could be trusted to be discreet, though Ysobel was reluctant to call upon him unless absolutely necessary. A man might well hold his tongue in the face of scandal but be unable to resist sharing the news that he had treated the emperor. If Lucius were alert, he would likely have no wish to reveal his true identity, but if he were out of his mind with fever, who knew what he might let slip?

She pushed open the door and saw that the emperor was asleep, with Burrell sitting on the floor next to him, just as she had left them both.

"How is he?" she asked.

Burrell rose to his feet and drew her over to the window.

"Much improved," Burrell said, but his face was wary. "He was sick when you left, but woke an hour ago, drank his fill, and ate a bowl of soup before falling back asleep."

"Good." It seemed she'd been worried for naught.

"It doesn't seem natural," Burrell said. "To go from being that sick, to being merely tired, in the space of a few hours."

He'd been uneasy with Lucius ever since the emperor had called upon his magic, and this was no different. Burrell would suspect magic in anything the emperor did.

"You think he healed himself," she said, intending to point out why this was absurd.

"I've done it before," Lucius said, interrupting her carefully planned speech. "My efforts may have sapped my strength for a time, but as my powers recovered, so have I."

She turned as Lucius sat up, then swung his legs over the side of the bed. He braced himself for a moment, then stood up.

He looked unkempt, as they all did, after their ordeal at sea. But he no longer appeared to be sick.

"I need to piss," he said.

His crudeness was intended to discomfit her, but she had spent most of her life at sea. It would take far more than mere words to disturb her sensibilities.

"There's a pot here, or Burrell can show you to the privy downstairs," she said. She handed Burrell the bundles that held clean clothing for the two men. "Here, you'll want to put these on."

Lucius looked at the clothing and shook his head. "After I've bathed."

She gritted her teeth. "I'll see what can be arranged," she said.

Her own skin itched with dried salt, but she'd far more important matters than her own comfort on her mind.

Lucius, it seemed, had different priorities.

Still, it would cost nothing to indulge him.

"I'll see if I can find a servant to bring up a basin of water and clean towels," she said. "And when you've changed, we'll talk."

Lucius nodded his agreement, then walked over to the chamber pot.

The servingwoman was old enough to be Ysobel's mother and inclined to be surly, but several coppers inspired her to bring water to Lucius's room and the adjacent room that Ysobel had claimed for herself. Dinner had been ordered as well, so she made quick work of stripping her clothes off and sponging herself down with the rags provided.

She longed for a proper bath and a chance to wash her hair. She'd been spoiled by living in Ikaria so long and promised that tomorrow she'd find an opportunity to visit the public baths for a proper scrub down.

The tunic was slightly too long, but the leggings fit well enough. She tied her hair back in a knot, then knocked on the door to the emperor's room.

"I've taken the room to your right. It has a table and chairs for us all," she said. "Dinner is being fetched. Join me when you're ready."

She returned to her room. The first knock was the servingwoman, this time accompanied by a young boy, who between them brought three trenchers of sausage and stuffed grape leaves swimming in sauce. A pitcher of heavily watered wine and three battered cups completed the service.

It looked heavenly. She forced herself to wait until there was a second knock, and Lucius entered, followed by Burrell.

Mindful for the first time of protocol, she waited for Lucius to sit first, but instead he stood there, watching her.

Burrell eyed the two of them, then, with a sigh, he pulled out the chair in the middle and sat down. The stalemate broken, she and Lucius took their own places.

The food was plain, but hot and filling, reminding her that her last meal had been the pressed barley cakes offered by their rescuers. The wine was sour, but it chased away the taste of salt water that had lingered throughout the day.

Lucius was the first to finish. Pushing away the trencher, he drained his cup, then turned it over.

At the imperial palace, this was the signal that the feast was over, and all guests were required to stop eating. But since he was apparently not standing on protocol, neither would she. Ysobel took her time finishing the last bites of her own dinner.

"Whom have you told of my presence?" Lucius asked.

"No one."

"And why should I believe you?"

Ysobel shrugged. "You were so sick when we arrived that I feared you might die, and suspicion would fall on me."

"So now that you know I will live, what happens next? Did you plan to kill me? Or hold me for ransom?"

In truth she didn't know. Her goal had been to find Lucius and ensure that he wasn't preparing to break the truce between their countries. Having found him, she didn't know what to do.

Emperor Lucius was valuable to her—he was the one who had agreed to the truce between their countries, and he would be the one to decide if the peace held or if there would be war. But an emperor-in-exile, potentially fleeing his homeland, was a different matter.

"I could take you to the federation, to see what you are worth," she said, just to test his reaction.

"I would advise against it."

Lucius was remarkably calm for a man who was at their mercy. This was not the diffidence of the monk nor the arrogance of the man that she had negotiated with, but rather some strange blend of the two.

Was this yet another mask that she was seeing? Or was this, finally, the true face of the emperor?

"Why? Because no one will pay your ransom?" Burrell asked. He spoke the truth, but phrased more cruelly than his wont. She wondered if the two had exchanged words in her absence.

"How do you intend to take me back to the federation?

By sea?" Lucius bared his teeth in the grimace of a predator. "Tell me, are you willing to match your command of your ship against my command of the waves? Or perhaps I will merely call upon the lightning to strike you down."

She jumped as she heard the low rumble of thunder, then realized it was merely someone dragging a heavy chest down the corridor.

Still, Lucius had made his point. His magic made him too dangerous to hold for long.

"What would you propose?"

"Leave me here," he said. "Go on your way and tell no one that you have seen me."

"And where will you go?" she asked.

"Xandropol, perhaps?" Burrell asked.

Lucius glared at Burrell, then turned back to face her. "It is no concern of yours. I am no use to you. Go back to Karystos and play your games with Zuberi if he has a mind."

Zuberi would not treat with her. For all his devotion to the late Empress Nerissa, Zuberi could not countenance any other woman who held power. Even if she returned to Karystos, she could do nothing to help her countrymen. They'd be better served by their ambassador.

"Why must you go to Xandropol?" she asked. Burrell must have discovered something earlier, or he would not have mentioned it otherwise.

"I have my reasons," Lucius said.

Interesting. Xandropol was neutral, and it held nothing of note except the great library of the Learned Brethren. Which explained why he was traveling as a monk but not what drew him there. Was he hoping simply to disappear?

But if so, why not pick somewhere else? A monk would be welcomed in any civilized realm. So why this insistence on Xandropol?

There was more here than met the eye. And having found Lucius once, she was not willing to let him disappear. Not until she knew for certain what he intended.

"In good conscience, I cannot allow you to travel alone. I can offer our protection, and access to swift ships that will cut your journey time in half," she said.

"And what if I do not want your help?"

"Then I will tell everyone that Emperor Lucius was seen in Skalla, on his way to Xandropol."

"If you come with me, you will swear to silence, agreed?"

"Agreed," she said. "As long as you are under my protection."

They exchanged the polite smiles of the court. Both would honor their agreements, but the truce between them was as fragile as the truce between their countries. She fully expected Lucius to try to lose them at the first opportunity.

As for herself, she had promised not to reveal Lucius's destination. But she could still tell her people what they needed to know without breaking her bargain. Namely that the emperor was no longer in Ikaria, and while he did not appear to be plotting war against the federation, there was no telling what his advisors might do in his absence.

Thus warned, her people would be vigilant. As would she.

Chapter 8

The city of Skalla was a study in contrasts. The official buildings were constructed of stone in the imperial style, but the rest of the city was constructed of yellow brick or even timbers, as she'd heard was common in the interior of the northern provinces. The blended architecture reflected the diversity of the inhabitants. As the northern-most imperial port, Skalla was a frequent stopping point for traders from the northern countries, as well as Ikarian merchants who came to meet them.

In winter, with the shipping lanes closed, three strangers would stand out. But in high summer no one paid any attention to them.

Ysobel had used her credit to acquire more suitable lodgings for their party, as well as new clothes. Lucius continued to exhibit a strange blend of arrogance and modesty. He assumed that she would make all the necessary purchases, then insisted that he would dress neither as noble nor merchant, but rather in clothes fitting for a scholar.

At last she'd found clothing suitable for him, as well as richer garb for herself and Burrell. She dressed as befit a Master Trader—discarding tunic and leggings for embroidered shirts and linen pants—some with wide legs, others cropped short for ease of movement when on ship. Burrell, too, found clothes in a similar style, though he preferred more sober fabrics.

Lucius would have been happy enough if she'd found another monk's robe for him, but allowed himself to be convinced that it would raise fewer questions if he dressed as a clerk, in plain tunics of cotton or linen, depending on the occasion.

She'd also found the city baths, and spent a luxurious morning soaking away the accumulated grime of their voyage. Lucius and Burrell had spent equally long in the men's bath—and when Lucius emerged she saw that he'd had his hair cropped short.

Clearly at some point he intended once again to disguise himself as a monk, most likely so he could make his own way, without their aid. But he was not as clever as he supposed. If he did manage to elude them, it would be far easier to track the progress of someone with the distinctive look of a monk than it would if he merely blended into the general populace.

Though how much he would blend in was a question. Blond hair and light eyes were not common in this part of the empire, and once he left the empire he would be immediately spotted as a foreigner. Whether traveler, trader, or monk, he would be noticed.

Though perhaps not recognized. As he walked the streets of Skalla—in carefully supervised excursions—no one gave him a second glance. Few, if any, of the citizens here had ever been south to the great capital Karystos, and of those who had made the journey, if they'd seen the emperor at all, it would have been at a distance.

Even if he stood in the central market and shouted his name, it was doubtful that any would do more than stare at him in pity.

She, at least, could prove her identity. But as a master trader, with five ships sailing under her banner, it was expected that she would travel throughout the Great Basin. The federation traders' guild had outposts to serve its traders at every major port and was expected to handle anything from routine inquiries to the arrival of a master trader who'd lost everything at sea.

If the local factor had heard that Lady Ysobel was serving as envoy in Karystos, she must have assumed that the assignment had come to an end. Trade ruled all in the federation, and even the prestige of being named an envoy would be seen as of lesser status than the prestige of managing the affairs of one's house. Naturally the factor would send word back to the trade guild that Lady Ysobel had been in Skalla, but by then it would not matter.

Lady Ysobel had already sent letters to the ambassador in Karystos and to Lady Felicia, head of the king's council, who had named Ysobel as envoy to the Ikarian Empire. To each she had explained Lucius was not at either of the two imperial retreats, and she was attempting to determine his ultimate destination. She did not believe that he was personally intending to attack the federation, but prudence dictated that precautions should be observed.

She suggested the ambassador could continue to handle the negotiations related to the truce until Lucius returned—or circumstances changed.

Her readers would understand that she meant a change in government. If Lucius were overthrown, there would be no need for Ysobel to return to the capital.

She'd been chosen as envoy not because Lucius trusted her but rather because she'd worked closely with him during his ill-fated rebellion against Empress Nerissa. The king's council had assumed that her knowledge of Lucius would give her an advantage in any negotiations.

She'd thought so as well, but in their first meeting she'd realized how wrong she was. They'd been able to hammer out a truce that both countries could live with, but it had been as if she was negotiating with a stranger who wore Lucius's face.

From the first he'd confounded her. He'd led a bloody rebellion against the empress, then, inexplicably, he'd surrendered, betraying all those who had once professed their allegiance to him.

Confined to Nerissa's palace as a royal prisoner, he'd somehow turned circumstances to his advantage, vaulting from obscurity to become the most unlikely of emperors. Now, at presumably the height of his power, he appeared to be abandoning the throne he had fought so hard to take.

It was a puzzle, but one whose answers lay not in

Skalla, but rather in Lucius's ultimate destination—wherever that might lie.

She found Burrell and Lucius in the common room, the remnants of a plate of olives and bread lying between them. Hooking her foot around a nearby stool, she dragged it over to their table and sat down.

She waved to beckon over the server. "I'll have the same, and we'll have whatever is planned for dinner."

The server frowned at her. "The lamb won't be ready for at least two hours. There's fish from lunch—"

"We'll have fish. And a pitcher of yellow wine, if you have any," she said.

"You found a ship," Burrell said

Ysobel nodded. "There's a merchantman that will suit our needs. I've already been aboard—she's clean, in good repair, and carrying a consignment of cloth bound for Tarsus."

Their other alternative had been a ship of similar size, but that ship was carrying clay jugs of olive oil—a heavier cargo that would result in a slower journey.

"Will we be sharing deck space with caged fowl?" Lucius asked.

The server returned, setting down the wine and a plate of dark olives and fresh bread. Ysobel ate a handful of the small, nutty-tasting olives before tearing off a chunk of bread.

"No ducks," Ysobel said. "They have cabins set aside for use by traders, which they make available to passengers when there are no family members aboard."

The bread was still warm, and she chewed it slowly,

knowing it would be some time before she savored fresh bread again.

"We need to eat, then make our way to the docks. The captain plans to sail at dawn and wants us on board before sunset," she informed them.

They'd spent three days here already, waiting for a suitable ship. After their recent experiences she'd been understandably reluctant to take just any ship. She'd passed on those that were too old, too slow, or whose reputation was tarnished in any way.

It would have been easier if Lucius had allowed her to book passage on a federation vessel; she knew all of the trading houses and their reputations by heart. But Lucius, fearing to find himself completely in her power, had insisted that he would only sail on an Ikarian ship or one from a neutral country.

Their dinner arrived—fillets of a plain fish that had been seasoned with spices, then baked with cheese and raisins. It was a bit dry, but better fare than they could expect aboard ship. After they ate, Ysobel refilled the emperor's wine cup and made a show of topping off her own and Burrell's, though neither had drunk more than was needed to slake their thirst.

"*Griselda* is a good ship, but she's Taresian," Ysobel observed. "We'd make faster time if we had a federation ship."

Sea trade was the lifeblood of the Seddonian Federation, and for generations their captains had jealously guarded their sailing routes—and the secrets of navigation that allowed them to reliably find the swiftest currents, sailing across the breadth of the Great Basin without depending upon landmarks.

"And we'd be swifter still if I could hire a vessel to take us directly to Xandropol," she added.

Chartering such a ship would take all her available credit and a talent for persuasion. But it could be done—and there was a chance that either the ministry or the Ikarian Empire would ultimately see fit to repay her generosity.

Lucius drained his cup. By her count it was at least his fourth, and who knew how many he had consumed before she had arrived. But his eyes were clear and his voice steady as he replied, "If speed were my sole concern, I could navigate for the captain myself."

Her eyebrows rose in disbelief. Rumors claimed Emperor Lucius had been the one who'd discovered the secrets the federation had guarded for so long, then taught them to his own navy. Perhaps she'd been hasty in dismissing those rumors.

"What, you think me unable to perform simple math? Even an emperor can reckon his sums," he added.

"If he wanted the Taresians to share his hard-won knowledge," Burrell said.

Lucius shrugged. "True, there is that to consider. I think it best for all of us if we let the captain of *Griselda* chart his own course."

"As you wish," she said.

Burrell paced the deck, taking advantage of the fair weather to stretch his legs—and to keep his eye upon the emperor, who sat leaning against the capstan, his back cushioned by the coiled ropes. Ostensibly the emperor was their clerk, but he avoided their company whenever he could, and they paid him the courtesy of allowing him his solitude. None of the crew had seen fit to question why he and Ysobel shared one cabin, while their clerk had the other to himself.

The emperor was in the habit of spending most of each day on deck, observing their passage or simply enjoying the fresh air. While in Skalla he'd acquired several books to replace the one he'd lost, and they consumed his attention.

They'd been at sea for four days, and the weather had been near perfect. Burrell carefully avoided thinking about whether such weather was due to good luck or some other influence.

At noon there'd been a faint shadow on the horizon, and as the day wore on it grew clearer until even a landsman could tell that they approached the shores of Tarsus. *Griselda* was bound for the city of Rauma, where they would have to find another ship to take them the rest of the way to Xandropol.

He noticed that the sun had shifted so that it shone full on the emperor's face, which would make it difficult to read. Usually the emperor would change his position throughout the day, so that he was always in the shade, but he hadn't moved for the past hour.

Burrell made a circuit of the deck, pausing to speak to the helmsman, who confirmed that they would arrive in Rauma sometime tomorrow. Then he made another circuit.

The emperor still had not moved.

Before he'd even realized that he'd made up his mind, Burrell crossed the deck. The emperor blinked as Burrell's shadow fell across him, his face flushed from the sun's rays.

Burrell crouched down next to him, putting one arm on the capstan for balance.

"You can see Tarsus on the horizon," he said. "We'll be in Rauma tomorrow if the weather holds."

The emperor nodded, closing the book that he held open on his lap. "I've never seen Tarsus," he said. "When I sailed before, we took the southern route."

Burrell kept his face carefully blank. The emperor's whereabouts during his years of exile was a matter of much speculation. Was it possible that he had spent that time in Xandropol? Was this the reason why he was so anxious to return—because he'd found safety there once before?

Lady Ysobel swore she had encountered Lucius on Txomin's island, which was part of the empire, at a time when he was calling himself Brother Josan and living as a lighthouse keeper. But that did not mean he couldn't have first journeyed to Xandropol.

"Did you wish to return to your cabin? It is almost time for third meal," Burrell said.

The ship's day was divided into four watches, with meals being served before each watch. The only concession made for passengers was that their meals were brought to their cabins. If they weren't there to receive them, they had to wait until the next meal.

The emperor tilted his head slightly and flexed the fingers of his right hand.

"Perhaps I prefer it here," he said.

"Or perhaps you can't move," Burrell said. "Prove to me that you can stand."

"I'll not be treated in this fashion," he said. "Leave me alone, or—"

"Or what? You'll summon the crew? They'll be happy to help me discipline my clerk."

The emperor glared.

"Come, strike me if you dare," Burrell goaded him.

The emperor continued to glare at him for the space of several heartbeats, then his expression changed to one of ruefulness. "Would that I could," he said, his voice softer than it had been before.

Burrell nodded slowly, his suspicions confirmed. "Shall I summon help?" A ship of this size wouldn't have a healer, but there would be one of the mates assigned the task of caring for the crew's ills—splinting broken limbs, sewing up cuts, and treating them for whatever ailments they caught while in port.

"And what can he do that all of the imperial physicians could not?"

Burrell rocked back on his heels. He was not used to feeling so helpless. If the emperor were suffering from a malady, there was little that they could do to help.

"Leave me alone," Lucius commanded. "This will pass. It always does."

Lucius's words were brave, but surely that must be a mask. If Burrell were the one who was paralyzed, he would be terrified.

"If I help you stand, can you walk?"

Lucius thought it over for a moment, looking hard at his feet. First one, then the other leg, twitched. "Maybe," he said. "But I'd rather wait."

"If you wait here, you will fry in the sun," Burrell said. "And then you'll be of no use to any of us."

He rose, and found one of the crew idling. Explaining that his clerk had been overcome by the heat, he enlisted the man's help. They pulled Lucius upright, then slung one of his arms over each of their shoulders, bearing most of his weight. With their help, the emperor was able to walk slowly to his cabin.

Burrell settled him into bed, thanking the sailor for his help.

"This will pass, you say?" Burrell asked, after the sailor had departed.

"It always has before," he replied. He did not thank Burrell for his help.

The emperor turned his face to the wall and Burrell took the hint. Closing the door to Lucius's cabin behind him, he went to find Lady Ysobel. If Lucius's illness was getting worse, then she needed to be informed.

He will tell Lady Ysobel, Josan thought.

Tell her what? That we are ill? She knows that already.

Lucius's voice was clear in his mind, though his body was still gripped by a chill numbness. He had been able to feel Lucius's spirit, but Lucius had not been able to take control. It had been Josan who spoke to Burrell, and

Josan who managed to stumble back to the cabin with the aid of his two helpers.

They are lovers, you know. Can't you picture the two of them together? I wonder if she is as commanding in bed as she is out of it? Lucius mused.

The images that came to mind stirred both of them, in different ways. This body had never lain with a man, but Josan still remembered what it felt like, and to himself, at least, admitted that he would enjoy letting his hands reacquaint themselves with firm muscles and silky flesh.

Lucius, though he despised Lady Ysobel's politics, nonetheless was intrigued by her exotic beauty—a rare combination of strength and grace, her dark hair and golden skin an exotic delight.

Do you think they would take us to bed?

Josan was shocked. *Which of them?*

Both, of course, Lucius retorted. *Then each of us would have what we wanted.*

Josan swallowed, hard. It had been so long since he had felt the touch of a lover ...

And then realized that Lucius had used his own longings to distract Josan.

Enough, Josan thought. *I will not be so easily distracted. You've been using magic to speed this ship's passage, haven't you?*

And what of it? The journey is taking too long. We should be in Xandropol by now.

He could taste Lucius's frustration, and underneath it fear. This was the first time since leaving Karystos that he and Lucius had been able to converse, though Lucius had taken control of their shared body at least twice. First when they'd been shipwrecked and it had been Lucius who'd summoned the wind that bore them to land. Later he'd surfaced in Skalla, when Josan had been lost in fever dreams, healing their shared body. But since then his possessions had been brief, lasting minutes rather than hours.

Lucius was growing weaker. Josan could feel his spirit fading. But as Lucius weakened, so did his body.

If Lucius's spirit were to disappear entirely, Josan might be free . . . But he swiftly squashed that shameful thought. It was more likely that this body would wither and die once Lucius's spirit faded.

You must save your strength, Josan told him. *Once we are in Xandropol, we will unravel this spell.*

And then what? Will I be free to return home? Will I still have an empire to rule? Or do you plan to live there, as Brother Josan of Xandropol?

It was the question that haunted them both. Josan did not like Lucius, but he respected him enough not to offer hollow reassurances.

If you exhaust yourself before Xandropol, I will make those decisions without you, Josan pointed out. *If you wish to reign once more as Emperor Lucius, you would be wise to hoard your strength.*

You are neither my father nor my elder brother, to order me about, Lucius said. But his presence diminished, and Josan could feel his nerves tingling as sensation returned once more to his limbs.

By the time a seaman arrived with dinner, Josan was fully recovered. He ate heartily, then pulled out a blank parchment and his writing case. They would soon arrive in Rauma, and he had his own preparations to make. Ones that did not involve being dependent upon Lady Ysobel's charity.

Rauma was a bustling port, far larger than Skalla had been, with ships of all sizes and descriptions tied up to her wharves. *Griselda* waited in harbor for several hours until a berth was freed for her. As soon as they could, Josan and his companions made their way off the ship, dodging sailors who were opening hatches and rigging hoists to unload their cargo.

After Josan's attack yesterday, Burrell had stopped by that night to inquire after his health, and Josan had been careful to give the impression that he was recovering, but still weak. He'd feigned the same at breakfast this morning. As he descended the gangplank, it was with a slow, hesitant gait.

Lady Ysobel watched him when she thought he was not looking. Burrell simply moved close and offered his arm. Emperor Lucius would have been affronted by such liberties, so Josan made certain to glare at Burrell before reluctantly accepting his support.

He was tired of playing the part of Lucius, but it was what they expected of him. And he dared not risk their discovering the truth.

"We need a ship for Xandropol. A fast ship, not a coastal trader that will pause at every inlet and cove for the next hundred miles," Josan said.

"I know what we need," Lady Ysobel replied. "I will go to the harbormaster to find out what ships are available.

He will not welcome a crowd, so you and Burrell may wait for me."

She thought him too weak to continue. At their mercy. And if he stayed with them, she would be right.

Josan scorned the first two taverns that Ysobel suggested as too disreputable before agreeing to the suggestion of a teahouse, which had tables both outside and in, where merchants and ships' officers sat sipping hot spiced beverages and conducting their affairs.

Ysobel left them, promising to return shortly. Josan felt his hands shake. This would be his best chance for escape. Burrell must have mistaken his nervousness for illness. Without prompting he suggested that they hire a private room rather than waiting in the common room.

Josan settled himself, sending Burrell out to fetch a mug of spiced kava and the sweet nut rolls for which Tarsus was famous. But when Burrell returned with the treats, Josan fumbled with the roll with his right hand, rather than tearing it apart with two hands as was customary. Petulantly he tossed it aside.

Burrell's face was carefully blank, as he took in the evidence that the emperor was once more paralyzed.

It was not long before Ysobel joined them. She and Burrell exchanged glances, communicating without words. It seemed more proof for Lucius's theory that the two were lovers, though Josan was not certain. Perhaps they were, or perhaps they had merely been together for so long that they could anticipate each other.

"There are two choices in harbor—a merchantman bound for his home port in Tyrns who swears he will arrive within the fortnight, and we can find another ship there to take us the rest of the way. Or there's a pilgrim ship with a Taresian captain bound for Xandropol, but they have four ports of call along the way, and will take at least three weeks," Lady Ysobel said.

Josan frowned, pretending to think over the choices. "What are our chances of finding a ship when we reach Tyrns? Is it a well-frequented port, or will we have to wait for days to find a suitable ship?"

Ysobel shrugged. "His home is one of the smaller ports, so there is no guarantee," she said. "Or there's the federation ship *Hypatia*, leaving this afternoon for Vidrun. I do not know her, but she's a three-master, and looks to be a fast ship. I'm sure I can persuade her captain to stop in Xandropol."

"No," Josan said. "Not *Hypatia*."

"Then I recommend the merchantman," Ysobel said. "And we can take our chances in Tyrns."

Josan gave a one-shouldered shrug. "So be it," he said. "When does she sail?"

"Tomorrow. I'll go make the arrangements," she said.

That left him alone with Burrell. Josan closed his eyes and leaned up against the wall. "We'll need a place for the night," Josan said. "Ask our host if he can recommend somewhere. Clean, but not too far from here."

He did not move, careful to give the impression of great frailty.

He heard the door open, then close again. Josan waited for the space of two dozen heartbeats, then opened his eyes.

He was alone.

Swiftly he stood, crossing over to the corner where

Burrell had placed their meager luggage. Opening Burrell's journey bag, he took out one of Burrell's embroidered shirts. Stripping off his tunic, he pulled the shirt over his head.

It was a decent fit. He hunted till he found a pair of trousers with cropped legs, then put them on. The cropping would make it less obvious that they were made for a man who was two inches shorter than he was.

Shoving Burrell's pack behind Ysobel's, he grabbed his own and moved to the door. He cracked it open and peered into the corridor, but there was no one to be seen. He longed to run but instead walked down the corridor with measured stride, until he reached the door that led to the terrace outside.

There he disappeared into the crowds—just another Ikarian merchant going about his affairs. He walked for ten minutes before he stopped a sailor, and asked, "Do you know the federation ship *Hypatia*?"

The sailor shook his head, though he gladly took a copper to bring a scroll to the harbormaster's office.

He tried a merchant next, but the man refused even to hear him out. At last a dock laborer nodded, holding his hand out for a coin. Josan dropped a copper in his outstretched palm, wincing as he noticed that the laborer was missing two fingers on that hand.

"She's tied at the end of sixth wharf," his informant said.

"Which one is sixth wharf?"

The laborer shook his head, amazed by such ignorance, and spit over the rail into the filthy harbor. "Same as in any civilized port. Sixth from the dawn side," he explained.

Josan thanked him, handing over another copper for the man's troubles.

At any moment he expected to hear voices raised in pursuit, but he reached the sixth wharf without interference. There were four vessels tied up alongside, and at the end, a ship with the head of a fantastic beast carved out of its prow. *Hypatia* was painted in gold leaf along the bow, an ostentatious sign of wealth.

Even to his inexperienced eyes, the ship had the look of one that was ready to sail. There were no laborers loading or unloading cargo, and the hatches were all closed shut. A gangplank connected the ship with the wharf, and Josan made his way to the top.

A white-haired woman barred his way. "We're done with trade for this trip. The captain doesn't care how important your cargo is," she said.

"I have no cargo," he explained. "Nonetheless, I beg a moment of his time."

She looked him over. "Your name?"

He hesitated. He hadn't thought of this, but he needed a name to give these people.

"Josan," he said. It was foolish, but having lived as Lucius for so long, he was not willing to relinquish his own name. "Josan of Karystos."

"Wait," she said.

She disappeared below and returned a few moments later accompanied by a middle-aged man, who was built like one of the ship's masts, his solid bulk topped with a surprisingly intelligent face.

"Captain Zorion, of *Hypatia,* in service to the house of Arles," he said.

"Josan of Karystos," he said. It was nearly true. "May I have five minutes of your time?"

"Five minutes, no more," Zorion said. "As soon as my first gets back with our sailing papers, we leave."

"Agreed. But in private," Josan said.

Zorion's expression did not change. "Amelie, five minutes, and if Edmond isn't back by then, fetch him yourself."

Captain Zorion led him over to the wheelhouse, which was empty while they were tied up to the wharf.

"What do you want?" he asked.

"Passage for myself, to Xandropol," Josan said.

Zorion shook his head. "I don't take passengers, and I'm not going to Xandropol." His eyes moved past Josan, caught by some activity on deck, and he began to move away.

"Wait," Josan said, grasping Zorion's arm. "I am prepared to pay."

Reaching inside his borrowed shirt, he pulled at the cord that was tied around his neck and pulled up a small leather bag. Opening the bag, he tipped a pair of rubies into his palm and held it out.

Zorion's gaze traveled from the rubies to Josan's face, then back again. "I need no trouble with the law," he said. "Not here, and not in Xandropol."

"I am not a criminal," Josan said. "The reasons I travel are my own. I must reach Xandropol without delay. These are yours if you agree to take me."

Zorion picked up the rubies, holding each up to the light in turn.

The stones were flawless, fit for an empress. Most of Nerissa's jewelry was still held in trust by the functionaries, but a few pieces had remained in her suite, overlooked in the chaos of preparing for the new emperor. When Josan had found the necklace he had first hid it, later surreptitiously taking it apart, gathering a dozen dark rubies. Other pieces yielded brilliant diamonds and polished amber luck stones.

Burrell had searched Josan's pack and found his purse—which was all the coin Josan could lay his hands on. An emperor did not need coins of his own, after all. But jewels were another matter, and Josan had hidden them within the thick cord that he wore around the waist of his monk's robe, carefully teasing them free when he was in his cabin on *Griselda*.

"For a few more of these, you could hire any ship," Zorion said.

Josan had a handful of gems, but had only placed three rubies in the pouch. He did not want to give an appearance of wealth, but rather one of a man who was bargaining away the last valuable things that he owned.

"Do we have a bargain?" Josan asked.

Amelie's head appeared in the doorway. "Edmond's back," she said. "We're ready to cast off."

Zorion's fist closed over the rubies. "Tell Edmond that he's bunking in with the sailing master. We've a passenger joining us."

"Thank you," Josan said.

"Your word that there's no trouble," Zorion said.

"I swear by all that I am that I am a free man on lawful business," Josan said.

"That's good enough for me," Zorion replied.

That, and a pair of rubies that might or might not make their way onto the ship's manifest. Though perhaps not all Seddonians were as mercenary as Lady Ysobel had shown herself to be.

Josan allowed himself to be led belowdecks, and accepted Amelie's admonishments that he was to keep out of the crew's way. He need only endure a fortnight longer, he promised his twin selves. Then they would be in Karystos.

Somewhere within the great library there would be the answers they needed.

Chapter 9

"Ysobel! Ysobel!"

She turned at the shouts and saw Burrell waving at her from the upper tier of the docks. He waited until she waved back, then dodged to his left, pushing folks aside as he clambered down the stairs that led from the upper tier where the merchants were located to the wharves themselves.

"He's gone," Burrell said, breathing hard and sweating from his haste.

"When?

"A few minutes after you left," Burrell said. "He asked me to find a room for the night where we could rest—I thought he wanted to sleep. I was gone no more than ten minutes, I swear, but he had vanished."

Ten minutes was nine minutes too long. If Lucius had been feigning his illness, he could have simply walked out.

"No one saw him leave, but the place was so busy it's

doubtful they would have noticed. I've been looking for him ever since," he said.

It had taken her over an hour to find the captain of the merchant ship and negotiate passage for three. Lucius could be anywhere in Rauma by now.

"Is there a monastery here?"

"No. The Learned Brethren are known here, but the closest monastery is two days' ride inland."

He would not have gone inland.

"Then he is hiding from us. Or trying to find his own passage," Ysobel said.

"Or both."

"I'll check the pilgrim ship, and with the harbormaster again, in case he makes his own inquiries," she said. "You check the taverns and the hostels, anywhere he might seek shelter. Ask for him by description and remember he may have resumed his monk's robe."

"At once," Burrell said. "I'll send word to the teahouse if I find him. If not, I'll meet you there—at sunset?"

"At sunset," she agreed. If they had not found him by then, they would need a new strategy.

She searched the docks till her feet grew weary, but no one recalled seeing anyone matching Lucius's description. He'd probably donned his tattered robe as soon as he could and pulled the cowl over his face, though those she questioned did not recall seeing a monk.

The harbormaster was not pleased to be disturbed as high tide approached, when dozens of ships were demanding his permission to set sail. His clerk was even busier, but at last unbent enough to swear that she was the only one who had asked about ships bound for Xandropol.

She searched the pilgrim ship herself, claiming to be in pursuit of a runaway apprentice, but he was not there. Though he might be waiting, elsewhere, planning to board before they left tomorrow.

And what would she do when they found Lucius? Obviously reasoning with him had failed, and she could hardly kidnap him—not without a ship of her own to hold him on.

He was too old to be claimed as kin or apprentice, that ruse only worked if no one had seen him. If she claimed he was a clerk who had stolen from her, they would likely insist on imprisoning him here rather than releasing him to her custody.

They would have to follow him—buy passage on whatever ship he chose. He had coin enough to book passage on a ship bound for Xandropol, but not enough to hire a ship to suit his desire.

If he was still bound for Xandropol. As her search continued to be fruitless, she wondered if he had ever intended to go there or simply allowed them to believe that was his destination. Perhaps he didn't care where he went, so long as he left Ikaria, and the long reach of his enemies.

She knew that Burrell would blame himself, but the fault was hers as well. Burrell had felt sorry for Lucius, and in his pity had forgotten to be suspicious. It was only at times like this that she was reminded that he had not been born into a trader's house. From birth, a trader's child learned that no fruit was ever as fresh as the seller claimed, no gem as rare, no silk as soft. There was deception everywhere, as much in what was not said as what was.

She would not have left Lucius alone, not for any reason. Not even if he appeared to be unconscious.

Lucius had seen Burrell's weakness and exploited it.

But where had he gone? She thought about offering a reward, but already her persistent questions had drawn more attention than she was comfortable with. She did not want the harbormaster or guild representatives to begin asking questions about her presence here.

Returning to the teahouse, she saw that the patrons had changed. Serious business had been put aside in favor of dinner, as small plates with a variety of delicacies crammed tables that had earlier been covered with account books and bills of lading.

The host chased after Ysobel, demanding a silver for keeping the private room longer than the agreed-upon time. The room was empty, but surprisingly their possessions were still inside, so Ysobel paid the silver.

The host, who could probably have been bargained down to half a silver if she'd had the patience, shook his head when asked if he'd received any messages for her. But he did come back with fresh tea and three ceramic cups, insisting that they were included in the price of the room.

Burrell joined her a quarter of an hour later.

"No sign of him," he said. "I checked every tavern house and lodging on the upper tier, and in the lanes nearby. There are other places in Rauma where he might go—"

"But we can hardly search an entire city," Ysobel said.

Burrell's face was grim, as he ran one hand through his hair in an unusual sign of nervousness. "I'm sorry to have failed you," he said.

"I should have warned you he might try something—"

"And I should have known that he was not as ill as he claimed," Burrell interrupted.

A thought occurred to her. "Do you think he was feigning his illness all this time?"

Burrell considered her suggestion for a long moment. "No. We both saw how weak he was after the shipwreck. And the emperor's attacks were well-known in Karystos."

"Assuming he is well for the moment, where will he go?"

"To the monks?" Burrell offered.

If Lucius had been a monk, he could expect the Learned Brethren to offer him shelter and arrange passage to the next monastery along his route. It would be a slow way to travel, but one that did not require riches, merely the ability to convincingly pass himself off as a monk.

He could hide himself anywhere that the Learned Brethren held sway. And as long as he stayed a monk, within the cloistered walls of scholarship, it would be difficult if not impossible for an outsider to find him.

It was likely that this was how he had passed the years of his exile. But she did not think he intended to do so again.

If she assumed Xandropol was his destination, the question was why? Merely to visit the great library and to live with the scholars there?

"What if he is going to Xandropol to meet someone?" Ysobel mused. "Brother Nikos was exiled to Xandropol, at the emperor's command."

"Brother Nikos never arrived there," Burrell said. "Or so our intelligence has reported. And why would an emperor travel the length of the Great Basin simply to meet with one of his old enemies?"

Why indeed?

"When the old king was ill, Prince Bayard sent for a physician trained at the college in Xandropol. What if Lucius is bound not for the library, but to consult with the physicians there?" Burrell suggested.

"Why wouldn't he send for a physician, as Bayard did?"

Burrell shrugged. "Perhaps there was not time? Or perhaps his enemies prefer him weak. A dying emperor could well be exactly what Proconsul Zuberi wants."

It made a strange kind of sense. Nothing less than the prospect of his own death could have made Lucius leave his empire behind. Her mistake had been in thinking that he was fleeing *from* the threat, rather than fleeing *toward* his salvation.

It was a cruel choice. Keep his throne and die as emperor, or give up everything in hope of finding a cure in Xandropol.

Strange that a man who ruled over countless subjects should have to flee with no one by his side, not even a single trusted servant to help him in his time of need. She felt the first inklings of pity but swiftly brushed them aside.

She would not let her feelings blind her.

"The tide is slack and no ship will be allowed to leave

before dawn," Ysobel said. "So in the morning we check the docks again and find out which ship he plans to take."

"At least we still have our packs," Burrell said.

Though replacing the contents of the packs would have been merely inconvenient—anything that they could not live without they carried on their persons. The packs merely held changes of clothing, soap for washing, and a cup and bowl for shared meals.

Lucius had taken his pack with him, with its added burden of books and writing materials, while hers was still in the corner, with Burrell's showing underneath.

She drained her tea. "We need a place for the night," she said.

"The host gave me suggestions earlier," Burrell said. "I've already visited them, looking for Lucius."

"Then we check them again," Ysobel said. "In case he has ventured out of hiding."

Burrell picked up her pack and handed it to her, then picked up his own.

As he lifted it, the flap fell open.

He set it on the table, and swiftly sorted through the contents. "One of the shirts is missing. And a pair of pants."

Laughter welled up inside her.

"The viper. He's wearing my pants," Burrell said, his face darkening with anger.

Ysobel laughed aloud at the absurdity of it all. The emperor of Ikaria, fleeing in stolen pants. It was better than any farce—and she had to laugh, or scream with frustration.

Burrell glared, his outrage undimmed, until at last she sobered, wiping her eyes.

"We asked the wrong questions," she explained. "We asked after a clerk, or a monk."

"If they saw him, they saw a merchant," Burrell said. "They wouldn't know him for an Ikarian, not wearing those."

Lucius was cleverer than she had imagined. Or more desperate.

And suddenly she realized. "He's not here. He's already left, on *Hypatia*," she said.

How could she have been so blind?

"He swore he wouldn't sail on a federation vessel," Burrell said.

"With us. He wouldn't sail with us."

It wasn't the whole of the federation that he mistrusted—merely her. The captain of *Hypatia* would have no reason to suspect that his passenger was anything other than he claimed to be.

"Lucius had coins for Vidrun, but not enough to persuade the captain to add Xandropol to his ports of call," Burrell said.

"Maybe he had more coins than we knew, or he found another way to persuade the captain to do his bidding," Ysobel said. It did not matter.

"So what now?"

"We find our own ship. We've come too far to stop now. We may not catch *Hypatia,* but we'll be hard on her heels."

And since Lucius had broken his agreement, she was no longer bound to silence. She could tell her countrymen where to search for the missing emperor—and ensure that whatever he planned, they were not caught unprepared.

Septimus arrived at Proconsul Zuberi's office just as the fifth hour was struck. The clerk, scribbling away at his accounts, did not even look up as Septimus approached.

"The proconsul is expecting me," he said.

"Of course, admiral," the clerk said, his eyes still fixed on his work. "If you would sit . . ."

Septimus moved to one side but did not sit. He did enough sitting in his own offices. Last year, when Emperor Lucius had offered him command of the imperial navy, Septimus had anticipated a life spent largely at sea. But while he had led a squadron to a remarkable victory over the federation ships that had encroached upon their waters, since then he had spent more time landbound than he had aboard a ship. He might as well be one of Zuberi's clerks.

Certainly Zuberi treated him as such. Zuberi had set the time for this meeting, but it was his custom to make Septimus wait. A petty trick, meant to remind Septimus of their relative importance. The proconsul spoke with the voice of the emperor, while Septimus was tolerated because Zuberi could find no other to take his place.

Though Septimus knew he could not complain overmuch. His own father, Septimus the Elder, had been executed for treason in the central square not far from here—one of the dozens put to death by Empress Nerissa for conspiring to overthrow her and restore the rule of the old blood.

Though innocent of treason, Septimus had fled Nerissa's wrath. It had taken guarantees of his safety from both Lucius and his council to persuade Septimus to return to Ikaria and accept their offer of command over the imperial navy. Since then, Zuberi did everything he could to remind Septimus that he owed his very life to the indulgence of the council.

If Zuberi's illegitimate nephew Chenzira had had the experience to match his connections, he would have been named admiral instead. But Chenzira was too young and too inexperienced. He had only recently been given command of his own ship, and it would be years before the fleet would willingly follow him.

Though Chenzira was likely out of his uncle's favor as well, since it was on his ship that the emperor had disappeared.

Such musings occupied Septimus as the bells signaled the quarter hour, then the half. As the last chime of the half sounded, the clerk rose and opened the door to Zuberi's private office.

"You may go in," the clerk said.

As Septimus had expected, Zuberi was alone when he entered the inner office. There'd been no reason for the delay, but Septimus would not give Zuberi the satisfaction of responding to the insult. He simply stored it away in his memory. When the tide turned in his favor, he would repay Zuberi threefold.

"No news of the emperor?" Zuberi asked.

Septimus took a seat opposite the proconsul, arranging the folds of his robe around him. Custom dictated that the admiral wear the robes of the court while in Karystos; his uniform was only worn aboard ship, or in times of war. In practice this meant that he was indistinguishable from any other member of the emperor's court, merely another face among the crowd.

Generals wore their uniform on all occasions of state, but the empire had long favored the army over the navy, though at least Lucius did not seem to share his predecessors' blindness.

But Lucius was not here, which was why Zuberi had summoned him.

"No news of the emperor," Septimus agreed. If there had been news, he would have rushed here at once, not bothering to wait for an appointment. "The last of the ships in question has been found—or rather, we know what happened to it. *Tylenda* was spotted off the keys, but when approached, she tried to run for shore. She wrecked on the shoals, and many aboard drowned before the rowboats from our ship were able to approach and bear off survivors."

Zuberi's eyes sharpened. "Why did they attempt to flee?"

"Smugglers," Septimus said. "They'd a cargo of untaxed oil on board. The captain was hanged, and his officers imprisoned."

"And you are certain the emperor was not aboard?"

"As certain as I can be. The survivors were all questioned, and there were several passengers who were lost in the wreck, but none fit the description of the emperor," Septimus said. "Nor of Lady Ysobel."

At the mention of Lady Ysobel, Zuberi frowned.

"*Tylenda* was a mere coastal trader, her passengers from the lower classes who could afford no better," Septimus said. "It is unlikely either the emperor or Lady Ysobel would have been aboard."

"So we do not know where the emperor is," Zuberi said.

"It would be better if we had some idea of his destination," Septimus said. "Or if you would allow me to inform my captains that they are seeking the emperor? A mere description isn't quite the same, especially if he has altered his appearance."

"No," Zuberi replied. He had refused this request before. All Septimus had been able to do was give his captains a list of vessels that had sailed from Karystos on the days in question along with their destinations, and request that each of those vessels be boarded and searched.

A half dozen men had already been escorted to Karystos, simply because they happened to be tall, with blond hair, blue eyes, and a noble visage. Septimus had apologized to each man and let him go.

If the emperor had left Karystos by sea, he must have disembarked before his ship was found and searched.

Or, as Septimus suspected, he could have left the city by horseback, or simply walked out through her gates.

If he had left at all. The ugly possibility of assassination weighed on his mind, though Zuberi seemed convinced that the emperor was alive. Perhaps he had proof that he would not share.

At first, Zuberi had implied that the emperor might have been kidnapped by Lady Ysobel, but his later remarks had led Septimus to suspect that the emperor might have left of his own volition. But why he would simply disappear was a mystery. Chenzira would have sailed the emperor anywhere he wished to go, and surely the functionaries would have been equally as willing to arrange a journey for him overland.

Unless, of course, the emperor did not trust them.

"You will inform me the moment you have news," Zuberi said.

"Of course," Septimus replied. "I will not rest until I know the emperor is safe."

Lucius was terrified. Never before had he felt so helpless, at the mercy of malicious fate. He gathered all his will together and called out to Josan, but the monk did not respond.

His body was lying in his bunk, as *Hypatia* sailed toward Xandropol. It was midday, but the monk had yet to stir. The tiny cabin was hot and airless, but he did not move to open the porthole. He had not even left the bed to empty his bladder.

This was not the seasickness that had plagued him during his earlier voyages. This was something else, something that paralyzed them both.

Lucius could feel nothing, it was as if his mind swam in a void. He could see, and hear, but he could not so much as turn his own head.

Nor could he feel the monk's mind presence. It was as if he had vanished.

He wondered if the monk was experiencing the same sensations—cut off from their shared body, his mind drifting helplessly.

What would happen if neither could take control of his body? Would he starve because he was unable to feed himself?

Would he die because he forgot to breathe?

Lucius strained, but he could not banish himself. The unknowingness that had once been his refuge had also forsaken him. He could not act, but neither could he rest.

It was torture, one far more insidious than any performed in the bowels of the imperial palace. There was neither the respite of unconsciousness nor the chance to bargain for relief. He had simply to endure, hour after hour, knowing himself to be completely at the mercy of whoever might come into his cabin.

Knowing, too, that he was dying.

They were dying. For if this body perished, both their spirits would be set free.

He had once hoped for such death—better that this body died than having the monk take sole possession, banishing Lucius to the unknowingness in which he had passed the years of his exile.

But he had pictured a quick death, not the uncertain agony of wondering if each breath would be his last.

He tried again, straining to reach out, to connect with his limbs. Cursing the monks who had done this to him. To them both.

But there was nothing. He was too weak.

He could do nothing but wait. Wait, and hope that the monk recovered before this body failed them.

And hope that no one decided to see how many more gems their passenger had brought aboard.

It would be simple to kill him—a mere hand over his mouth, and he would die, helpless as any babe.

If only the monk had closed their eyes before he lost control. He had no desire to watch as death approached.

They were two days out of Rauma when his passenger made his first appearance on deck. Captain Zorion watched from the wheelhouse as Josan of Karystos made his way to the prow of the ship, noticing that he clutched the rail with his left hand, and his right leg dragged with each step.

He hadn't been lame when he came aboard.

Edmond, who was first in command after the captain, looked up from the charts to see what had caught Zorion's attention.

"He wasn't at morning meal," Edmond said. "Nor at midday, or so I have been told."

Passengers were a rarity on *Hypatia*. If Josan had been a member of the house of Arles or one of its allies, he would have been served meals in his cabin, or, more likely, invited to join Zorion in the captain's quarters. Those few others who took passage were expected to eat in the watch room with the junior officers, Edmond among them.

"Perhaps the sea has distressed him," Zorion offered.

"A trader who becomes unwell at sea?" Edmond scoffed.

"He did not claim to be a trader."

"He speaks the trade tongue as one born on Navar," Edmond said. "And he wears the clothes of a merchant rather than those of a landsman."

"Which means nothing."

"It is not the landsman's sickness. It is some other illness that plagues him," Edmond insisted.

He was probably right.

"You have our course?" Zorion asked. "Be careful not to let the current pull us too far south. We're headed for Xandropol, not Vidrun."

"Our cargo is due in Vidrun by the new moon," Edmond said. "My father will not like it if we break the contract."

Zorion cuffed the back of Edmond's head for the impertinence. "And your father would like it even less if we turned aside the chance for profit," Zorion said. "We can bring our passenger to Xandropol and still have the cargo in the warehouses at Vidrun before the new moon."

"Of course, captain," Edmond said, ducking his head.

Zorion bit back a sigh. Edmond was a good lad, but he was just that. A boy barely grown into manhood. Too young and lacking in self-confidence to serve as captain, which was why the house of Arles had hired Zorion, who'd been a captain on the Great Basin before Edmond was born.

It seemed to be Zorion's fate to train up the young. Lady Ysobel had been even younger than Edmond when she'd come into possession of her first ship and hired Zorion to take command. She'd sailed that season with him, first as apprentice, then as mate, ending it as first. The next season she'd sailed the first trading voyage as captain with him a watchful first at her side. Returning to the federation, she'd purchased a second ship, starting a fledgling trading house as she captained one ship, while he commanded the other.

He'd done a fine job training her up—he'd taught her everything she needed to know. Including how to release him from her service when he'd displeased her.

And now his duty was to another house. To train this boy into a man and make sure that nothing went wrong on a routine voyage. Which meant he needed to speak to his passenger.

"Likely it is nothing more than a bellyache, from too long spent ashore, indulging himself in port," Zorion said. "But it does no harm to be certain."

As he left the wheelhouse, he was approached by Merle, one of the seamen inspecting the spare topsail that was currently spread out on the foredeck.

"Captain, looks like rats got into it since we checked it last—perhaps in harbor," Merle said, fingering two small tears. "I think we need to check all of the gear stored in that hold."

A good catch by a conscientious sailor, but Zorion said nothing.

"Captain?" Merle repeated.

"Edmond has the watch—you should discuss it with him," Zorion said.

"Of course," Merle said. "Just thought you should know, since you were here and all."

"Tell Edmond," Zorion repeated.

He knew why Merle had stopped him. It was not merely because Zorion was walking by, but because Merle, like many of the sailors, had yet to put their trust in Edmond. When faced with an issue that could mean life or death, they would ignore the protocol that said they should speak with the watch officer first, and he would determine what and when to tell the captain.

If it had been Amelie on the watch, Merle would have gone to her without hesitation. But Edmond had still to earn his crew's trust

Time. It would take time, and demonstration of competence. In a way, this was a good test. Removing the gear from the hold, inspecting it, and stowing it back was a labor-intensive task that would require him to rouse sailors who were off watch to help. If Edmond came to Zorion before issuing those orders, it would be a clear sign that he still lacked confidence in his own judgment.

As he made his measured way to the prow, Zorion listened with one ear. Just as he neared their passenger, he heard the bell that summoned those off duty to the deck.

Zorion smiled.

And then felt the grin slip from his lips as Josan turned to face him.

Josan braced himself against the side of the ship, clutching the rail with both arms to steady himself.

"Captain?" His voice was steady, but his face was pale, his eyes sunken.

"My crew was concerned that you might be unwell," Zorion said. "You have missed your meals today."

Josan shrugged. "I wasn't hungry."

"So this is a sudden illness? Or did you know you were ill before we left Rauma?"

If this man had brought a plague aboard his ship—

"I am no risk to you, nor your crew," Josan said. "My troubles are mine alone. I thank you for your concern, but I assure you it is not needed."

He released the rail and took a step away, considering the conversation at an end. But Zorion caught his arm, unwilling to let him go so easily.

"It is my concern if you die aboard this ship," Zorion said. Death at sea was part of a sailor's life, but it was considered bad luck to have a passenger die. Their spirits were said to linger, rejected by the Sea Witch as landsmen, unable to find rest.

Zorion did not believe in spirits, but he knew there were those of his crew who did.

"I will not die."

"Can you be certain?"

Josan opened his mouth, and then, with a sigh, closed it.

At least his passenger was an honest man.

Zorion took his measure, as if this was the first time they had met. Could Josan have really changed so much in the span of two short days? Or had Zorion overlooked the signs of illness, blinded by the gems that Josan had offered?

He had thought he was taking advantage of a desperate man. He had not realized he was taking advantage of a dying one.

.

Josan must have sold everything he had to pay for his passage.

"I can put you ashore in Thuridon," Zorion said.

"No," Josan said. "I paid for passage to Xandropol, and I expect you to honor your contract."

"And if you die en route?"

"I will die if you set me ashore."

Zorion shivered, despite the warmth of the day.

So death *was* stalking his guest.

"Bring me to Xandropol, as agreed," Josan said. "If what I have given you is not enough—"

"No," Zorion said. He did not want to hear this man beg for his life.

It was a terrible burden to be captain, balancing the fate of one passenger against the well-being of his crew and his duty to the house that he served.

Edmond would have turned for shore and set Josan off at the first port they came across.

Edmond would have been right.

But Zorion was far closer to death than young Edmond. He had seen too many fall prey to its clutches, struck down before their time.

He would not condemn another. If there was even the chance that the physicians in Xandropol could cure him . . .

"Your passage is paid," Zorion said. "*Hypatia* honors her obligations."

"Thank you," Josan said. He looked down at his feet, then his gaze rose back to meet Zorion's.

"If . . . if anything happens," Josan added. "There is a

letter in my pack, addressed to...my people. It will tell them what they need to know."

He'd been about to say something other than "my people." Family? Or the name of a trading house, as Edmond suspected?

Zorion hoped that he would never have cause to find out.

Chapter 10

Septimus looked over the harbor wall at the ships anchored inside the moles. He categorized them at a glance—from the tiny lighters that ferried goods and people between the ships and shore up to the massive freighters that could sail the length of the Great Basin without needing to stop for provisions. A handful of warships were anchored just beyond the western mole, his own flagship among them. Officially anchored there because space inside the harbor was too valuable to waste on the navy, the warships could rapidly move into position to close off the harbor at need.

Vessels from all of the civilized countries could be seen, though there were fewer federation ships than there had been in times past, when he'd served as harbormaster. Last year, during the undeclared war, there had been none at all. The sight of federation-flagged vessels meant that the truce was holding.

Though if Lady Ysobel had anything to do with the emperor's disappearance, the truce would soon be over.

He hoped it would not come to that. He did not want to go to war. Even with the weapons the emperor had provided, there would be no easy victory. The imperial navy was outnumbered by their federation counterparts, and, in a pinch, any federation merchant ship could be pressed into service. If it came to war, it would be a long, bloody affair.

And if Zuberi became emperor, he would not care how many in the navy perished. While the newcomers had long flocked to the army, which offered prestige and rapid advancement, service in the navy had been the last honorable refuge for the sons of the old blood, who lacked patrons and connections at court.

The old nobility had borne the cost of Prince Lucius's aborted rebellion. Ironically it was those who had remained loyal to Empress Nerissa who still held their commissions in the navy, and thus would be the first to die if war came. Men like himself.

Septimus had accepted the post of admiral not out of loyalty toward Lucius but rather because it was the only way in which he could serve the empire. But gradually he'd grown to respect the new emperor. Lucius had demonstrated his courage by sailing with the fleet, and seen firsthand the cost of war. If Lucius were here, he would not carelessly throw away the lives of Septimus and his men.

But Lucius was missing—and there was no telling what Proconsul Zuberi would do in his absence.

Septimus turned away from the seawall, and began

walking back toward the navy's headquarters, which was sensibly located in the lower crescent rather than within the maze of imperial bureaucracies that swarmed the palace compound. He was still surrounded by spies, of course, but even the illusion that he was out from under the constant watch of Proconsul Zuberi was welcome.

Someone jostled his elbow.

"Excuse me," a voice said.

Then, a moment later, the same voice said, "A thousand pardons, admiral, I didn't realize it was you."

He turned and saw Captain Chenzira at his side. The bruises had faded from Chenzira's face, but his left arm was still splinted. He had a large pack slung over his right shoulder, which swung as he walked.

"A fortunate encounter. If I might have a moment of your time?" Chenzira said.

"Of course," Septimus replied. "I was just making my way to the harbormaster's office, if you'd care to join me."

The harbormaster had two offices—one in the palace, which was seldom used, and the second located precisely in the middle of the docks, an oft-rebuilt wooden building two stories tall that allowed the harbormaster to look down upon his domain.

Chenzira cheerfully babbled of trifles as Septimus led the way to the office, then climbed the stairs to the second floor.

His successor, Donato, was busy talking to one of his clerks. As he glanced up, Septimus said, "With your leave, we will borrow your balcony."

He did not wait for an answer but rather continued

across the landing, out the door that led to the balcony encircling the second story.

"See those ships there and there?" Septimus said, as he walked outside, deliberately pitching his voice to carry as he pointed at two federation trading ships. "Donato is careful to keep them separate, to prevent mischief, but in case of trouble we need only move the navy ships like so, and we can cut them off."

He continued to speak and gesture as they walked around the balcony until they reached the spot that was farthest from the door. He moved to the rail, where the constant breeze from the harbor tugged at their clothes . . . and blew their words out to sea.

They could be seen, but no one would hear what they said.

"What do you want?" Septimus asked. He knew better than to suppose that Chenzira had stumbled across him by chance.

"Proconsul Zuberi read a message from the emperor today," Chenzira said. "The emperor continues in good health and is enjoying the tranquillity of his time in the countryside."

Would that it were true. Strangely there was not even a hint of gossip saying otherwise. The court speculated on the cause of the emperor's illness, but so far, it seemed, only a handful knew that the emperor was missing—perhaps taken, perhaps dead.

He wondered how long Zuberi would continue to issue misleading statements. Surely, in time, some would grow suspicious and demand to see the emperor for themselves.

"I could have heard this from any," Septimus said.

Chenzira bit his lip and nodded. He shifted the pack off his shoulder, into his left hand, winced, then placed it on the ground.

Rumor had it that Chenzira had spent several days as a guest of the torturer Nizam—presumably at his uncle's command. But Chenzira had said nothing of his ordeal when he'd finally made his report to Septimus, merely apologizing for being detained.

Left to his own devices, Septimus would have stripped Chenzira of his command. But such would have required the consent of Zuberi, which was not forthcoming. And any lesser discipline paled beside what Chenzira had already endured. Instead Septimus had merely questioned Chenzira at length, forcing him to recount every moment he'd spent in the emperor's presence, then dismissed him.

He'd not expected Chenzira to seek him out.

"I've been making my own inquiries," Chenzira said.

Septimus made a noncommittal noise. He could not forget that Chenzira was his uncle's man, and it was likely that his presence here was a test. Proof that Septimus was disloyal might well restore Chenzira to his uncle's favor.

"The monk was not chosen at random," Chenzira said.

"I know that. You told me that the emperor summoned him aboard your ship." Septimus did not bother to disguise his impatience; it was too late for Chenzira to be making excuses.

"Did you know that the monk was about to leave on his own journey? One that the emperor had specifically requested?"

Septimus's own inquiries had revealed as much. "He wanted books. Books from the library at Xandropol."

Emperor Lucius had shown a mastery of obscure knowledge—he had personally taught Chenzira the secret navigation techniques that Chenzira had then shared with the rest of the navy. And it was Lucius's research that had resurrected the Burning Terror, a weapon once thought lost to the ages.

It was not surprising that he would seek out even rarer volumes.

"I am convinced that he journeyed in Brother Mensah's place," Chenzira said.

"To do what? He could have a dozen monks fetch him all the books he required."

"He sought a different kind of knowledge," Chenzira said. "A cure for his illness."

"He admitted to being fatigued—" Septimus began.

"It is more than that. I have spoken with his servants, his clerk, even Eight, who watches over him at night."

"Eight?"

"The emperor gave all the functionaries numbers, since they refused to accept names. Eight is the oldest of them and was given the task of watching the emperor at night since it is the least demanding time."

Septimus blinked. How was it that a mere captain was privy to this information? Was it his family connections? Or something else?

"They all told me he was ill—far more seriously than he'd let anyone know. A wasting sickness that sapped his strength, and neither his own magic nor the healer's art could aid him."

From the first, Septimus had suspected that the emperor had been tricked or taken by force. It made no sense that he would abandon his empire. But if he were truly ill and desperate for a cure . . .

"We've stopped and searched all vessels that left that day, and he wasn't on any of them," Septimus pointed out.

"Would your captains recognize him?"

"They had a full description—"

"He would not look like an emperor, or even a noble. We spent long hours together when he was teaching me, and when he is tired, he forgets himself. He fetches his own water, and will send his servants to bed and do their work himself. If he were dressed as a servant, no one would look at him twice."

Chenzira's words made a terrible kind of sense.

If only he'd been allowed to send men who personally knew the emperor to aid in the search for him. But Zuberi had refused—for sending the men would involve telling them that the emperor was missing.

"You think he sailed in the monk's place, taking his passage to Xandropol," Septimus said.

"I do."

"*Tylenda* wrecked off the keys," Septimus said. "No one matching the emperor's description was among the survivors."

"They did not know whom they sought," Chenzira argued. "He has his own powers. If any survived, he would have been among them."

It was the optimism of youth.

"What would you have of me?" Septimus said.

"Send me to Xandropol," Chenzira said. "The emperor will need men who are loyal to him, and a ship for his return home."

If he was right, it was the least that Septimus could do for the emperor he had sworn to serve. But even if this were not an elaborate trap, he could name a half dozen captains that he would send for this errand rather than picking Chenzira.

"One of my captains will go—" Septimus began.

"I will go," Chenzira said. "Who among your men has spent days in his company? Who else will be certain to know him at a glance?"

Septimus could feel his resolve wavering.

"And I have something he needs," Chenzira added, kicking the pack that he'd placed at his feet.

His curiosity aroused, Septimus picked up the pack and unbuckled the flaps.

He saw a silk-wrapped object inside.

"Careful," Chenzira warned.

Septimus had started to lift the object out, but instead he merely pulled at the layers of silk, until he caught a glimpse of the treasure within.

"In the name of the triune gods," he breathed. "What have you done?"

Chenzira grinned. "He may need to look the part of an emperor."

"And if your uncle finds out you have this, he won't wait to hang you for treason. He'll kill you himself."

Inside Chenzira's pack was the lizard crown—the imperial crown of Lucius's ancestral line. He dared not ask how it had come into Chenzira's possession.

The crown convinced him that this was no trap. And it was proof that Chenzira was insane. He'd risked everything on his conjecture that the emperor was bound for Xandropol. If Chenzira was wrong, he would pay for his mistake with his life.

"Well?" Chenzira asked.

Septimus drew a deep breath. Chenzira had made his choice. It was time for him to choose, as well.

"Go to your ship," he said. "Orders will arrive within the hour, bidding you to Xandropol. I'll send another ship with you, the fastest I can find. If you find the emperor—"

"When I find him."

"*If* you find him, the second ship will bring word to me," Septimus said, ignoring the interruption. "You will stay with the emperor. Obey him in all other matters, but do not leave him. Not for a single hour."

Chenzira saluted. "It will be as you say."

"And may the triune gods watch over us both," Septimus said. Officially he was a follower of the twin gods, as Empress Nerissa had been. But it was the religion of his ancestors that called to him now. If there were any gods that looked after fools, it would be they.

"The emperor of Ikaria is too great a prize to be kept secret for long," Zuberi argued. "If the federation had taken him, we would have heard something by now."

"Or maybe they are holding him in secret, waiting until we declare him dead. Then they will reveal him, and we will be made to look fools," Demetrios said.

It was an argument they'd had before, in the weeks since Emperor Lucius had walked off *Green Dragon* and vanished. With each day that passed, Zuberi's frustration grew, as did the temptation to act.

"What of it? We'll deny their claims, say the man is an impostor. They'll never be able to prove otherwise," Zuberi said.

An assassin could be dispatched, under the guise of sending a delegation to confirm or deny the impostor's claims. Thus neatly solving the problem of succession and embarrassing the federation.

If Lucius was alive, and being held captive in the federation. But if he was not . . .

"There's no need to act in haste," Demetrios said. "We must wait until we are certain."

What he meant was that Zuberi should be patient, while Demetrios prepared to launch his own bid for power. Zuberi's spies had reported that Demetrios had been in communication with General Kiril, leader of the imperial army. So far, it seemed Kiril was ignorant of the emperor's disappearance, but he surely must be wondering why Demetrios was making overtures of friendship.

Zuberi had made his own overtures as well. Subtler than Demetrios, he'd thought to court not just Kiril, but also Kiril's brother-in-law Commander Anatoli, who commanded the legions of the south. Both men owed him favors for advancing their clients and had cause to think favorably of him.

If necessary, he would inform Kiril of the emperor's disappearance, then make an immediate bid for his support. The key was to secure the backing of Kiril and his legions before the general realized that he could gain a greater advantage by playing Demetrios off against Zuberi, making the would-be emperors bid against each other for his services.

"It is not my patience, but that of the court," Zuberi said. "The emperor cannot stay hidden away in the country forever."

Though there was precedent—Aitor the Great had been confined to his bed for the last five years of his life, spending more time in his country estates than he had in the capital. But at least there had been proof that Aitor was alive and still in command of his wits.

Zuberi and Demetrios could make excuses for only so long.

"Agreed. In a month's time, if there is still no word, then we will decide what to do next," Demetrios said.

In a month's time, Demetrios might be humbly offering himself to stand in the emperor's stead. Or his body might adorn a funeral pyre in the sacred groves, the victim of his overreaching ambitions.

The same could be said for Zuberi.

"We will wait," Zuberi said. "And I will take no action without consulting you."

The lie slipped smoothly from his lips.

"And I the same," Demetrios said, smiling back with equal falseness. He extended his right arm, and Zuberi took it in the grasp of friendship.

"Between us we will keep the empire safe," Demetrios vowed.

Zuberi merely nodded, and left. A litter was waiting

outside Demetrios's town house, and Zuberi directed his bearers to take him home.

No breeze stirred in the crowded streets, so he let the curtains of the litter fall shut.

Demetrios was not his only concern. There was Admiral Septimus to consider. His bloodlines made his loyalties suspect, though nothing had ever been proven against him. It was unfortunate that Septimus had to be informed of the emperor's disappearance, but the navy had been needed for the search. At present, self-interest would keep Septimus quiet. He had no friends at court, and if Lucius were to fall from power, so too would he. But he would bear watching.

Petrelis, head of the city watch, also knew that Lucius was missing, but there Zuberi had no worries. Petrelis was personally loyal to him and would do as he was told.

Demetrios. Septimus. Petrelis. Chenzira. The torturer Nizam. And, of course, himself. Zuberi ticked over the names in his mind. Six men who knew that the emperor was missing. If each of them had shared the news with only one other—

It would not be long before the whole of Karystos knew as well.

Zuberi must be ready, so that when the emperor's disappearance was inevitably revealed, all eyes would turn to him as Lucius's natural successor.

Lost in his thoughts, it took a moment for him to realize that the litter had paused. A servant parted the curtains, revealing a scene of chaos, as porters swarmed a mound of luggage outside his residence.

Standing in the center, an island of calm amidst the

storm, was a petite woman, wearing the ankle-length day gown of a modest Ikarian matron.

His wife, Eugenia, who was supposed to be in the countryside for at least another month.

He took a breath, then another, until he could greet her without letting the frustrations of the day color his words.

She took no notice as he emerged from the litter.

"No, those crates are for the kitchens," she said. "Fresh produce from our estate. The trunks are for my rooms."

"Honored wife," he said.

She turned and smiled. She looked well, immaculately attired with not a single hair out of place, despite having just endured a long journey.

"Honored husband," she replied, stepping around the crates to take both of his hands in hers.

Their eyes met, then he kissed her on each cheek. A formal greeting; they would save more affectionate gestures for when they were alone.

Releasing her hands, he looked around. "Where is our son?"

"Still in the country," she said. "Bakari wanted to see the grape harvest, so I agreed that he could stay with his friend Antonius."

Antonius was the son of Antonius of Caspia, a retired senator who owned the estate that adjoined Zuberi's own. Though no longer active in politics, the family was still held in high regard. It was a suitable friendship for his son.

And likely safer for his son to be removed from the intrigues of the capital. Still, Zuberi could not supress a pang of disappointment.

"A poor wife I am, letting you stand here in the heat," she said. "Go, and wash away the dust of the city. I will join you presently."

He obeyed with a meekness that would have surprised any who knew him from the court, allowing himself to be shooed away as the chaos slowly ordered itself under his wife's commands.

Entering the house, he summoned a servant.

"Send my regrets to Matticus of Alondra, and tell him that I won't be joining him tonight," he said.

Matticus was a former client who held the post of inspector of the imperial roads. He was important enough not to offend, but Zuberi could alleviate the slight by inviting Matticus to join him the next time he held a select dinner party.

With Eugenia returned to Karystos, he would once again be expected to host such gatherings.

Retiring to his private chambers, he bathed, then dressed in fresh clothing. He could hear voices from his wife's adjoining rooms—the cheerful sound of her maids as they unpacked their mistress's garb.

He still wished she had seen fit to remain in the country, but had to admit that the house would be more lively now that she had returned.

They shared an intimate dinner that night, dining on a single couch, their arms entwined as if they were lovers rather than husband and wife. She offered him the choicest morsels, while he complimented her beauty, which despite the years was undiminished. Each time he looked at her, he felt pride, knowing that he was the envy of his peers.

After her third cup of wine, Eugenia confessed that she'd been bored in the countryside. Senator Antonius was a widower, and there were no women of her rank living nearby.

"Of course, if the emperor had gone to Eluktiri, we could have had a summer court," she said. "What fun that would be."

"I met you at the summer court, when you were handmaiden to Nerissa," he said, offering the expected response.

She laughed. "Nerissa was the only one who spoke in your favor. Everyone else thought I was mad."

In the formal atmosphere of Karystos they would have never met, but in the relaxed atmosphere of the summer court, the strict separations between unmarried young women and the men of the court had been relaxed.

Eugenia's father had not been pleased by his daughter's friendship with a clerk—a man who seemed destined to rise no higher than a petty bureaucrat. But his daughter would not be denied, and eventually he'd consented to the match.

He'd lived long enough to see Zuberi named as proconsul, second in power to the empress herself. It had been a heady day for Zuberi when the man who had formerly despised him had come to beg his favor.

"A shame that the emperor's illness confines him to Sarna," Eugenia said, continuing her earlier thought. If she noticed Zuberi's inattention, she was too kind to point it out.

"He was fatigued when he left," Zuberi said. "It is hoped that his time away will restore his spirits, when he returns for the convocation of the senate."

The convocation was traditionally held after the harvest season, before winter made the seas too perilous for travel. On that day an emperor must stand in front of the senate and bless the opening of debate.

This year it might be Zuberi's turn to wear the purple robes and say the ritual words.

An emperor for a husband, and her son an emperor-to-be. His wife had chosen more wisely than any might have dreamed, that long-ago summer.

"And what of my nephew?" she asked. "May I invite him to dine with us this week?"

"Captain Chenzira is away at present, on the business of the navy," Zuberi said. "But when he returns, of course."

Chenzira had been given orders for an extended survey trip, charting the currents that ran through the heart of the Great Basin. As their most experienced navigator he was a logical choice for such a task, though Zuberi suspected Septimus had sent Chenzira away to make sure he didn't have the opportunity to talk to anyone.

Or, possibly, to shield him from Zuberi's wrath.

He was still angry with Chenzira, though relieved by the discovery that his nephew was merely incompetent rather than treasonous.

Chenzira was the only son of Eugenia's late brother, who had died before he could breed a legitimate heir. He occupied a special place in her affections, and for that reason Zuberi had done what he could to advance his nephew's career.

A politician's wife, Eugenia would have understood if he'd had to have Chenzira killed, but understanding was not the same as forgiveness. If Chenzira had been executed, it would be a long time before Zuberi felt welcome in his own home.

"So tell me, what gossip is there?" Eugenia asked.

"There is little to tell. With so many gone from the capital, I have lived a dull life."

The lie slipped smoothly from his tongue. He trusted his wife—trusted that she would remain faithful to him, and that she would die to protect their son. But she was a woman, after all, and could not be trusted with matters of state.

"Well, now that I am here, your life will be more exciting," she said.

"Of that I have no doubt."

Chapter 11

Josan nodded cordially as he entered the cramped cabin that served as the dining hall for the junior officers. Amelie was present, as were Edmond and the sailing master, Bryan. Only Pascal was missing, and since this was the middle of the day, it was likely that Pascal was sleeping in preparation for the night watch, while Captain Zorion had the current watch.

A bowl was at his customary seat, sunk into the carved indentation that held it in place in rough seas.

"That's the last of the fresh vegetables," Edmond said.

The bowl held long strips of brightly colored peppers interspersed with round slices of gourds, which had been fried in oil, then mixed with rice. He dipped in his spoon and tried a mouthful. It was subtly spiced with saffron and other herbs.

"It's good," he said, taking another bite. Amelie filled

his wine cup with one part wine and three parts water, as was the custom on this ship.

"Starting tonight, it will be dried meat and lentils. And maybe fish, if we're lucky," Edmond groused.

"You complain, but I've yet to see you send a meal back," Bryan observed.

Josan let their words flow over him as the crew bickered amiably, responding only when asked his opinion. Mindful of his presence they spoke only of inconsequential things—when Edmond mentioned a problem with a seaman, Amelie abruptly changed the subject.

Josan merely took another sip of his well-watered wine and pretended he hadn't heard. He was not offended. They knew only what the captain had told them—that their passenger was a traveler who suffered from bouts of the landsman's sickness. They had no reason to trust him.

"It is a calm day if you wish to take the air, Josan," Amelie said.

"Thank you, that would be pleasant," he agreed.

It had been a long time since he had been allowed to simply be Josan. To be called by his own name. For two years he had lived as Prince Lucius—first as a prisoner, then ruling as emperor. His life had depended upon others believing that he was Lucius, and so he had done his best to act the part of a prince, burying his own nature underneath the role he was forced to play.

But the crew of *Hypatia* had no such expectations of him. They called him Josan without the mockery that he had heard each time Lady Ysobel used his name. They did not expect princely airs, nor did they seek to punish him for crimes committed by the man whose body he now wore. Their acceptance of him was a gift—one he was careful not to abuse.

He finished his meal and rose, leaving them alone so they could discuss the business of the ship.

Venturing up on deck, he saw that Captain Zorion was indeed in the wheelhouse. After a week at sea, Josan had memorized the rhythms of this ship. Four watches a day, the five officers rotated the schedule among them, so that the burden of the night watches was shared by all. As soon as lunch was finished, Zorion would be relieved by Edmond, and he in turn would be relieved by Bryan, then Pascal, and finally Amelie.

Amelie held the post of cargo master, apparently equal in rank to the sailing master. It was strange to see a woman commanding men, stranger still to see young women scrambling up the rigging alongside boys. He'd never before sailed upon a federation vessel, where women served in nearly equal numbers to the men.

Some tasks seemed reserved for men alone, but he had yet to determine how these had been decided. Was it by the captain's decree? Or a matter of long-held custom? Would they be done differently on another federation vessel?

He could ask, but such questions would raise suspicions. A trader would be expected to know these things, particularly one who could speak the trade tongue with the cadence of the islands.

Intellectually he'd known that Lady Ysobel was more than a politician—she was reputed to be head of her own merchant house and an experienced sea captain. He wondered if she had ever captained a ship such as this. Was this the life she'd led as a girl—going to sea in one of her family's ships, learning to raise and lower the sails, splice ropes, and spend endless hours scouring the brasswork?

The life of a sailor was full of tedium, but it also offered endless opportunities for learning and adventure. He wondered why anyone would leave it behind for a life of scheming and political intrigues.

He took a turn around the foredeck, where he would be in no one's way. Their course had taken them deep into the Great Basin, so there was no land to be seen, but the blur he saw on the horizon soon resolved itself into the shape of sails.

"It's two ships, maybe three," he heard the lookout call down to the deck.

The message was dutifully passed on to Captain Zorion in the wheelhouse, where he had been joined by Edmond.

They'd sighted other ships during the week they'd been at sea, but never more than one at a time. A convoy, perhaps. All federation traders, of course, for few others dared sail this deep into the heart of the Great Basin.

Zorion left the wheelhouse and paused to nod to Josan before continuing below to his cabin. He must have been pleased that his passenger had shown no signs of an illness that might threaten his ship.

Josan had had one more attack in the week that he'd been aboard ship, but it had been at night, with none to witness it save himself. Fortunately, he'd recovered by morning.

He lacked the instruments for proper calculations, but by both his informal reckoning and Edmond's statements they were halfway to Xandropol. They would arrive in another week, then the final race would begin. Could he find the information he needed before this body failed him? Or would he have risked all, simply to die in a foreign city?

It would not be easy. The study of magic was not forbidden in Xandropol the way it was in Ikaria, and thus the great library would hold numerous tomes on the subject, of varying quality. It would be a daunting task to search through them all, trying to winnow out the truth from lies and legends.

If he could confide in another, it would speed his search. But he dared not. It did not matter that Josan and Lucius were both victims; what had been done to them would be seen as an abomination. At best he could expect to be imprisoned, left to wither as his fate was debated by scholars and politicians.

At worst he would be handed over to the priests for cleansing—which would mean his death.

His fear was a constant thing, itching under his skin. Always present, but never overwhelming. It might even be Lucius's emotions he was sensing rather than his own. But a man could not live in a constant state of terror. Intellectually he knew he was dying, but at the moment his body felt fine. And the day was too fair for melancholy, with the sun shining and a brisk breeze speeding the ship along.

At last he found a quiet spot against the rail and sat on the deck, in no hurry to return to his cramped and airless cabin. He meditated, bringing to mind what he could remember of the great library from his previous visit. As he planned his research, his surroundings faded into the background.

A shout from the lookout roused him from thought. He blinked, surprised to see Edmond leave the wheelhouse. He watched as Edmond swiftly climbed the center mast and joined the lookout at his post. The two conferred for a long moment, looking through a long glass. Edmond gestured, then began his descent. He began calling out orders before he'd reached the deck.

His commands meant nothing to Josan, but the urgency of his tone was unmistakable.

Josan stood. The tiny sails he'd seen earlier had come into view—it appeared they were three ships, in close formation.

Was the lookout concerned that they might be pirates? But such usually plied the coastlines, darting out of sheltered harbors to take their prey, then disappearing again before they could be detected.

Captain Zorion appeared on deck, accompanied by the sailing master, Bryan, and they joined Edmond in the wheelhouse. Zorion pulled out his own long glass and looked at the ships, then nodded decisively.

Josan drifted closer, watching as they conferred among themselves. He could tell the moment Zorion reached his decision, for Edmond saluted, then left the wheelhouse.

Edmond summoned a sailor. "Find Amelie and tell her to issue swords to those who are on defense," Josan overheard him say.

This order needed no interpretation. The sailor scurried off.

"What's happening?" Josan asked.

"I've no time," Edmond said brusquely. "Go below, where you won't be in the way." Edmond looked above, cursed, and began bellowing orders.

Josan had thought that *Hypatia* had already been carrying all the canvas she could, but under Edmond's profane encouragement, the sailors raised a sail along the boom that projected from the bow.

Spray flew as the ship sliced through the waves. She seemed to be sailing much faster than before, but surely the sensation was from his nerves rather than the effect of a single added sail.

Josan waited, but their course did not change. It seemed Captain Zorion had chosen to sail toward whatever was happening up ahead rather than fleeing from danger.

A girl carrying a bucket of sand with both hands shoved him aside. "Get below if you can't get from underfoot," she said.

Josan merely retreated, watching as the girl and several other youths placed buckets of sand at key points around the rail. He wondered at the purpose of the sand—would they sprinkle it for traction on a slippery deck?

Or was it in case of fire? But that made no sense. Fire ships and flaming missiles were risks associated with close-packed harbors and shore-based catapults.

He grew cold as he remembered that fire was also the weapon of the Ikarian navy. A gift that he himself had given them.

Josan pushed his way through a knot of sailors, who were tucking swords into their belts.

"Josan—" Amelie began when she caught sight of him.

He ignored her. He did not bother to knock, but simply entered the wheelhouse.

"What did you see?" he asked.

Captain Zorion turned and his face was cold. "Go to your cabin; I've no time for you."

"What did you see?" Josan repeated.

"I'll have you dragged below, and you'll spend the rest of the trip in chains," Zorion said. His tone was mild, but his eyes were those of a man who was fully prepared to match deeds to words.

But Josan had faced far more frightening men in his time. He would not be intimidated.

"Answer my question, then I will leave."

"Two ships of the Ikarian navy, attacking a federation trader," Bryan said.

Josan shook his head. "No. They are not Ikarians."

"How can you be certain?" Zorion asked.

"I *know*," Josan replied, trying to convey the force of his convictions with his voice. They would hardly believe the truth.

"See for yourself," Zorion said, handing him the long glass.

Josan took the glass, turning it in his hands to extend it, then sighted through the piece. It took him a moment to find the ships, and another to focus the optics.

Zorion was correct. There were two vessels with the red-bordered sails of the imperial navy, flanking a ship with the plain white sails of a trader. He could not tell the merchant ships of one country from another, but Zorion's haste meant that it was likely a federation trader, as Bryan had claimed.

Josan closed the glass, and handed it back to Zorion.

"What do you plan to do?" he asked.

"They've pinned her between them, and are likely boarding as we speak," Zorion said. "Our arrival will change the odds."

Even so it would be an unequal fight. Merchant ships carried cargo, while naval vessels used that space to house marines and weapons. *Hypatia*'s crew would be heavily outnumbered.

"Now go," Zorion said, giving Josan a push. "Or do you still insist that they are not imperials?"

"They are not," Josan said. "But you will see that for yourself soon enough."

Bryan snorted with disbelief, and Josan left the wheelhouse though he did not go below. He knew that those ships were impostors. Admiral Septimus would never have broken the truce without direct orders from the emperor.

Josan knew that he had not given such orders. Nor would Proconsul Zuberi have done so without at least informing the emperor of what he intended.

He had only been absent a few weeks. Surely everything he had accomplished could not have been undone in that time.

Around him the frantic pace of activity had slowed, as preparations were completed. Each sailor apparently had a place to be and a task to perform. Several shouted at Josan for his presence—to each he nodded, then simply moved until he was out of their sight.

Hypatia raced through the water, but to his eyes the battle was growing no closer. Strange to think that ahead of them men were fighting, even dying, and they could do nothing.

By the time they arrived, it might well be over.

"I told you to go below." Zorion's voice came from behind him. "This is no place for the curious."

"I need to be here," Josan said. "I can help."

Zorion shook his head. "I will not give you a sword," he said. "And my sailors need no help from a man who does not know one end of a line from another."

"How long will it take us to reach them?"

Zorion looked at the horizon, then up at the sails, which had begun to flap, first billowing out, then collapsing.

"Wind's shifting," he said. "Will take us at least two hours, longer if the wind dies. But unless you're a friend of the Sea Witch..."

Josan grimaced. Perhaps it would be best if the wind died—he had no wish to experience another battle first-hand. The people on that distant merchant ship were not his subjects; he had no responsibility toward them.

But the attackers wore the colors of his fleet. If they were Ikarians, then he needed to know. And if not—then he needed to know that as well, and to have Captain Zorion bear witness.

"Would a storm help?" Josan asked.

Captain Zorion laughed. "Do you have one in your cabin, tucked away with your books?"

Josan felt light-headed, and took a deep breath, then another, but it was not enough. His senses swam. Was it only days ago that he had chastised Lucius for this very sin? But Lucius had been reckless. This was not recklessness, this was his duty.

He wondered if the storm winds would come to him, without Lucius to call them.

He wondered how he would explain himself if this worked.

Josan closed his eyes and reached deep inside himself. He could not feel Lucius, but he felt the first stirrings of power within.

"Tell your crew to prepare for a storm," he said.

Josan turned so that he faced the direction they must go, then braced himself.

"Come," he said.

Zorion watched him for a long moment, then laughed. "You almost had me convinced," he said.

Josan did not respond. He focused every bit of his will on nurturing the power within him, calling it into being.

He did not know how Lucius made the magic obey his bidding. Whatever he summoned might be too little, or it might escape his control and wreck this ship.

Ruthlessly he pushed his doubts aside.

Wind, he thought, calling to mind the feel of a storm against his skin, the way strong winds would tug at his clothes, buffeting his body.

The grin slid off Zorion's face as the sails above them filled with a resounding crack.

Josan brushed the short fringe of hair from his eyes, feeling the first drops of rain splattering against his skin.

"Your storm, captain," he said.

Zorion reached out as if to touch him, then pulled back his hand.

It was Josan's turn to laugh. He had done as Zorion

had asked, but now he was cursed, unclean in Zorion's eyes.

A part of him knew he was being unfair, but the rational part of him was overwhelmed by the sensations from without and within. Outside the storm was growing, and he clutched the rigging to keep his balance. While inside, the power rose within him, whispering that this was only the beginning. He could do anything. Anything.

He'd been wrong all this time. Lucius was right. If they had power, why shouldn't they use it? The power wanted to be used—his very flesh tingled as if it was being stroked by a lover.

He never wanted it to end.

Zorion gave him one last look, then began giving new orders to the crew.

Josan let him go. The rain fell harder as the sky grew dark above them. He could not see the ships ahead of him, but he did not need to.

His mind called out—and the lightning answered.

Josan woke to a pounding head, and a body that ached all over. His bed moved beneath him, as if he were still drunk.

He could not remember the night before—had he truly drunk himself insensible? Or was this some new poison?

He opened his eyes, but could make no sense of what he saw. He was not in his bedchamber, but rather in a narrow wooden room, illuminated by a single lantern which hung from the ceiling above him, swaying crazily in time with the pulse that pounded in his head.

A white-haired woman sat in a chair next to his bed. As his gaze met hers, she smiled.

"You're awake," she said.

"What happened?" he asked. It seemed a safer question than where am I, or who are you? Better not to reveal the extent of his ignorance until he was among friends.

He tried to push himself up to a seated position, but his arms refused to cooperate.

"I'll get the captain," she said. "He wanted to know the moment you awoke."

She left before he could protest. Captain?

Mere moments later the door opened, and a man stepped inside.

Zorion. Josan's memories returned in a rush. He was not in his palace—this was *Hypatia,* and the man before him was her captain.

From the weakness in his limbs, he realized that he must have had another one of his attacks. But he could not remember.

"What happened?" he repeated.

Zorion sat in the chair that Amelie had earlier occupied. "Do you mean the battle? Or before that, when you fell to the deck?"

"*Hypatia* is safe?" he asked.

He remembered that they had sighted distant sails, then realized that a merchant ship was being attacked. After that, nothing.

But they must have survived the battle—elsewise Zorion would not have time to talk to his troublesome passenger.

"*Rhosyn* was lucky," Zorion said. "Before we reached

her, one of her attackers was destroyed by lightning. The other sailed off, abandoning their fellows. By the time we came alongside, the boarders had been overcome, and we picked survivors of the first ship out of the water."

Josan swallowed hard as his memories returned. He remembered the taste of frustration, of knowing that they would arrive too late to discover the truth. He remembered thinking that he could use Lucius's magic to call a wind that would carry *Hypatia* before it.

He remembered promising Zorion that a wind would come.

How could he have been so foolish? It was tempting to blame this folly on Lucius, but there had been no voice in his head urging him on. This folly was his, and his alone.

Josan swallowed hard, wondering what price he must pay for his moment of madness.

"Fortunate indeed," Josan said.

Zorion frowned as if he'd expected something more, then rubbed his chin consideringly. "Do you remember earlier, when you insisted that the ships were not from the imperial navy?"

"Yes. I was right, wasn't I?"

Josan held his breath.

"I'll answer your question, if you answer mine. An even trade," Zorion proposed.

"If I can, I will," Josan said.

"Did you call this storm? Summon the waves the way another might call his dog?"

If Josan denied his powers, he would never know the truth of the encounter. Never know if his own navy was committing acts of piracy. Zorion's crew would follow his lead. If the captain willed it, no one else would tell Josan what had happened.

But if he acknowledged that he had called the storm—what would Zorion do with such knowledge? A man who could command the weather was more valuable than his weight in gold—it would be an irresistible temptation to one who made his living at sea.

Josan was wholly at Zorion's mercy. He could not so much as twitch his arm to defend himself.

The risks were grave, but despite everything, he had to know.

"If one bears the curse of power, he can call a storm, if he wills it," Josan said. "But not without cost."

He could tell from the astonishment on Zorion's face that the captain had expected him to lie.

"They were mercenaries from Vidrun," Zorion said. "The attack was staged for our benefit. They meant to sink *Rhosyn* and enslave her crew. We would have seen it all, but arrived too late to save them."

"Why?"

"What would happen if we brought news to port that the Ikarians are once more attacking federation ships?"

"War," Josan breathed. One report would be dismissed as rumor, but if enough such encounters happened, the truce would be shattered.

"Some might say I owe you," Zorion said. "Thanks to the storm, *Hypatia* is unharmed—neither ship nor crew suffered so much as a scratch."

Here Zorion showed his race. He did not say that there was a debt between them, merely that some might consider that there was. There was no promise of payment, merely the hint that he might consider himself in Josan's debt.

He wondered whether honor or greed would win out. How much did Zorion covet the advantages that a pet magician could provide? When Lady Ysobel had proposed taking him prisoner, Josan had threatened her with retaliation. But he was far weaker than he had been, and if Zorion sensed this . . .

"I paid for passage to Xandropol," Josan said. "I expect you to honor that agreement."

"Not for a bit," Zorion said.

Josan's heart sank at these words.

"*Rhosyn* was damaged. She won't make it that far, and alone she's easy prey. I've promised to escort her to Tyrns."

"And then?"

"And then I hope that the house of Arles understands why I broke their contract by choosing to deliver a passenger first, rather than sailing directly to Vidrun to deliver their cargo," Zorion said.

So he was not a prisoner, after all. At least for the moment.

"Rest," Zorion said. "There's a boy outside, who will fetch you whatever you want."

Josan nodded and closed his eyes. Let Zorion think that he was merely resting, rather than that he was incapacitated by his recent exertions.

The weakness had always passed before. It would again.

He hoped that both his selves had learned their lesson—he could not risk using magic again, not in any form. Not unless it was to save his life. Zorion had promised to set Josan free, but once he thought it over, he might change his mind. When the ship reached Xandropol Josan would need all his wits about him—and a body that would obey his bidding.

Anything less would doom him.

Chapter 12

Xandropol was a city of wonders, from the great library that dominated the heart of the city to the marketplaces where you could find rare goods from every known land. Protected by both treaty and the armies of Volesk, the streets of Xandropol teemed with peoples of every race, speaking a dozen different languages. Impoverished scholars in tattered robes jostled wealthy merchants wearing embroidered silks, while traders from Tyrns looked on, their voluminous wraps making it impossible to tell if they were male or female, young or old. Any were welcome in Xandropol, as long as they kept the peace and paid their taxes.

This was Burrell's first visit to Xandropol. As a marine he'd had no reason to come here. But Lady Ysobel had been here often; Xandropol was a popular destination for merchants offering their wares in return for goods from the north that had been ferried down the Bronze River.

If it could not be found in the markets of Xandropol, then it likely didn't exist.

Though so far, at least, they had no luck in finding what they sought.

Their journey from Tarsus had been swift. Rather than waiting for an appropriate vessel, Lady Ysobel had drawn upon her own credit to hire a ship to take them directly to Xandropol. She'd bargained fiercely, but the agreed-upon sum had still been more than Burrell would earn in a year.

It had been on that journey that she'd finally invited him to share her bed.

It was something that would never have happened if they'd remained in Karystos. Whether commanding one of her ships, or serving in the embassy, Ysobel still thought of herself as a captain, foremost. And thus she would not lie with one under her command.

No matter how much Burrell had wanted her to.

He'd given up hope of ever being more than her friend, but during the fortnight it took to sail from Tarsus to Xandropol they'd become lovers. He'd always known that she was beautiful, and was not surprised that the passion with which she embraced everything else carried over to the bedchamber as well. She was as likely to pounce hungrily upon him, stripping him in her haste to join together, as she was to enjoy slow, tender embraces that lasted until dawn.

He did not fool himself into thinking that it was anything he had done that had changed her mind. It was rather that their circumstances had changed. Forced once again into a passive role, with nothing to do until they reached Xandropol, Ysobel was using him to forget.

While they dallied, they were simply a man and a woman, the burden of their responsibilities temporarily laid aside.

When they'd arrived in Xandropol a week ago, he'd known without having to ask that the brief affair was over.

At first, they'd not been surprised to have outpaced *Hypatia*. But as day after day passed without any sign of their quarry, their doubts had grown.

With nothing to do but wait for *Hypatia* to arrive, Ysobel had grown increasingly short-tempered. Burrell shared her anxiety though he hoped he was better at concealing his frustrations. From the beginning, their course had been a gamble. If Lucius had never boarded *Hypatia*, or if he had sailed with her to some other destination, then they would have failed.

And the news he was bringing her would only serve to add to her unease. He hesitated outside her room, then squared his shoulders before entering.

"Any news?" she asked. "The ambassador asked me this morning how much longer we intended to stay."

Dorinda of Navar served as the federation's representative in Xandropol. A cousin of Lady Solange, the minister of trade, Dorinda styled herself ambassador though her official title was that of liaison. Dorinda had not been pleased by their arrival, especially when Lady Ysobel invoked her status as envoy to demand lodging.

Dorinda likely viewed Lady Ysobel's presence as an attempt to assert her power—a reminder that Ysobel outranked her both in the court and in the halls of trade.

In truth they stayed here because their purses were flat—they could afford a room, but not servants to run errands for them. And, if news from Ikaria came to Xandropol, it would come here first.

They had taken their turns scouring the markets and docks for information, sending Dorinda's servants to fetch daily lists of newly arrived ships. This morning it had been Burrell's turn to visit the docks, while Ysobel chivied Dorinda's clerks.

"No news of *Hypatia,* but she's not the only ship that is late," Burrell said.

"A storm at sea, or contrary winds?" Ysobel suggested.

It was possible—no two captains sailed precisely the same course. Their ship might have had the advantage of favorable currents, while a ship sailing even just a point north or south of that course might have found itself becalmed.

Or so he had suggested every time Ysobel fretted over *Hypatia's* failure to arrive. He'd almost believed it himself.

Until now.

"*Lily* is a week overdue, and was just posted as missing," he said.

Ysobel's face tightened. "That's one of my father's ships," she said.

He'd known as much by the name, even before he saw confirmation. The house of Flordelis traditionally named their ships after flowers.

"And *Greenbow,* a single-masted ship from the house of Laurent arrived this morning, badly battered. They claimed they were attacked by a ship of the Ikarian navy. There were rumors of other attacks, but this is the first time a ship has survived to bring the tale to shore."

She winced as if he had struck her. During last year's war, both sides had used the pretext of pirate ships as excuses to launch their attacks. It was possible the Ikarians were trying the same ruse again.

"The captain is at the docks, even as we speak, but I'm certain he'll be making his way here before long, to tell the liaison what he knows," he added.

"Do you believe him?"

Burrell hesitated. He'd seen *Greenbow* arrive, with her jury-rigged mast and tattered sails. She'd been in a fight, but it seemed impossible that such a small craft could have fought off a navy vessel, unaided.

"I don't know," he said. "Even an incompetent captain should have been able to take that ship. The captain may be lying because he can't reveal the truth of who attacked him, or why."

"Or he may be telling the truth," Ysobel said. "While I was chasing Lucius across the Great Basin, the Ikarians have gone to war."

"We don't know that—"

"We don't know anything," Ysobel snapped.

Burrell took a step toward her, then hesitated. At this moment she did not want a lover, nor would she respect one who offered mindless comfort.

"We may be at war," he said. "But you know as well as I that the house of Laurent has a spotty reputation. Talk to the captain yourself before you judge the truth of his tale."

And before you condemn yourself any further, Burrell thought.

If war had come, it would be none of Lady Ysobel's doing, though he knew she would blame herself. Each choice she made had been in service of her mission, but that would not matter to her.

Nor would it matter to those who had sent her to Ikaria. She'd fought one war at their bidding, emerging triumphant from a mission meant to ensure her death.

He could only hope they would be so lucky again.

Ysobel had been present when the *Greenbow*'s captain met with Dorinda—though the liaison had refused to allow Burrell to join them. He paced anxiously in his quarters, waiting for her to return.

His thoughts chased themselves in an endless circle— if the Ikarians were once more on the attack, it was imperative that he and Ysobel return to the federation. They had proven themselves in battle before, and given the opportunity would do so again.

Unless, of course, they were punished for incompetence, for not having foreseen the Ikarians' aggression. Some might even see Ysobel's decision to leave Karystos as a reckless abandonment of her sworn duty.

And what could they say? "Emperor Lucius disguised himself as a monk and took passage on a common trader so we decided to follow him"?

With no proof, the truth would condemn them as fools.

He threw himself into a chair, looking longingly at the sweat-beaded decanter of chilled wine that sat on the table, left over from their earlier lunch.

But he had not drunk a glass then, and he would not now.

At last, Ysobel returned.

"Well?" he asked, rising to his feet. "What did he say?"

Ysobel showed fewer scruples than he, for she crossed to the sideboard and poured two cups of wine. She handed one to him, not bothering to add water.

Ysobel swallowed half the cup, then said, "I wouldn't buy so much as a rusty nail from him."

He breathed a sigh of relief and took a sip of his own wine.

"But—" Lady Ysobel began, and he felt his heart sink. "He is not lying about this. He was attacked, and the description he gave sounds very much like an Ikarian ship."

"The federation must be informed."

"Dorinda is seeing to that," Ysobel said, with a grimace. "And I will send word as well."

"What of us?"

"We will wait," she said. "The monthly courier ship is expected in two days' time. We can board her for her return to Sendat."

A courier ship would be faster than any merchant that they could hire. But he was not looking forward to spending two more days kicking their heels ashore.

"And what of *Hypatia*?"

Ysobel laughed. "By now she's unloaded her cargo in Vidrun and picked up a new load. I doubt Lucius was ever on board."

If Lucius had been on board, headed for Xandropol, then the *Hypatia* should join the list of overdue ships, so the guild could be notified. But privately he agreed with Ysobel; it was unlikely that Lucius had boarded *Hypatia*.

He had simply disappeared in Tarsus, and they had chased an illusion.

And for that they would pay the price.

Ysobel strode impatiently back and forth across the pier, as a harbor pilot guided *Hypatia* into an open berth. To her eyes the ship appeared undamaged, but there must be a reason why the captain had signaled for a berth rather than simply dropping anchor in the harbor.

She could see the courier ship, loading supplies in preparation for the return voyage back to the islands. She and Burrell had planned to board later today. But instead of a summons to their ship, a servant had brought the news that *Hypatia* was in harbor, preparing to dock. It was only sheer luck that she'd found out—she'd intended to tell Dorinda's clerks that they no longer need watch for *Hypatia,* but in her anger over being deceived by Lucius she'd forgotten.

Burrell leaned against a support pillar, pretending to watch *Hypatia*'s approach, but she knew his gaze rested on her when he thought her attention elsewhere. His mood was in direct counterpoint to her own. As her frustration grew, Burrell became visibly calmer, which served to irritate her even more.

At last *Hypatia* was tied to the pier, and a gangway put in place. The customs clerk and his assistant were the first to board, with Ysobel nearly treading on their heels.

Ysobel had her second shock of the day, when she saw Zorion standing next to a middle-aged woman. She'd known he was sailing for the house of Arles, but hadn't realized that *Hypatia* was his ship.

"I need to see your bills of lading and your registration certificates," the clerk was saying. "You're liable for the daily docking fee plus a tax on all goods that are bought, sold, or delivered."

"I have no cargo, merely a passenger to disembark," Zorion replied.

So Lucius *was* on board. Her hands clenched into fists.

Ysobel stepped around the clerk and Zorion's eyes widened as he saw her.

"This is Amelie, my cargo master," Zorion said. "She will provide you with whatever you require."

Amelie drew the customs officials to one side.

"Where is he?" Ysobel demanded.

Zorion's lips twisted in a rueful smile. "Not even a greeting? I thought we'd parted on better terms than that," he said.

"Our apologies, Captain Zorion, but the matter is too urgent for pleasantries," Burrell said, pitching his voice low so none could overhear them.

"Where is Lucius?" Ysobel asked.

"Lucius?"

"Josan, or Brother Mensah, or whatever he calls himself these days. The passenger you took on board in Rauma."

"Below," Zorion said.

Ysobel started to move past him, but he placed his bulk in front of her. "I'll not have you disturbing him," he said. "Not until you tell me what business you have with him."

"Do you know who you have on board?"

"He's a passenger who has paid his passage twice over, once in coin and again in service to this ship," Zorion said. "So I ask you again, what business do you have with him?"

She wondered if this would have been easier if the captain was a stranger to her. Zorion knew her too well. With a few words, he could make her feel like the awkward young woman she had once been.

"The emperor of Ikaria is in your guest cabin," she said, and had the satisfaction of watching Zorion's face pale. "And as we are likely at war with his empire, I need to have a word with him."

"They weren't Ikarians," Zorion said.

His words made no sense.

"Who weren't Ikarians?"

"The ships that attacked *Rhosyn*," Zorion replied. "They had Ikarian sails, but the ships were built in Vidrun and crewed by mercenaries."

"*Greenbow*?" Burrell asked.

Zorion shook his head. "Not *Greenbow*, it was *Rhosyn*. Which is why we're late. *Rhosyn* was damaged, so we escorted her to Tyrns."

Rhosyn had not been on the list of overdue ships, but the list only encompassed those ships that were expected in Xandropol. But if she had been attacked by someone posing as Ikarians ...

"And you are certain they were not Ikarians?" she asked.

"I would swear it on my life," he said. "On your life."

Which was his way of reminding her of the history that lay between them. She had let Zorion go from her service for precisely that reason—because he valued her life over his duty to his ship. He would not have uttered such an oath lightly.

"We need to talk," she said, just as Zorion uttered the same words.

"Come below," Zorion said. He nodded to Amelie, who was still conferring with the customs officials, then led them below to his cabin. There was a neatly made bunk in one corner, and a large table which could serve for mapping routes, or hosting a half dozen at dinner. Zorion took a seat at the head of the table, and she and Burrell sat on either side of him.

She had seen no sign of Lucius, but he must be nearby.

"Tell me of this man you think is Lucius," he said.

"I do not think he is Emperor Lucius, I know it," she said. "And he is behind what has happened."

It was too much of a coincidence that he had disappeared at the same time that his navy had begun attacking federation ships.

Zorion shook his head. "You may be right about his name, but you're wrong about the other. I told you I owe him a debt—without him we never would have reached the *Rhosyn* in time to help. Somehow he managed to call a storm from a clear day and called lightning to strike his attackers."

She and Burrell shared a long look. "It is him," she said. "Emperor Lucius has the magic of his ancestors, and we have seen him call the winds to do his bidding."

Zorion still did not appear convinced. "But what is he doing here? Aboard my ship?"

"I intend to ask him that very question," she said.

She knew her smile wasn't a pleasant one. But she had grown tired of Lucius's prevarications and had not forgiven him for breaking faith with her when he had fled in Rauma.

"You'll go easy," Zorion said. "I'll have your word on that."

"He is our enemy."

"I *owe* him," Zorion said.

She knew better than to expect that he would lightly set that debt aside. It did not matter whether or not Lucius was deserving of such consideration. If Zorion believed that he owed Lucius, then he would insist on repaying that debt.

"I will not harm him," she said. It was the best she could offer.

"Very well, I'll have him fetched," Zorion said. "There's not room for all of us in his cabin."

Zorion stepped outside and spoke to a sailor.

A few moments later, two sailors entered, supporting Lucius between them.

His appearance was a shock—he was thinner than she recalled, and his legs dragged uselessly on the ground as the sailors maneuvered him into a seat.

He had feigned weakness once, but she doubted very much that this was a show put on for her benefit. He had the look of a man who was gravely ill, and she could see why Zorion had been hesitant to disturb him.

But whatever pity she might feel was overbalanced by the harm he had done to her, and to her people.

"Lady Ysobel," he said. "Captain Burrell."

She waited until the sailors had left, shutting the door behind them. "Emperor Lucius," she said.

Lucius nodded in acknowledgment, then turned to Zorion. "How long have you known?" he asked.

"She's spent the last quarter hour trying to convince me that I had an emperor aboard. But I did not believe it till this very minute," Zorion said.

"Is an emperor any more unlikely than a magician?" Lucius asked.

Zorion chuckled. "I'll grant you that."

The ease between them grated on her nerves. They were conversing as old friends, leaving it up to her to remind them that this was not a social occasion.

"Tell me, emperor, how long have you known that our countries were at war?"

Lucius abruptly sobered. "The attackers were not Ikarians, they were mercenaries from Vidrun," he said. "Captain Zorion will tell you as much."

"So he has said. But he has no proof except his own word. And other ships have told a different tale," she pointed out.

"Not just my word," Zorion began, but Lucius interrupted him.

"I cannot be responsible for what other men say," Lucius replied, speaking over Zorion's protests. "I know the truth, and that is enough."

Could he really be so naïve?

"It will not be enough for the federation," she said. "Already messages have been sent telling them that the Ikarian navy is once more on the attack. They will not wait; they will take action."

Lucius still did not appear to comprehend the danger, but Burrell's face grew grim.

"What will your people do when the federation navy attacks one of your own?" Burrell asked Lucius. "They will not wait to ask why. They will simply respond in kind."

"And then it will be war, whether just or not," Ysobel said. "Once it starts, it will be beyond any of us to stop it."

Lucius swore under his breath. She did not recognize the language but could guess the meaning.

"What would you have me do?" he asked.

She hesitated, not having expected him to capitulate so easily.

"Put an end to this before it is too late," Burrell said.

"How?" Lucius demanded. "I have no ships, no armies, no one to do my bidding. I cannot even command my limbs to obey me."

Her face showed the neutral mask she wore when trading, but his scorn cut her to the quick. Lucius, for all his faults, was right. In her obsession to find him, she hadn't thought what she would do with him—or what he could do for her. A poor strategist indeed, to pursue a prize with no idea of its worth.

But just because she could not immediately think of a use for him did not mean that he was without value.

"If you sent orders to your navy—" Burrell began.

Lucius slammed his hand on the table. "Those were not my ships. Whatever ills you think were done, they were not done by my men."

"The attackers were mercenaries from Vidrun,"

Zorion said, drawing all eyes to him. "We'd the luck to capture one of their officers. He confirmed what his sailors had told us, that they'd been hired to pose as Ikarians to attack our ships."

"Where is this officer?" Ysobel said. "Where is your proof?"

"With *Rhosyn*," Zorion said. "She was the injured party, and she had the claim against them. They were put ashore with her in Tyrns."

It was her turn to swear. Lucius's words were suspect, but she trusted Zorion. If he said that the attackers had been mercenaries posing as Ikarians, she believed him. But others would not share her belief, and any proof was hundreds of miles away in Tyrns. If the mercenaries were even still alive. *Rhosyn*'s captain might have asked the authorities to execute them as pirates. He would not have known that other ships had been attacked, nor how important it was to prove who was behind these attacks.

Meanwhile, Captain Pepin from the house of Laurent had sworn that he'd been attacked by Ikarians, and Dorinda would send the account of his attack back to the federation as a warning.

It was likely that Pepin had been tricked by the same vessels that attacked *Rhosyn*, but without proof, the ministry would be left to judge the tales of two captains. Zorion's reputation for honesty might have carried the day—

If the recent war with the Ikarians was not still fresh in everyone's memories.

Faced with a tale from Zorion that could not be

proven, and a growing list of missing ships, it was likely that the council of ministers would err on the side of caution.

They would launch an attack, hoping they could inflict sufficient damage before the Ikarians' new weapons turned the tide of battle against them.

"You could come with us," Burrell said. "We sail for Sendat this afternoon."

Zorion shook his head. "I cannot abandon *Hypatia,* nor my duty to the house of Arles. I have already stretched that duty as far as I can. And I doubt they'd find my tale any more convincing in the flesh."

"Not you," Burrell said. "Him."

And he pointed to Emperor Lucius.

They did not know what they asked of him.

Josan had been stunned by Burrell's absurd request, then shocked when Ysobel took him seriously. She'd asked—no, demanded—that he go with her to the federation.

Where presumably his presence would be enough to convince the federation that the Ikarian Empire was not behind the recent attacks.

Or that they could use him to bargain for peace.

It was absurd. Anything he said would likely be contradicted by Proconsul Zuberi and his allies. They might be preparing to crown a new emperor even as he sat here, hiding in his cabin, pretending that he was safe on board the ship of his enemies.

He knew that was not strictly fair. Not all in the federation could be judged by Lady Ysobel's standards. Captain Zorion had dealt with him honestly. It had been Zorion who put an end to Ysobel's badgering, insisting that Josan, as he still called him, be allowed to think over her request in private. He'd personally helped Josan back to his cabin and sworn that Josan would not be disturbed.

But neither was Josan free to leave. He could stand on his own, for a few minutes. But he could not leave this ship without help. Nor without Zorion's permission.

Even if Zorion was willing to let him go, Lady Ysobel was not. He'd be set upon the moment his foot touched the dock.

He was trapped, and he knew that all had sensed his fear.

They thought him a coward—willing to chance a senseless war rather than risking his own life by journeying to the land of his enemies.

Ysobel had sworn over and over again that he would be safe, under diplomatic protection. She might even believe it to be true, but he knew better. Politicians had no honor, and the emperor of Ikaria was a prize that would be too tempting to resist.

But he did not fear the Seddonians. Nothing they could do to him would be worse than his current fate, trapped in a body that was slowly failing.

If a cure was to be found, it would be here. In Xandropol, somewhere within the complex of buildings that formed the great library, and the tens of thousands of volumes stored within.

He had little time left. And if he turned aside now—

There would be no cure. Just death—perhaps swift, perhaps slow. He had only his own conjectures on how long it would take this body to fail completely. He might be trapped within a paralyzed shell for days, months, or even years, at the mercy of those around him.

When the time came, he hoped they'd have the kindness to kill him.

He suspected they would want him to suffer first.

It was not cowardice, was it, to want to live? He'd never asked for any of this—never asked for the spell that had taken his soul from his own dying body and transplanted it into the body of a prince.

Never asked to be emperor.

He'd never wanted power, nor fame, nor riches. Just to be allowed to live the life of a scholar in the peaceful pursuit of knowledge.

It was not fair, he thought, with a child's overwhelming sense of injustice. I do not deserve this.

But what he deserved was a double-edged sword. Many would say that he did not deserve to be alive, living in this borrowed body. And what of Lucius? If there was any hope of restoring his soul, it would be found here. If Josan gave in to Ysobel's demands, he would be condemning both of them to death.

In Xandropol there was hope that at least one of them might be saved. If they went to the federation . . .

They might even die before they reached the islands. In which case, his sacrifice would be for naught.

His thoughts chased themselves in endless circles, but

as his temper cooled, reason came once more to the forefront.

He'd told the others that he could not be held responsible for the attacks. If mercenaries chose to pose as ships from his navy, then the impostors were the ones who should be caught and punished for their deeds.

But it was troubling that the mercenaries were from Vidrun—a powerful kingdom with a long history of enmity toward Ikaria.

Among Empress Nerissa's accomplishments had been bringing an end to the interminable wars with Vidrun—though she had not achieved victory, merely a stalemate that was declared to be peace.

The question to ask was who would benefit if Ikaria and the federation went to war?

The federation would not attack their own ships. They did not want war, not because they were opposed to it, but because they saw no profit in it. The risks posed by the newly armed Ikarian navy were too great.

As for himself, Josan had been sickened by killing. The fire weapons he had taught his navy to make had indeed lived up to their name—the Burning Terror. But the ingredients for the Burning Terror required a rare earth element, so their supply was limited. And conventional sea warfare still favored the federation, with their larger fleet. If the two nations went to war, it would be a long, deadly struggle that would weaken them both.

Which might well be what was intended. Vidrun's expansion to the north had ended at the Bronze River, stopped by the armies of Volesk. Her expansion to the south had halted, in part, because the imperial legions had offered their assistance to Kazagan, which their king had reluctantly accepted, becoming a vassal state of the Ikarian Empire.

But if the empire was weakened by war, then Vidrun could attack unopposed. And best of all, they need risk nothing beyond hiring a few ships of mercenaries to incite the conflict.

It was a clever plan. And he had an ugly suspicion that he knew who was behind it.

Brother Nikos. Once head of the Learned Brethren in Ikaria, and one of Empress Nerissa's principal advisors.

And the man who had orchestrated the foul spell that had joined Josan's soul to Lucius's body, in an attempt to create a puppet that would be under his command.

Nikos had deserved death for his crimes, but he could not be executed without revealing what he had done, which would have meant Josan's own death. Instead Nikos had been exiled from Ikaria, sent to join his brethren in Xandropol. But he'd never arrived. Spies had reported his presence in Vidrun, where, it seemed, he was up to his old tricks.

Josan sighed. Even if Nikos was not behind this, he could not let it go unchallenged. If there was anything he could do to prevent a conflict from erupting, he must do it.

Lucius, he called, listening intently for any trace of the prince's mind voice. *Lucius,* he called again, but there was no answer.

He would have to decide for both of them.

Strange—he had known of Lucius's existence for over two years, ever since he'd discovered that this body was not his own. They'd argued, fought, and struggled for supremacy, before finally learning to cooperate. When Lucius was present, he could hear what Lucius was thinking, sense his feelings, and at times he'd been able to draw upon Lucius's memories and skills.

But he still did not know Lucius. He did not know what Lucius would choose if the decision was his to make.

Lucius had agreed to this journey, seeing it as his last chance to restore himself to health and to sole command of his own flesh.

It was tempting to take the path of cowardice and claim that this was what Lucius would have wanted.

But Lucius also saw himself as an emperor in the tradition of his illustrious ancestors. Given the opportunity, he might choose the path of noble sacrifice, rather than self-interest.

Josan knew what he must do, but he continued to weigh the options over in his mind, pretending that his fate was not already sealed.

He'd been in his cabin for at least two hours when at last a knock sounded on his door. Lady Ysobel's patience had held out longer than he'd expected.

"Enter," he called.

Zorion entered, carrying a tray. "You missed lunch," he said.

It was a kindness to have fetched it. Zorion set the tray on the bed next to Josan. He'd no appetite, but picked up the cup, which was filled with plain water, and drank it down.

"You can trust Lady Ysobel," Zorion said. "I served her for a decade, and she never broke her word to me. If she says she'll protect you, she will."

Josan shrugged. "I'm sure you have found her to be fair," he said.

He did not doubt that she'd dealt honestly with Zorion, and had likely done the same with others that she encountered in her role as Ysobel of Flordelis of Alcina—captain, ship owner, and head of her own trading house.

But that was not the woman he had had dealings with. Ysobel the spy, Ysobel the conspirator, Ysobel the politician, was quite a different creature. That woman's loyalty was to her own advancement first and her country second. She was more than capable of promising one thing to Emperor Lucius while intending something else entirely.

But he would not argue the matter with Zorion and risk antagonizing the only one who'd showed compassion for him.

"Even if she is true to her word, do you imagine she speaks for all of your countrymen?" Josan asked.

Zorion rubbed his chin with one hand. "Her word should be enough," he said.

"But it won't be," Josan finished for him. "If I survive the trip, it's likely my presence there will accomplish nothing except providing a target for their wrath."

Zorion's gaze had sharpened as Josan mentioned the possibility that he would not survive the trip. It was a fear he'd not shared with the others, but then, they had not been witness to his steady decline in the way that Zorion had.

"I could fetch a physician," Zorion offered.

Josan's mouth twisted in a bitter grimace. "I don't need a physician. I need a miracle."

"So you've made your decision, then?" Zorion asked.

Josan nodded. "Tell Ysobel she's won. I'll go with her, for all the good it may do us both."

To his surprise, his capitulation did not appear to make Zorion happy. Instead Zorion frowned, and stared at the floor of the cabin, as if seeking guidance from the scarred planks.

"There's something you should know before you make your decision," Zorion said. "Two ships entered the harbor a few moments ago. They bear the colors of the Ikarian navy."

"The mercenaries are here?" Josan pushed himself up, swaying as he tried to stand.

"Easy," Zorion said, grasping his forearms and lowering him back down when it became clear that Josan's legs would not support him.

Josan flushed, humiliated anew by his weakness.

"They don't have the look of pirates," Zorion said. "They could be exactly what they seem to be, though what brings them this far east is a mystery."

It was possible, if unlikely, that they had come looking for him. Even if not, if they were true navy vessels, then perhaps he was no longer at Ysobel's mercy.

Though he must first find a way to speak to their captains. Hopefully there would be at least one of those he had helped train—otherwise, it might be difficult to convince them that the frail man dressed as a common merchant was indeed their emperor.

"Bring their captains to me," Josan said. "I will know if they are my men or impostors."

He held his breath, knowing that Zorion held his fate in his hands. He could not help but wonder at the impulse that had prompted Zorion to tell him of the Ikarian ships. If he'd kept silent, Josan would have sailed with Lady Ysobel, never knowing that there might have been another choice.

"How shall I fetch them? They'll hardly believe me if I say I have Emperor Lucius aboard," Zorion said.

"Tell them the truth," Josan said. "Tell them that there've been reports of pirates masquerading as Ikarian ships, and you want their help. If they are mercenaries, they'll come because they need to find out what you know. And if they're not, then they'll come because that is their duty."

"And what will you say to them?"

"Whatever I must," Josan said, growing impatient. "I will not argue with you. You were the one to bring me this news. Summon them or not, it is up to you. But I'll wager even Lady Ysobel will want to know what these captains know, and I am the only one who can get that information for you."

"I can recognize a mercenary," Zorion said, but his tone was mild.

"And if the mercenaries and my navy are working together, how will you discover that?"

"There's that," he admitted. "Very well, I'll send them

a message. If they come, they come. If not, at sunset I'll give Lady Ysobel your answer."

"Thank you," Josan said.

He felt like a condemned man given an unexpected reprieve. Hope returned, but it was almost too painful to bear.

Chapter 13

Zorion had visited Ikaria often enough to expect that both captains would be men. There were no women in their navy, nor indeed in any positions of authority. One was young for his rank, something perhaps explainable by his dark hair and pale complexion that showed his connections to the new Ikarian nobility. The other was a middle-aged man, with the light brown hair of the old Ikarians who were more typically found in the navy.

He was surprised at how quickly they had answered his invitation—and that they'd come in person rather than sending junior officers. Either they were truly concerned over a possible threat to the truce between their countries, or they were both involved in whatever was going on.

"Your message mentioned pirates, disguised as one of our ships?"

Curiously it was the younger captain who was doing the talking. His uniform was new, the fabric unweathered, while his companion's uniform showed signs of wear, the brass insignia worn down from repeated polishing.

The pirates that had attacked *Rhosyn* hadn't bothered with uniforms, except for the officer they'd captured, who'd worn a belted tunic with leggings rather than the customary pantaloons.

If he'd met them anywhere else, he would have taken them to be what they said they were. But these were perilous times, and he was interested to see what his passenger would make of them.

"If you'll follow me, there's someone below that you need to speak with," he said.

The two captains exchanged glances. Going below meant putting themselves at risk, since the sailors that had rowed them over would be unable to see or hear any disturbance.

Then again, only a fool would attack a captain while his ship—and its heavily armed crew—swung at anchor only a few hundred yards away.

Zorion had put Josan in his own cabin for this meeting, where he'd be able to sit upright in the backed chair, giving the illusion of strength.

As the door to his cabin swung open, the younger captain stopped so abruptly that his companion ran into him.

"Emperor Lucius!" he exclaimed, then dropped down on one knee. "It is good to see you again."

"Chenzira. Rise and tell me what you are doing here."

"I've come for you," the young captain said, scrambling to his feet. "I swore to the admiral that I could find you, and I did. Your calculations were exactly right.

Following the new route, we made the voyage in less than half the time it would have taken before."

Josan—no, Lucius—smiled. "You've shown yourself an apt pupil."

Zorion realized that, up until this moment, he'd not really believed that this was Lucius, emperor of Ikaria. Even after Ysobel had identified him, and after Josan had agreed with her, he'd still thought of him as simply Josan, the man who had begged for passage to Xandropol.

But imperial captains would not kneel for just any traveler.

"This is Captain Eugenio," Captain Chenzira said.

"Emperor Lucius, I am honored," the second man said. He'd remained kneeling even after Chenzira had advanced.

"Rise," Lucius said. "This is Captain Zorion's ship, not the throne room in Karystos. Come, sit."

Chenzira took the seat closest to the emperor, while Eugenio sat next to him, his back as stiff as a plank. Zorion sat opposite them so he could watch their faces as Lucius questioned them.

"Why did you leave *Green Dragon*?" Chenzira asked. "I would have sailed you anywhere you wanted. I would have rowed you here myself, if only you'd asked."

So Chenzira was not just any captain. He was the emperor's personal captain, which explained why his comrade deferred to him.

"I had my reasons," Lucius said. He did not bother to explain himself, the first sign that he was accustomed to command. "Did Captain Zorion tell you what happened?"

Chenzira shook his head. "Only that there was a suspicion that one of our ships had turned pirate."

"I saw the attack with my own eyes," Lucius said. "Two ships, with the red-bordered sails of our navy, attacking a federation merchant ship."

"They were not ours," Captain Chenzira insisted. "They could not have been."

Captain Eugenio eyed Zorion, then turned back to his emperor. "May I speak freely?" he asked.

"I command you to do so," Lucius said.

Eugenio swallowed. "Last year, there were...incidents," he began.

"You mean honest ships and their crews were destroyed by your navy," Zorion interrupted. Good men and women, along with their ships, had simply disappeared at sea, their fates a matter for conjecture.

The federation might have begun the practice, but the imperials had perfected it.

Eugenio shrugged. "There was much to regret on both sides," he said. "But Admiral Septimus has given strict orders, and none would dare disobey him. Whatever you saw, those ships weren't under the command of one of your captains."

"They were crewed by mercenaries," Lucius said. "Is it possible that the navy is using mercenaries to mask our involvement?"

"No," Eugenio responded. "The admiral would not defile our fleet in that way."

Lucius turned to Chenzira. "What of your uncle?"

Chenzira's lips thinned. "The proconsul no longer

shares confidences with me," he said. "But if he had given such orders, we would have known."

Lucius sighed.

"I thought you'd be pleased that they were not ours," Chenzira observed.

"If they were my ships, I could order them home," he said. "Or whoever has taken my place could do the same."

"You are still emperor," Chenzira said. "No matter where you are."

"So we're back to where we were," Zorion said. "With no proof, and no way to stop them, the empire will take the blame for these attacks."

"Unless I convince them otherwise," Lucius said. "I have not forgotten my promise. You may tell Lady Ysobel that I will accompany her back to the federation."

"No," Chenzira said.

Lucius's eyebrows rose. "You wish to advise me?"

"I have my orders," Chenzira said. "I am not to leave you. If you need to travel, then you will do so aboard my ship. Lady Ysobel may join you there."

Zorion did not like this, and he knew Lady Ysobel would like it even less. It was one thing to sail aboard a federation courier ship, but if the emperor was on his own ship, he could change his mind at any time.

"You already agreed," Zorion said. "And in our waters you will be far safer in a federation vessel than on one of your own."

"Not to mention Lady Ysobel would prefer her own ship," Lucius said.

"You cannot ask her to travel aboard one of yours, surrounded by her enemies," Zorion said.

"Of course not," Lucius countered. "After all, I've already agreed to travel to the country of my enemies in order to try and stop a war I did not start. Clearly it's too much to ask that she should inconvenience herself in any way."

It was more than a mere inconvenience, but Lucius had made his point. Of the two, he was taking the far greater risk.

"Lady Ysobel will be as safe on my ship as she would be on one of her own," Captain Chenzira said.

Zorion doubted that. But short of kidnapping Lucius, he could not force the emperor to do anything. If he were in Lucius's place, he'd want to be on one of his own ships, surrounded by his own people.

Especially if he thought he was dying.

"Agreed," he said. "I'll inform Lady Ysobel of your decision."

"Thank you," Lucius said.

He rose, noticing that Captain Eugenio appeared troubled that he did not wait to be dismissed. No doubt the Ikarians expected courtly manners, but *Hypatia* was his ship, and while he was on her, he deferred to no one.

Not even an emperor.

Ysobel pulled her cloak tightly around her against the midnight chill. By habit she glanced up at the stars, noting that they continued to steer a southwesterly course, toward the islands of the federation.

So far, it seemed, Emperor Lucius intended to live up to his promises.

It was strange being aboard a ship of the imperial navy, where the crew insisted on treating her as if she were a delicate lady of the court, despite the fact that she owned—and had captained—larger vessels. She'd been given the cabin assigned to the first lieutenant as her own, and Captain Chenzira had offered to allow her to bring a maid on board, but Ysobel had declined. Unless she was dressing in the formal attire required for the court, she was well able to serve her own needs.

She'd cheerfully have shared the cabin with Burrell, but knew the suggestion would have shocked her hosts, who'd assigned Burrell to bunk with their officers.

Both she and Burrell had been observing their hosts closely. The ship appeared to be on course, but for the past two evenings the emperor had left his cabin to meet with Captain Chenzira up on the deck. Burrell had been unable to get close enough to overhear what they discussed, so tonight Ysobel was trying her hand at spying.

The few crew on night watch gave her a wide berth—indeed only the officers would look her in the face. The common sailors glanced away if they caught sight of her, and would not speak to her unless she spoke to them first. On Captain Chenzira's orders, she suspected.

Lucius and Chenzira were standing next to a high table that had been brought up onto the deck—so tall that a man could write without having to sit down. Two scrolls were weighted down against the breeze, and beside them was a navigator's quadrant—an object she knew well.

A thin beam of light from a shuttered lantern illuminated the scrolls, as Lucius wrote and Chenzira observed.

She realized he was reckoning their position.

"This way is quicker," Lucius was saying. "See here? You can replace these two equations with this."

Chenzira murmured something she could not hear.

"It's easier for a beginner to follow the equations step by step, till they understand the process," Lucius was explaining. "But once you've done enough of these, you'll have memorized the sets and can use Jennivar's transformations instead."

"Not all of us have swallowed a library," Chenzira said, with a laugh. "Show me again, slowly."

Lucius smiled, absently brushing the hair from his eyes. As he looked up, he caught sight of her.

"Good evening, emperor," she said, as if she had every right to be here.

"Lady Ysobel," Lucius said. "Curious, or merely unable to sleep?"

"Perhaps a little of both," she said.

He gestured for her to approach.

"I'll wager Ysobel has been reckoning these sums since she was a child," Lucius said. "She can probably tell our position without needing paper for her calculations."

Ysobel shook her head. "It's been a while," she said.

Far too long since she'd sailed as captain. In the brief war last year she'd commanded ships, but as leader of a task force rather than as captain. Navigation had been left to others; Ysobel had plotted tactics instead.

She glanced down at the table and saw two sets of equations. The ones by Chenzira followed the forms she was familiar with—proof, if any was needed, that the Ikarians had learned the secrets of navigation from someone in the federation.

The emperor's scroll, on the other hand, was less than half the length of Chenzira's and included symbols she did not recognize.

Interesting. She'd never imagined the emperor as a teacher, though it had long been rumored that he was the one who had brought his navy the stolen secrets. And from Chenzira's ease, it was clear that this was not the first time the emperor had instructed him.

She walked around the table, so the scrolls were no longer upside down, but still could make no sense of the writing upon Lucius's. Though the final line on both scrolls was the same—a set of numbers that referred to charts based on *Aeneades*' map of the Great Basin.

Both positions were the same—a point approximately halfway between Xandropol and Grayza. Precisely where they should be.

"We'll need your guidance to sail the inner passage," Chenzira said. "Or we can skirt the islands and arrive from the west, but that will add days to our trip."

"When it's time, I'll give you the course," she said.

She waited for a moment, but Lucius showed no signs of resuming his instruction. Pity. She would like to have understood the meaning of the symbols that he'd so carelessly scratched. It was possible that his knowledge was in fact superior to the federation's, which left her once again wondering who had taught him.

At least she had found out what she needed to. Odd as it might seem, the emperor's midnight excursions were not a sign of conspiracy.

And whatever illness he had been suffering from in

Xandropol seemed to have passed. Lucius had told Zorion that he was dying, but other than being thinner than he had been, he showed no signs of imminent collapse. His voice was strong, his body relaxed as he stood next to Chenzira, cheerfully correcting his sums.

She bid them both good night and returned below. She knew Burrell would be interested in what she had discovered, but seeking him out this late would surely offend the Ikarians' rigid sense of propriety. If she'd uncovered a plot, she would not have cared for their offense, but good news could safely wait until morning.

Owing perhaps to his late night, Lucius did not make an appearance the next day. The following day she met with Chenzira to plot out their approach to Sendat. Foreign vessels normally skirted around the islands, but with no time to waste, she had agreed to guide Chenzira's ship through the inner passage. They'd likely pick up an escort as soon as they were sighted, but a single Ikarian navy vessel under a flag of truce should be safe enough until then.

She wondered where the second Ikarian ship had gone—was it secretly rendezvousing with an Ikarian fleet somewhere at sea? Or was it returning to Karystos, as Captain Chenzira had claimed?

She wondered how Zuberi and the rest of the Ikarian government would react to the news of their missing emperor. Would they rejoice that he had been found? Or had they already begun the process to replace him?

Speed was of the essence. The emperor was akin to a cargo of exotic fruit. Rare and highly prized, his value nonetheless rotted a little each day that he had been away from his empire.

Mindful that they could not afford mistakes, she made Chenzira trace the course she had shown him on the map, proving that he had understood her directions. At last she pronounced herself satisfied.

"And Emperor Lucius, will he dine with us tonight?" she asked. "I wish to speak with him about his intentions once we arrive in Sendat."

She had her own plans for Lucius, of course, but it would be easier if he cooperated.

Chenzira shook his head. "It's unlikely. The emperor is unwell."

"He appeared fine the other night," she said.

"The emperor is not accustomed to sea travel," he explained.

Strange. Lucius had just spent weeks at sea—some in tolerable conditions, others less so. If he was suffering from anything, it wasn't from being at sea.

Lucius had appeared fine the other night, but she remembered Zorion's voice as he shared with her Lucius's conviction that he was dying. She'd not forgotten that he'd tricked her once by feigning illness, and had assumed this was simply a ploy for sympathy, especially when the physician they'd summoned found nothing wrong with him other than a lingering weakness which the physician had ascribed to a summer ague.

But what if he was genuinely unwell?

She made her way to Lucius's quarters, which were a suite of two rooms adjacent to the captain's quarters. Less luxurious than she'd expected, it was likely that *Green Dragon* had been designed as an admiral's flagship, rather than the emperor's personal ship, which would have been large enough to accommodate both the emperor and his numerous attendants.

A single functionary was aboard, who oversaw the two crewmen Chenzira had assigned to serve the emperor. They had little enough to do. If Chenzira had thought to bring a wardrobe fit for an emperor, there was no sign of it. Instead Lucius continued to wear the clothes she had purchased for him after the wreck.

She wondered how the Ikarians would react if she were to present them with a bill for all she had spent on Lucius's behalf.

The crewman who stood outside the door to Lucius's room stiffened as she approached.

She observed him carefully. Unlike the federation navy, which was comprised of sailors and marines, the Ikarians did not distinguish between those who served on ships and those who were trained for boarding enemy vessels and land attacks. Both were called sailors, and both wore the same uniform. This man had the sunburned skin and callused hands of one who pulled lines, rather than one who practiced with the cudgel and short sword.

A sailor, rather than a guard. This would make her task even easier.

"The emperor is not to be disturbed," he said.

"I need to speak with him."

"He asked to be left alone," the sailor insisted, his eyes darting down the passageway, looking for someone with the authority to dismiss her.

She advanced, projecting an air of absolute confidence. She knew that the sailors were under orders not to touch her.

At the last moment, he stepped aside.

"I'll summon the captain," the man said.

"Do so."

She unlatched the door and pushed it open.

The Ikarians' prejudice against women was a weakness. A federation sailor would have stood his ground, but this sailor judged her little threat. He was more afraid of disobeying an order by striking her than he was of any harm she might do his emperor.

She had previously been in Lucius's sitting chamber, which had a large window cut into the bow of the ship and a table where they had dined. This room was smaller, with merely two small portholes for fresh air and lanterns to provide light.

Lucius sat in the room's sole chair, still dressed in a linen sleeping robe. The blankets on his bed were disarranged, suggesting he had only recently arisen.

"Lady Ysobel, I would say this was a pleasure, but I recall asking not to be disturbed," he said.

His face was flat, unwelcoming. This was not the same man who had joked with Chenzira under the stars.

"I heard of your illness and was concerned," she said.

"Concerned that I might die before you can trade me

for something of worth," he said. "Since you're here, you might as well fetch me water."

He gestured toward a small table, where she found a pitcher of warmish water and a cup. She filled the cup and brought it to him, wondering where his servants were. Surely there should be someone here attending to him?

"I sent them away," he said. "I wished to be alone."

She ignored his words and the glare that accompanied them.

"We will arrive in Sendat in a few days," she said. "I came to ask what you intend."

Lucius drank the water, and then held out the cup for more.

She heard voices in the hall, then a brisk knock at the door, followed by it swinging open.

It wasn't Chenzira, but rather his first lieutenant, Federico, whose quarters Burrell was sharing. Federico bowed low.

"Emperor, I apologize. This won't happen again," Federico said. Then he turned to Ysobel and gestured for her to come.

"Let her stay," Lucius said, showing one of the rapid mood changes that had been the subject of so much gossip back in Karystos. "When she no longer amuses me, I will command her to leave."

Federico bowed low, and when he straightened his cheeks were flushed. She knew just how Lucius's remark had been interpreted.

"Of course," Federico said. "I will see that no one else disturbs you."

He backed out and closed the door behind him. He must have thought that he'd interrupted the two of them as they were preparing for a tryst.

Lucius had meant to insult her, but she refused to be distracted.

"What do you intend?" she asked.

"*He* has a plan," Lucius said, finishing the cup of water.

"He?"

"Josan. The monk," Lucius said.

He did not look feverish, but his words made no sense. "I do not understand."

"Of course you don't. I don't understand myself—we were in Xandropol. We could have sought a cure, but *he* decided to turn aside."

Was the emperor insane? Was this the secret behind his so-called illness? The reason for his flight?

How could she have missed this?

"What is Josan's plan?" she asked, speaking softly as if to a child.

Lucius laughed, an ugly sound. "You'll have to ask him." He looked around his cabin. "Is there wine?" he asked.

"No," she said, without even bothering to look.

"I suppose you think me mad," he said.

She said nothing. Let him interpret her silence as he would.

Lucius rose from his chair and sat on his bed, leaning back against the wall. "Sit," he said, gesturing to the chair. "Let me tell you a story."

He waited until she had sat down before continuing. "Years ago, in the time of the first rebellion against Nerissa, there was a monk named Brother Josan. He'd been at the library in Xandropol collecting rare knowledge, but on his journey back to Ikaria he was struck down by the breakbone fever. By the time he reached the collegium it was too late; there was nothing the monks could do for him."

"So you took his identity?" She'd long suspected that Lucius had lived under the brethren's protection during his exile.

"Patience," he said. "At the same time there was a young man. A prince—arrogant, ambitious, and so naïve that he placed his trust in those who wanted to use him for their own gain, regardless of the cost."

His words stung, and her hands curled into fists at her sides. "I did not come here to be insulted. Or to rehash all of our dealings."

"Ah, but you've never heard the rest of this," he said. "Only two people know the full story—three if you count Josan."

How did one count a dead man? She nodded for him to proceed.

"The prince, realizing that the rebellion was doomed, fled to his old tutor, Brother Nikos. And Nikos saw an opportunity. The rebellion had shown him that Empress Nerissa was vulnerable. The prince, alas, was too weak, but with Nikos's backing the proper candidate might succeed. Nikos sent for a monk who had spent his life studying forbidden magic. The monk promised that he could take the soul of the dying man and place it in the body of the prince—creating someone who wore the face of a prince but was sworn to loyalty to Nikos."

She leaned forward, intrigued despite herself. "What happened?"

"Brother Nikos handed me a cup of wine, to help me sleep. The next time I woke, it was five years later."

"The spell failed?" Of course it must have—what he was saying was impossible, the delusions of a deranged mind.

"Yes. And no."

"I don't understand."

"Neither did I. Nor Brother Josan, who woke to find himself confused, his wits damaged from his illness. His body so clumsy that he needed to relearn how to write, and a hundred other tasks most men take for granted. Of course, it was not his fault. How was he to know that the body he wore was not his own?"

"That's impossible," she said, slowly shaking her head. Surely the emperor was lying. This was a symptom of the madness that she had only just begun to suspect.

"I wish it were," he said. "It took years for my soul to find its way back to my body. I still do not know if it was the passage of time or mortal peril that brought me back. Since then we've shared this body. Sometimes he is in command, sometimes I am."

She stared at him, but he did not have the look of a man who was mad, merely one who was tired.

"You have no proof," she said.

"I don't need proof. You've met Josan yourself. You

knew from the first that he was not the same man that you'd known during the rebellion."

"Men change," she said. "You were younger then. We all were. And if this were true, what of Brother Nikos?"

"The spell did not work as he had planned. He thought us too damaged to be of use, so sent us into exile. When we finally returned to Karystos, Josan confronted him. Rather than a willing puppet, Nikos had created two implacable enemies. It's hard to say which of us hates him more," Lucius said.

It was monstrous, if it were true. To steal a man's body? To deliberately plot to destroy not his life, but his very soul? What kind of man could think up such a tale?

"If this is true, why tell me? Why now?" She knew he did not trust her—why would he confide in her, of all people?

Lucius leaned back against his pillows. "Because I'm tired of pretending," he said. "Because you should know that the soul spell is failing. As our link fails, so, too, does this body."

Her head was spinning. If anyone else had told such a tale, she would have dismissed him as a liar. And yet, Lucius's words held the ring of truth. He was not trying to convince her, merely relating a story.

The less he argued, the more she was inclined to believe him.

"That's why you went to Xandropol," she said. "Not to see a physician, but rather to consult with their magicians."

He shook his head. "Do I look a fool? I cannot trust anyone to help me. Josan had planned to do his own research, hoping that if he found the source of the soul spell, he could also find the means to reverse it."

She did not want to believe him. And yet his story explained so much—the strange fits she'd observed, his unpredictable temper, even his flight to Xandropol. As well as how one man could appear a spoiled noble on one day and a commoner on another.

But even if it were true, it changed nothing. It made no difference if he was mad, or if the body before her truly was inhabited by the souls of two different men. The body belonged to the emperor of Ikaria, and in the end, that was what mattered.

"I haven't been truly awake for weeks, now," Lucius said. "From time to time I surface, as if in a dream, but Josan has remained in control of my body."

"So the decision to come here—"

"Was the monk's," Lucius said. "I'd have stayed in Xandropol."

"But you will help us stop this war," she said. Was this all an elaborate ruse so he could claim that he was not truly bound, because he had not been the one to swear the oath?

"Doesn't matter. In a few minutes or hours at the most you'll be speaking with him again. He'll do as he likes; he always has."

If it was true, it was monstrous. To have your own body invaded—usurped by another? She could only imagine how helpless he must feel.

Something of what she felt must have shown in her face, for he patted the bed beside him. "I don't suppose you'd lie with me? One last wish for a dying man?"

"No," she said.

"Pity," he replied. He stretched out full length on the bed, closing his eyes. Then, after a moment, he reopened them. "If it were the monk's choice, he'd prefer your aide."

Chapter 14

Zuberi had forgotten about the functionaries. When he'd made his list of the men who knew that the emperor was missing, he'd forgotten the functionaries who ran the imperial household and accompanied the emperor everywhere. They knew that none of their number had accompanied the emperor to either Sarna or Eluktiri—and though they were forbidden to gossip, he'd not thought to tell them to lie.

It had been a simple enough matter that unraveled it all. Prince Hadeon lived in Ikaria as hostage to ensure the continued cooperation of his father, the ruler of Kazagan. When Hadeon had received news that his mother was ill, perhaps dying, the prince had sought permission from the emperor to return home.

If Hadeon had made his request in a letter, Lucius's clerks would have brought it to Zuberi, who would have dealt with the matter. But instead Hadeon had gone to

Sarna, apparently feeling that honor required him to make a personal plea for release.

But the emperor was not at Sarna. Returning to the capital, instead of going to the proconsul, Hadeon had instead approached one of the functionaries to request help in sending a message to the emperor's summer palace at Eluktiri.

Only to be told that the emperor was not at Eluktiri, either.

The functionary hadn't told Hadeon that the emperor was missing, but the damage was done. The prince had seen their refusal to tell him where the emperor was as a sign that he, and his kingdom, were unworthy of the emperor's attention. He'd complained loudly to his friends over the slight, and others, more cunning than he, had seen what the prince had not. If the emperor wasn't at either of his summer retreats, then where was he? He was too important to pass unnoticed for long.

Fortunately one of Zuberi's clients was among Hadeon's circle of acquaintances, and so he'd learned of Hadeon's indiscretion even before the rumors started to swirl through the city.

Zuberi realized that the time had come to put his plans into motion.

He chose the senatorial baths for the first part of his plan, arriving in late morning when the baths were quiet, so that his presence would be duly noted. He began by indulging himself in a long soak in the warmest pool, where the heat inspired only desultory conversation with fellow bathers.

When he left the pool, the attendants dried him, then

dressed him in a loose cotton wrap that belted around his waist and fastened rope sandals on his feet.

He left the bathing room for the antechamber, where patrons mingled as they sampled the delicacies on offer, or gathered on benches for conversation. He accepted a cup of chilled fruit juice and made his circuit of the room, pausing now and then to engage in conversation. At last he spotted Senator Columba sitting in close conversation with his companion.

Perfect. Columba was a known gossip, who would not be able to resist this tidbit. He paused to make certain he caught the eye of his aide Hanif, who'd been carefully observing his master from the periphery of the chamber. Hanif nodded, then held up his hand showing five fingers.

Five minutes, as they'd agreed.

Zuberi made his way over to where Senator Columba sat, then paused, as if by chance. Summoning a passing servant, he ordered "Run and find out if the barber Tomasso is free. I will wait here."

The servant disappeared, and Zuberi turned slowly, as if surveying the room.

As he caught sight of Columba he inclined his head. "Senator," he said.

"Proconsul, greetings of the day to you," Columba said. "And may I present my cousin Parnassus, who has just arrived in the city?"

"Parnassus," he said, inclining his head.

"I am honored," Parnassus replied.

"Will you join us?" Columba asked.

Zuberi shook his head. "I am waiting for the barber," he said.

Just then Hanif hurried over, panting as if he'd run a great distance. His face was red, covered in sweat. If Zuberi had not known otherwise, he'd have sworn that Hanif had run the length of the city to find him.

"Proconsul," Hanif said, gasping for breath.

"What is it? Have they found him?" Zuberi demanded, as they had rehearsed.

Hanif shook his head. "No, but the commander has returned and wishes to meet with you at once," he said.

"He was ordered not to return alone," Zuberi ground out. "If he has failed, and the emperor has been harmed—"

He bit off his words, as if suddenly recalling that they had an audience.

"Come," he said, taking Hanif by the arm.

He left, without a backward glance, but he knew that Senator Columba's eyes would be fixed upon him.

By fortunate coincidence, that night he'd already planned to host a select dinner party, for his most important clients and closest allies. Two additional invitations were sent out, and he informed his wife of the extended guest list, so she could alter the preparations accordingly.

As night fell, fourteen guests joined him for dinner, along with their wives and companions. They ranged from Matticus of Alondra, who held the obscure if lucrative post of inspector of roads, to Senator Demetrios and General Kiril, both men who could challenge him for the emperorship, if they dared.

As the guests arrived they were escorted to the inner courtyard, where hanging lanterns illuminated the statues and frescoes, while the perfumed waters of the bubbling fountain filled the air with the scent of flowers. A musician played the kithara, while servants circulated, offering glasses of wine and delicacies to whet the appetite.

Several of his guests eyed him closely, showing that rumors had reached their ears, but in the presence of the women the conversation was general.

Only Demetrios was bold enough to break with custom, drawing Zuberi aside.

"Have you heard the rumors?" he demanded. "It's all over the city that Lucius is dead."

"Only just," Zuberi lied. "This is not the time, but stay after my guests leave, and we will decide what must be done."

Just then Petrelis entered with his longtime mistress, Savina, on his arm, and Zuberi excused himself so that he could greet them.

When the last guest arrived, he nodded to Eugenia, who gave the signal that they should proceed inside. His wife's reputation as hostess was well earned, and for the next three hours the guests dined on a succession of exquisite dishes. Wine was offered freely, but no one drank to excess.

They spoke of the things that were oft discussed at such gatherings—high-minded discussions of intellectual matters mingled with the gossip of the court: which senator's wife had demanded a divorce, and which minister's clients had deserted him after he'd gambled away his patrimony.

Matticus of Alondra described his recent visit to inspect his new estate in the country, which was being rebuilt after an earthquake. There was general commiseration as he described his dismay when he realized that the builders had ignored his directions, allowing the laborers to simply rebuild the old villa, rather than tear it down and start anew. All agreed that his mistake had been in trusting a provincial factor rather than sending his own man to supervise.

Savina told a humorous story of her reception where both Senator Aeaneas's wife and his mistress had decided to attend, much to the horror of both women. The guests laughed, as they were supposed to, but their laughter had a brittle sound and soon died away.

At last, when the final savory was offered, none had the stomach for it. Eugenia caught his eye, and as he nodded, she rose from her couch.

"Honored husband, the evening grows late, and it is time I retired," she said, in accordance with custom.

"Honored wife, on behalf of my guests, my thanks for your splendid hospitality," he said, rising to his feet.

The rest of the party rose as well—some having to be helped to their feet after having reclined for so long.

The women followed Eugenia as she led them to her private sitting room, where they would drink tea and discuss the foibles of their men, before litters were summoned to take them home.

The men followed Zuberi, who led them back to the courtyard, where chairs had been placed around braziers to ward off the chill of the night. Some men paused to use the adjacent lavatory, but Zuberi had drunk only sparingly at dinner and did not join them.

Tables held pitchers of wine, along with crystal goblets, and his guests served themselves as they took their seats.

It was understood that the servants would not approach unless specifically summoned, so the guests could speak freely.

Demetrios maneuvered himself so he took the chair to Zuberi's right, while General Kiril took the seat across from him, so that he faced both Demetrios and Zuberi. When the last guest had found his place, they exchanged uneasy glances, no one wanting to be the first to break the silence.

It fell to Telamon, who'd replaced the murdered Simon as Chancellor of the Exchequer, to say what all were thinking.

"Three people came to me today, and swore that they'd heard the emperor was dead," Telamon said.

"Mere rumors," Demetrios scoffed.

"Rumors or not, they would not have dared say such a thing unless they were gravely concerned," Telamon replied.

"We cannot be responsible for every bit of idle gossip," Zuberi said.

"It's not just gossip," Matticus of Alondra said. "The emperor has been gone too long—and all know he was ill when he left. If he could be seen—"

He could not have asked for a better prompt.

"No," Zuberi said swiftly.

"Why not?" General Kiril asked.

"It's not possible," Zuberi replied.

Kiril leaned forward. "What is it that you're not telling us? How ill is he?"

Zuberi made a show of hesitating.

"We have a right to know," Kiril said. "*I* have that right."

Zuberi took a deep breath. "What I say must go no farther than this courtyard," he said. "I'll have your oaths."

His guests exchanged glances among themselves before pledging themselves to silence.

"Do you think this wise?" Demetrios hissed.

"They have the right," Zuberi replied, careful not to look at his onetime ally. "The emperor is not ill. He is missing. We believe he was kidnapped the night he was to leave Karystos."

There were shocked exclamations from his guests. Kiril did his best to appear surprised, though he'd had the news earlier from both Zuberi and Demetrios, though naturally neither had informed the other of what they had done.

"We've kept it quiet, hoping we'd be able to discover his whereabouts and free him," Zuberi explained.

"Who did this? And why?" Matticus asked.

Zuberi shook his head. "I have my suspicions, but no proof."

"There's been no sign of how he left the city," Petrelis said. "Neither by land nor by sea."

There was a long moment as the guests digested the implications of that.

"Who knew of this?" Telamon demanded, quick to see the implied slight.

"Myself, Demetrios, and Petrelis," Zuberi said. "And Admiral Septimus, whose navy helped in the search, though they know not for whom they were looking."

Septimus had left the city a few days before, sailing with his fleet on a mission that was both training exercise and a chance to show the imperial flag, to remind vessels whose waters they sailed in. He hadn't bothered to request permission, merely sending a report stating his intentions, but Zuberi was not unduly worried. The imperial succession would be determined on land, not by any act at sea.

If it had been the legions that were on the move, rather than the navy, then Zuberi would have had cause for concern.

"It's been two months," Kiril said. "How long did you plan to keep this news from his subjects?"

"Until we knew what to tell them," Demetrios said.

"And what if he was murdered? What if he never left the city?"

Once again it was Telamon who voiced the obvious.

"I am the emperor's loyal servant," Zuberi said. "I will not give up hope."

"Neither will I," echoed Demetrios, apparently determined to prove himself equally virtuous. "The proconsul and I were agreed from the start that we would keep silent until we knew the emperor's fate."

"It's been too long," Kiril said. "If the emperor was alive, you'd have heard from him."

"Or from whoever took him," Petrelis added, as smoothly as if he'd been prompted.

"The empire cannot be left adrift. This may be precisely what our enemies intended. We must have a new emperor," Telamon said.

"Zuberi, I know you refused this burden once before,

but this time you have no choice," Kiril said. "For the good of the empire, you must declare yourself."

He could not resist stealing a glance at Demetrios, who appeared thunderstruck by Kiril's declaration. No doubt he'd deluded himself into thinking that Kiril was his ally, just as Zuberi had intended.

Zuberi shook his head. "I say it is too soon—"

"You must," Telamon said. "We need an emperor. And there is no one more fitted to serve."

Zuberi looked at his guests, meeting each of their gazes in turn. "You are all in accord?" he asked. "I cannot do this without your support."

"I and my legions will support you," Kiril said.

"As will I," Telamon echoed.

The rest chimed in, Matticus gulping nervously as he realized that he was being asked to help decide the next emperor.

At last Zuberi turned to Demetrios. "Friend, I could not have held the empire together without your support. As you speak, so will the senate. What say you?"

Demetrios knew when he was beaten. "We must have an emperor," he agreed. "We will announce the emperor's death and name you as emperor-in-waiting. On the thirty-ninth day, if there is still no news, you will be crowned."

Zuberi frowned, then cleared his face, hoping that the others would think him merely hesitant to assume power. He'd hoped to take the crown immediately, but could not object to Demetrios's proposal. Propriety dictated a period of mourning for Emperor Lucius, and practically there was very little difference between emperor-in-waiting and emperor in fact.

Thirty-nine days was the traditional interregnum between an emperor's death and the coronation of his successor. He had waited this long. He could wait a little longer.

His guests soon took their leave, after once again vowing that they would remain silent until the official proclamation was made.

Zuberi thanked them for their support—and knew that they would not hold their tongues. At the very least Matticus would drop hints to his own clients, using his advance knowledge to impress upon them his close connection to the next emperor.

It was what he would have done in Matticus's place.

Demetrios stayed behind after the others had left. As soon as they were alone, he let his anger show.

"You planned this, all of this," he said, waving at the remains of the dinner party with one arm. "You betrayed me."

Demetrios was not angry at the betrayal. He was angry that Zuberi had acted first, before he could put his own plans in motion. But it was not the time to gloat, he needed Demetrios's support.

At least for the present.

"The rumors were none of my doing," Zuberi said. "As it is, I'm surprised that we were able to keep this quiet for so long."

"You didn't have to answer Kiril," Demetrios said.

"If not tonight, then it would have been tomorrow, or the next day," Zuberi said, holding to reason in the face of

Demetrios's ill temper. "The senate convenes in less than a month. We'll need an emperor by then."

"So you put yourself forward," Demetrios said.

"I'll admit I was flattered tonight," he said. "But in truth, it was always going to be me that they chose as the next emperor. I was the closest advisor to both Nerissa and Lucius."

He'd been Nerissa's proconsul for the last half dozen years of her reign. And as for Lucius—not only had he agreed to seat Lucius on the throne, he'd held the emperor's life in his hands. Every decree, every ruling, every appearance by Lucius had been first approved by Zuberi. For the past year he'd been the emperor in all but name.

Now it was time to take his rightful place.

"I meant what I said. I need your support," Zuberi said, as he approached and laid one hand on Demetrios's arm. "I will be emperor, but we will continue to rule Ikaria between us. On the day I am crowned, you will be named proconsul, if you so choose."

Proconsul, but not emperor-in-waiting. That title would go to his son, Bakari.

Demetrios shook his arm free. "And if I prefer to remain Senator Demetrios?"

Zuberi shrugged lightly. "Then we will continue as we have, and you will help me decide who should take my place as proconsul."

He needed Demetrios, needed the support of the senate. In return he was offering Demetrios the opportunity to become the second-most-powerful man in Ikaria.

The trick was to offer Demetrios enough to ensure that

he saw the value of remaining loyal but not so much that Zuberi seriously diminished his own power.

But if Demetrios was tempted to conspire against his new emperor . . . Well, once Zuberi had secured his grasp upon the throne, there were others who would be eager to take Demetrios's place and to prove their loyalty.

It would be unfortunate if he had to have Demetrios killed.

"Do you think he's really dead?" Demetrios asked.

"Who?"

"Lucius."

"Does it matter? If he's not dead, he may as well be," Zuberi said.

It had seemed a kidnapping at first, but with no demand for ransom, Zuberi had begun to wonder. Had Lady Ysobel kidnapped the emperor for revenge? Or had Lucius been killed, perhaps deliberately, perhaps accidentally as he tried to escape?

In any case, she'd gravely miscalculated. She'd thought to strike a blow against the empire. Instead, by ridding the empire of a weak ruler, she'd actually strengthened it.

But there would be time to deal with her later—and to decide if he wanted to seek vengeance against the federation for the loss of Emperor Lucius or simply blame a faceless assassin for the emperor's loss.

"Tell me that I can count on you," Zuberi said.

Demetrios gave a thin smile. "You can count on my support—just as I know that I can count on yours. I will be your proconsul, and together we will guide the empire back to greatness."

Zuberi embraced Demetrios as if he were a brother, then stepped back and called for the servants to fetch star wine.

They drank a toast to the future of Ikaria. And as each man swore his friendship, both knew that they were lying.

Chapter 15

Lady Ysobel was watching him. As Josan took his daily walk around the deck he could feel her gaze weighing upon his back, even as he knew that if he turned, he would find her attention elsewhere.

Ever since he'd woken to find himself missing a day's worth of memories, he'd found himself the subject of Ysobel's scrutiny.

She'd watched him before, but this was somehow different. Before she'd eyed him as a potential foe, looking for signs of treachery. Now he'd caught glimpses of something that might be mistaken for concern.

Questioning those assigned to serve him had been unrewarding. Apparently he'd dismissed them because he felt unwell, and at some point Ysobel had visited him.

But what had she seen? Had she seen him lying insensate, his body unresponsive?

Or had she spoken to Lucius? Was it possible that the prince had found the strength to take control of his body?

Josan could feel no trace of Lucius's presence, but that did not mean that he was gone. Merely that he was out of reach. If Lucius had been conscious, that was surely a good sign, wasn't it? It meant that he was not as weak as Josan had believed. Perhaps there was still hope for them.

Such optimism faded when confronted by reason. It was more likely that Ysobel had seen him helpless, reduced to a witless, drooling husk. Not wanting her pity, he had done his best to avoid her, but he could not do so forever. They were already within the islands, with Sendat only a day's sail away. And he still had yet to decide what he would do when he arrived.

Simply declaring himself and his empire innocent of ill intentions would hardly serve—though perhaps one as simple minded as Lucius might think so. No, he needed logic to win the federation over to his side, and there was little time left to plot his strategy.

And for that he would need Lady Ysobel's help. So when she approached him during his next circuit of the deck, he gestured for her to join him.

"I've been thinking about what you said the other day," she began. "About Brother Nikos."

He'd said nothing of Brother Nikos. Nothing that he could remember, that is. But perhaps Lucius had.

"What of him?" he asked.

"It seems incredible, that he should be capable of such a thing," Ysobel said, her words coming slowly as if she were weighing each one.

Nikos's recent treachery was nothing compared to his earlier deeds, but of course he could not tell her that.

"You must ask yourself who benefits if we go to war with one another," Josan said. "We would triumph, of course—"

"I would not be so certain," she interjected.

"But either way, we agree that the war is likely to be long and bloody, yes?"

"Yes."

"And even the winner will be greatly weakened," he said. "What better time for Vidrun to pursue its own ambitions? Your federation has no interest in the disputed territories, so if Ikaria loses, their armies can push west unopposed. And if Ikaria wins, well, even if we had the heart for another protracted war, our armies will be too busy pacifying your islands. So, once again, Vidrun can expand unopposed."

He waited, but there was no response. He looked to his left, but she was no longer at his side. Instead she'd abruptly halted.

He took two steps back to her.

"You think that Nikos is in Vidrun? That he is behind these attacks?" she asked.

"I know he is in Vidrun. As for the rest, it seems likely. He thrives best when he's in the middle of some intrigue, and he harbors ill will toward me and my empire. He'd use any opportunity he could find to strike against us."

He could not shake the sense that his words had surprised her.

"And the mercenaries—"

"Are safer than using their own navy," he said. "Their

ships disguised to look like my navy, their gold to buy mercenaries to crew them. Likely former pirates or those with equally low morals."

"Even if this was true, we have no proof," she said. "What do you intend to do when we arrive?"

She meant how would he prove his worth—and by extension prove hers. If his gamble failed, then she would be seen to fail as well. It was likely that they'd be the first two casualties when war was declared.

And while they were not friends, he did not want anyone to die over this foolishness. Not even her.

"I have an idea," he said. "And I'll need your help."

They arrived at Sendat without incident, and Ysobel breathed a sigh of relief as the familiar harbor came into view. After spending a fortnight surrounded by Ikarians, it would be a relief once more to be among her own people. Not that this made her mission any less perilous—she had as many enemies in the federation as she did without. But here, at least, she had the advantage of knowing who they were.

The harbormaster must have been warned of their approach, for he sent a boat out to guide them into harbor. *Green Dragon* was directed to drop anchor at the northern edge of the harbor, where, not coincidentally, she'd be flanked by vessels from the federation navy. Last year, Ysobel had shown the Ikarians how much damage could be inflicted by a single enemy vessel, and the federation was taking no chance of the Ikarians returning the favor.

A rope ladder was thrown over the side, and Ysobel

stood with Captain Chenzira preparing to greet their visitor. To her surprise, the harbormaster Neville had come in
person, rather than sending one of his numerous assis-
tants. A heavyset man, he wheezed as he climbed up onto
the deck, his face flushed from his efforts.

Neville's eyes flickered over her, but when he caught
his breath, his first remarks were addressed to Chenzira.

"Captain, may I ask your intentions?"

"I've brought an envoy to speak with your people, under a flag of truce," Chenzira responded. As agreed, he
did not name the envoy.

Neville frowned. "Lady Ysobel, have we no ships of our
own that could have brought you here?"

"This vessel was the most convenient, for me and my
guest," she said. "We travel together as a sign of mutual
good faith."

Neville shook his head. "These are difficult days. I
can't say I'm happy to have you here," he said. She hoped
he meant the ship, and not herself.

"But we are not at war with the empire," she ventured.

"No," he said.

So they were in time. The tightness in her chest eased,
though she did her best to hide the relief that she felt. By
virtue of his position, the harbormaster was often the first
source of gossip, and she would give him no reason to
spread doubts about her or her mission.

"If you need provisions, one of my clerks will arrange
for you to purchase what you need," Neville told
Chenzira. "Your crew will be expected to stay aboard
ship, but if Lady Ysobel vouches for you—"

"I do," she said.

"Then you may come and go freely," Neville finished.

"And my guest and his servants may come and go as they will," Ysobel said.

Neville frowned again. "How many servants?"

"Three," she said. This, too, had been negotiated with Chenzira, who'd originally wanted to send a dozen of his men to protect the emperor. The emperor had wanted none of this, so they'd finally compromised on allowing the functionary and two of Chenzira's sailors to accompany him.

With a heavy sigh, Neville granted his approval to this request as well. It only showed how much tension there was between the two countries. In the past, any ship with coin to spend or goods to trade would have been welcomed. From where she stood, she could see ships from a dozen different nations in port—though, naturally, the vast majority of vessels belonged to federation trading houses.

Then again, there was a difference between a trading ship and one meant for war.

After Neville took his leave, Chenzira arranged for them to be taken ashore, along with their luggage. The emperor could have stayed at the Ikarian embassy, but that would have revealed his presence before they were ready. Instead she sent a runner ahead to her father's house, instructing that the rooms allocated to Flordelis of Flordelis be prepared for a visitor.

It was seldom that she called upon her family connections, preferring instead to rely upon herself, as head of her own trading house. But in this instance she had no other choice. Though the emperor might well be content to share the same three rooms that she used whenever she had occasion to be in Sendat, once the emperor's identity was revealed, it would be expected that he would be housed according to his rank.

Even if he might have preferred otherwise. She'd shared closer quarters with him—or at least with the emperor's body. Whether the body had been guided by Lucius, Josan, or perhaps both, was a mystery that she was unlikely to unravel.

Strange as his tale was, she had become convinced that it was the truth. It was not the persuasiveness of his arguments, but rather that he didn't try to persuade her. In fact he seemed to have totally forgotten that he'd spoken of it to her at all. Which meant he was either a better actor than he appeared—

Or it was just as he had said. The man who had confessed to her was Lucius, while the monk Josan was the one who had spent the past days plotting with her.

So far as she could tell, the monk had no idea that his other self had bared all to her. She'd held her tongue—in part because this knowledge felt like an advantage, and one she was loath to give up. And in part because she wanted to see if the monk would trust her, as Lucius had apparently done.

Though perhaps Lucius had revealed himself not to win her trust but rather simply to spite the monk. He'd been bitter about what had happened to him, as was to be expected. She could only imagine how she would feel in his place. Mere anger seemed too small for such a violation.

Each time she looked at him, she was torn between pity

and horror. But she could not let her feelings distract her from what must be done. It was difficult enough dealing with one man. Now she knew that there were two—and that their goals might not be the same.

It had been the monk's decision to come here, Lucius had said, implying that he would have chosen a different course. She could guess how the monk would act, but as for Lucius? She could only prepare for all eventualities and be ready for anything.

When they reached the dock she hired a carriage for herself and the man she still thought of as Lucius, and a wagon to carry their scant luggage and his servants. Lucius insisted that his elderly servant, whom he referred to as Eight for reasons that passed comprehension, be allowed to ride in the carriage with them, so Burrell helped the emperor inside, and then assisted his servant.

She took advantage of the opportunity to draw him aside. "You know what we need," she said to Burrell. "The trader's guild hall first, then if my clerk Balere is not there, you must seek her out at the warehouses."

"And I'll check with the navy as well. Whatever news there is, you'll have it," he said.

She'd feel better if she could do her own intelligence gathering, but Lucius could not be left to his own devices. And Burrell knew what she needed to know—how many ships were missing? What rumors swirled regarding their fates? Were there any witnesses to the attacks, or were the reports that she brought the first news to reach the federation?

And most important, was Lucius still emperor of

Ikaria? If not, then he was merely a disposable pawn, and her plans would change accordingly.

Burrell helped her inside the carriage, then went off on his errands.

The seat of Flordelis was on the island of Alcina, but like other large trading families they maintained a constant presence in the capital Sendat. The mansion was in the old quarter of the city, a legacy of the time when Flordelis had been one of the great houses. A fine building of imported white stone, it housed those who supervised Flordelis's affairs in Sendat, as well as visiting captains and traders. The top floor was given over to apartments set aside for Flordelis of Flordelis and the senior members of house.

Ysobel had been born into the house, but unlike her siblings, she'd left to make her own way as a ship owner and master trader. She'd already been well established when her father had been selected as Flordelis of Flordelis. Since then their relationship had changed. They were not merely father and daughter but two master traders tending to the affairs of their own houses—which brought them into conflict as often as not.

She wondered how he would react when he discovered the use she had made of his hospitality, but then, as the carriage drew up before the mansion, she saw the pennant flying above. Lord Delmar was in residence, which meant she would have a chance to tell him herself.

The boy standing door watch, doubtless the child of one of her numerous cousins, opened the door to the carriage and helped her alight. She turned, and held out her arm for Lucius, who ignored it. Though after descending he then reached in and offered his arm to his scandalized servant. The servant shook his head, but did allow Lucius to take charge of his leather bag while he climbed down, then swiftly reclaimed his prize.

Ysobel wondered what made the bag so valuable. Did it contain the emperor's purse, perhaps? Or was it merely the servant's own possessions?

The boy's eyes took all of this in, but his face was as expressionless as any trader could wish. "Lady Ysobel, Lord Delmar bade me bid you and your guests welcome," he said.

So her father was not merely in the city, he had been here when her message arrived. Good.

"Our luggage is following on a cart. When it arrives please see that it is brought in," she told the boy.

Lucius looked around, his eyebrows raised. "Yours?" he asked.

"House Flordelis," she replied.

"In the literal sense, I believe," he said, his mouth quirking in a wry smile.

"Where is Lord Delmar?" she asked. She could have asked for her father, but the occasion called for formal manners.

"In his office, master trader," the youth said. "He is expecting you."

Lucius instructed Eight to remain behind until the cart with their luggage and the rest of his servants arrived, then followed her inside.

Her father's seldom-used office was on the ground floor, used only for the affairs of the family. When it came to meeting with other traders he had a table at the guild hall, as was customary, and a working office in the complex of warehouses owned by Flordelis.

She could not remember the last time she had been summoned there, but she knew where it was well enough. There were new frescoes on the walls, but the tiles under her feet were the same as they'd been when she was a child.

As they entered, Lord Delmar rose to greet them. He looked as she remembered him. His gray hair was perhaps a little thinner, the lines in his face a little deeper from the weight of his responsibilities, but his dark eyes were still bright, and he smiled to see her.

"Ysobel, I am glad to see you well," he said. He took her hands in his and kissed her on both cheeks, choosing to welcome her as family and not as one trader to another.

"The rumors in port have been troubling, and I've been worried about you," he added, with a glance toward Lucius. Naturally he was too discreet to mention precisely what those rumors were in front of a stranger.

"It is good to be home," Ysobel said. "As for the rumors, I have brought news that should shed light on recent events."

There was a pause as her father waited for her to introduce Lucius to him, as would be expected if her companion was the clerk he appeared to be. Instead she turned to the emperor.

"May I present my father, Lord Delmar Flordelis of Flordelis of Alcina?"

Lucius nodded gravely in acknowledgment.

"Father, this is Lucius Constantin Aurelius," she said. "The emperor of Ikaria."

The good news was that Lucius was still emperor of Ikaria. Reports said that he was resting at one of his villas in the countryside. Some said he was ill, others that he'd merely sought to escape the oppressive summer heat.

Unfortunately, they were not the first to bring news of ships being attacked. The guild knew of a half dozen missing ships, and Burrell's contacts in the navy had yielded the names of two more. Suspicion had fallen upon the Ikarians, but it had been mere speculation—until the captain of the *Greenbow* gave his damning report.

Ysobel had sent copies of Zorion's sworn testimony to both the ministry of trade and the king's council of advisors and requested an audience with each.

Lady Felicia, head of the king's council, was the first to respond, summoning Ysobel to a private meeting. She'd not been pleased that Ysobel had taken it upon herself to leave her assigned post in Karystos. Her frown only deepened as Ysobel made her report.

"You claim that those who attacked *Rhosyn* were not Ikarians, but you did not witness this for yourself," Lady Felicia said.

"No, but you have the sworn statement of Captain Zorion—"

"Who once sailed for you, did he not?"

"Yes, but no longer." She'd known that Zorion would be seen as partisan, but it was hardly the time to admit that she'd released him from her service because she no longer trusted his judgment. It would not help her case to admit that Zorion had previously set aside his responsibilities to others in order to protect Ysobel.

"If this is an attempt to hide your incompetence, it is remarkably weak," Lady Felicia said. "First you allowed the Ikarians to dupe you into thinking they would honor the truce, then once you realized that you'd been deceived, you try to hide your failure by blaming others for their aggression."

Ysobel's hands curled into fists but she kept her voice even as she responded. "If you thought so poorly of me, you would never have sent me as your envoy to the Ikarians," she said. "You asked me to bring you peace, and I did."

She let her words hang in the air. Unspoken was the knowledge that Lady Felicia and the council had been the ones to pursue the path of war until the Ikarians had made it unprofitable. Only then had they sued for peace.

Ysobel had accepted the role of envoy knowing full well that her own people were prepared to sacrifice her, if that was the price that Emperor Lucius demanded. But he, at least, had dealt honorably with her.

Would that she could say the same of her own people.

"I come before you because my goal remains unchanged—to prevent a war that will cost lives and treasure that none can spare," Ysobel said.

"Even if you speak the truth, how do you propose to do this?"

"I respectfully ask that King Bayard and his councilors meet with the envoy who accompanied me," Ysobel said. "Hear him before you decide upon any course of action."

Lady Felicia's eyebrows rose at the mention of the king. Ysobel had never met him herself; he preferred to leave the ordinary affairs of governance in the hands of his ministers. But it would be an insult to leave him out.

"This envoy, I've never heard of him. Neither has anyone else," Lady Felicia said.

"He speaks with the voice of the emperor," Ysobel said. Such was traditionally said of those who served as ambassadors or envoys, but in this case it was the literal truth.

"And you will not tell me what he wants?"

Ysobel hesitated. "It is for him to say," she finally said.

The gaze that raked over her was not friendly. "Perhaps you were wise to return," Lady Felicia said. "It seems you have grown too cozy with the Ikarians. You should strive to remember where your loyalties lie."

It was a perilous path that she walked. Reveal Lucius's presence too soon and lose the advantage of surprise. Yet the longer she delayed, the more it would seem to her enemies that she had chosen to put the emperor first and her own country second.

"I know my duty," Ysobel said. "And where my loyalties lie."

"For your sake, I hope you do," Lady Felicia said.

They'd decided that he was to feign illness as part of the tale that they'd agreed upon to explain his absence from his empire. But when the hour of the audience arrived, the weakness was all too real and the cause all too familiar.

Josan had awoken that morning to the sound of low

whispers, but the chamber he'd been assigned had been empty. At first he'd suspected that he was hearing conversations from an adjacent chamber, but gradually the whispers grew stronger, until he realized that it was the sound of Lucius's mind voice.

Lucius was present, able to speak to Josan clearly for the first time in weeks. But there was a price—Josan's entire right side was numb. He could barely stand, and his right arm swung uselessly by his side. He'd been forced to allow Eight to dress him as if he were a child.

After so long, the imperial robes felt strange on his skin—the silk slippery rather than soft, and the elaborate embroidery weighing as heavily on his body as it did on his spirits.

Trust Eight to bring along robes fit for an emperor—and then to scold his emperor for not taking better care of himself when Josan's infirmities were revealed. He did not know what he had done to earn such loyalty—by leaving the palace, Eight had risked his life. And he had compounded the risk by giving Chenzira the lizard crown, which Eight claimed had been given to him for safekeeping though doubtless others would say it was stolen.

Chenzira, too, had risked all, gambling that he could find Lucius where others had failed. Here it was easier to understand his partisanship—a bond had formed between them when Josan had taught the secrets of federation navigation techniques to the imperial navy. Chenzira had been his first pupil, and he still saw the emperor as a benefactor.

But that did not explain why Admiral Septimus had permitted Chenzira to embark upon his journey—nor

Septimus's instructions that the rest of the fleet would support this madness. By doing so, he had set himself in direct opposition to Proconsul Zuberi—a man who could not bear to be opposed.

It was humbling when Josan considered how many were trusting him—trusting that he was still their emperor, and that by helping him they helped Ikaria. But mixed with the humility was equal parts fear, at the realization that it was not just his own life that he had placed at risk.

We are their emperor. It is their duty to support us, Lucius thought, with the mental equivalent of a shrug. He took the devotion of others as his due—a birthright just as much as the lizard crown.

But Josan could not be so sanguine. Even if he was enough of an emperor that he would use their loyalty, regardless of his misgivings.

It took the combined efforts of both of Chenzira's seamen-turned-servants to help him descend from the third floor, while Eight followed behind, muttering about dire consequences should the emperor fall.

It was a relief to them all when he reached the bottom of the stairs. The seamen released him, and he stood for a moment, regaining his breath. Then he made his way unaided out to the central courtyard.

Lady Ysobel was already waiting for them—the impatience on her face changing swiftly to concern as she observed Josan's slow progress and the way his right leg dragged with each step.

But when he reached her, her only words were to ask if he was ready to depart.

Josan nodded. "I know what I must do," he said. "See that you play your part as well."

As they made their way to the palace where they were to meet with King Bayard, Josan found himself wondering why she had not asked about his illness. Not that he wanted her concern, nor did he want to brush away offers to send for a healer or physician, but it was out of character for her not to say something.

Even if it was only to worry if he would be strong enough for the upcoming audience.

I told her, Lucius thought.

What?

I told her about us. About Nikos, the spell, all of it.

If Lucius had been a physical being, Josan would have struck him. He was appalled; no, he was infuriated by Lucius's recklessness. How could he have done such a thing?

Why? he demanded. *Why would you tell her anything?*

Because I could.

You wanted her to pity you. You risked us both for the smile of a beautiful woman.

I would have slept with her, if she agreed, Lucius thought, fueling Josan's rage. *But do not cast me as wholly selfish. Someone must know of Nikos's treachery once we are dead.*

Josan would not have picked Lady Ysobel to confide in. Yet there was no one else.

You should have consulted me first.

As you did, when you decided to forgo our search for a cure?

He would have consulted Lucius had he been able to,

but logic was unlikely to sway the headstrong prince. Fortunately the carriage drew to a halt, bringing an end to the argument.

King Bayard's palace was not what he expected—merely a larger version of the mansions owned by the leading trading houses. It could have been dropped unnoticed into a corner of the imperial palace compound in Karystos.

Then again, the federation had no concept of a ruling dynasty. Their rulers were chosen from among the ranks of the nobility. King Bayard had been elected king thirty years ago, but before then he had merely been the minister of trade. And just as the heads of the trading houses were expected to step aside when they could no longer serve, the king was also allowed to retire gracefully, at a time of his choosing.

As opposed to Ikaria, where the crown passed only in the event of the death of its owner—peaceful or otherwise.

He had yet to meet King Bayard, but already he envied him.

Two soldiers guarded the iron gate that led into the inner courtyard. There was a brief delay as the seamen had to lift Josan out of the carriage, and he swayed as he stood on his own feet.

Burrell came forward, trailed by a man wearing a smock emblazoned with the seal of the federation.

Seeing Josan's weakness, Burrell quickly stepped forward to offer his arm, and Josan clutched it gratefully. He could not help wondering if his weakness was deliberate, another sign of Lucius's spite. But then he felt ashamed of his doubts. Lucius could be petty, but he was committed to the survival of his empire.

The soldiers swung open the gate, and their escort led the way, with Lady Ysobel at his side, followed by Josan's and Burrell's halting progress. Eight trailed behind them, carrying a cedar casket.

"What's in the box?" Burrell asked. He, too, did not comment on Josan's obvious weakness, nor how much effort was required to make it appear as if he lent his arm for courtesy's sake, when in fact he was supporting a substantial portion of Josan's weight.

"Diplomatic credentials," Josan replied.

Unlike Ikarian mansions, which were often built around a central courtyard meant for entertaining, federation mansions had a small courtyard barely large enough for a fountain. The royal palace was much the same, and it took only a few paces to pass through the courtyard and enter the mansion proper.

Lady Ysobel slowed as they approached a set of elaborately carved doors.

Unlike his own palace, no guards stood outside. Instead their escort simply rapped once on the doors, then swung them open.

Josan braced himself for what was to come.

As he entered, his eyes swept over the room. Ysobel had expected a full council of twelve, but he saw fourteen people in the room. King Bayard was easy to recognize, for he sat at the head of a long table, a platinum circlet nearly blending in with his iron-gray hair. At Bayard's right was a woman who must be Lady Felicia, the head of his council. On Bayard's opposite side was an elderly man with a shaven skull, likely Telfor, who'd he been told was Bayard's closest advisor, though he no longer held any official post.

Based on the information Ysobel had given him, he could make guesses at the rest who ranged themselves along each side of the table. Pity that they did not have placards displaying their names, so he would know which ones to be wary of.

Strange to see so many were women—six of the fourteen, including Lady Solange, who was minister of trade. According to Ysobel, this was the most important ministry, more powerful than even the ministry of war. He wondered what Nerissa would have made of such a gathering.

At the end closest to the door, there was a man whose eyes widened as he caught sight of them. Josan did not recognize him, but that meant nothing. As emperor, there were many who knew him by sight.

There were two seats vacant at the end of the table, but Josan made no move to take one of them.

Instead he released Burrell's arm. "Introductions," he said, making sure his voice would carry to the king.

It was a seemingly deliberate discourtesy, and he knew Ysobel well enough to know that she was angry, though a stranger might think her calm. Still, Ysobel did as he'd requested.

"Bayard of the house of Merlion, King of the Federated Islands of Seddon," Ysobel said, then proceeded to name the councilors in turn.

Josan nodded, acknowledging each introduction. The man who'd stared so hard at him was Hardouin, who'd served as ambassador to Ikaria before being expelled for his part in the failed second uprising. It was possible that he recognized the emperor, but in a few seconds that would no longer matter.

Josan gestured, and Eight came forward and opened the casket, his back to the council so that only Josan and his companions could see what was inside.

"Credentials," Burrell murmured. It sounded as if he were trying not to laugh.

Josan flexed the fingers of his right hand, and for a mercy they obeyed him. It would have been humiliating to have another perform this task. Reaching inside the casket with both hands, he lifted the lizard crown out and set it upon his head.

He could not see what had happened, but from the gasps he knew that the crown had glowed when it recognized its rightful owner.

The usurpers had been unable to wear this crown—Aitor and his descendants had instead worn a heavy jewel-encrusted monstrosity. But Zuberi had deemed Lucius unworthy of such treasure, and at Lucius's coronation he'd been crowned with the lizard crown of his ancestors—something that Zuberi swiftly regretted as the lizard crown responded to the magic inside Lucius. Each time he put it on, the filigreed crown would flash with light. And some swore that as he wore it, the lizards would dart between the twined olive leaves.

He'd never witnessed such for himself, but he knew it would make a lasting impression.

"Lucius Constantin Aurelius, Emperor of Ikaria," Lady Ysobel said.

There was a brief hush, then King Bayard rose to his feet.

"I bid you welcome," the king said. "Please, be seated. We have much to discuss."

In some ways, it had been very much like a meeting of his own council, from the early days of his reign. Then, as now, he'd been in fear for his life, knowing that the wrong word could see him imprisoned, or worse.

The risks here were actually less. While Zuberi had often threatened to send Lucius back to the torture chambers, it was unlikely that Bayard would order anything more drastic than imprisonment. Or a swift execution.

Which might be preferable to the lingering death by paralysis that Lucius feared.

It had taken all of Josan's strength to sit upright for the council meeting and appear in command as King Bayard's councilors argued with him and among themselves. Bayard, for his part, had said nothing, content merely to observe the debate. Until the end, when Telfor had whispered something that caused the king to announce that the council was over. Bayard had gravely thanked his honored guest and his councilors for sharing their wisdom, then taken his leave without reaching a decision.

Burrell had had to help Josan stand, and it had taken the efforts of both Burrell and one of Bayard's servants to support Josan as he made his way back to the hired coach. Once they'd arrived at the Flordelis's mansion, he'd been carried upstairs to his rooms as if he were a child or an old man.

At least this gave credence to the tale they'd spun for the council—that Emperor Lucius had been on a private voyage when he'd witnessed the rogue attackers, and Lady Ysobel had convinced him to set aside his own concerns in order to defuse the crisis.

It nearly passed belief that an emperor would leave his realm, but all understood that a dying man could be driven to desperate acts. And that he had turned aside from his own quest to help avoid this war would surely count in his favor.

If Bayard and his councilors were reasonable men. Which was yet to be proven.

Exhausted from his efforts though it was scarcely midday, Josan allowed Eight to chivy him into lying down for a rest.

When he woke, it was late afternoon, judging from the shadows on his walls. Once again he heard voices, but this time they came from outside his head.

"Come, you must rise," Eight said. "You have a visitor."

Josan pushed himself to a seated position with his left arm, but needed help to stand. He resigned himself to being treated as a child, as others dressed him, then combed his hair.

He'd seen little of Lord Delmar since his arrival, but when Josan entered Delmar's personal study, he found his host speaking with none other than King Bayard. Delmar waited until the servants had helped Josan to a chair before asking permission to leave, closing the door behind him.

Josan's studies had concerned mathematics rather than history, so he could be forgiven for not knowing if this was the first time that the ruler of the federation had held a private meeting with his Ikarian counterpart. But if this was not the first such meeting, it was surely a rare event.

He wondered what Bayard had to say to him that he could not say in front of his own councilors. It was fortunate that Josan spoke both the diplomatic tongue as well as the trade tongue—left to Lucius's efforts they would have needed an interpreter.

"I am told that you are unwell," Bayard began.

Josan shrugged, pretending to an ease that he did not feel. "A weakness plagues me from time to time," he said. "It will pass."

"I would gladly offer the services of one of my physicians—"

"No," Josan interrupted. "I do not need a physician, nor did you come here to inquire about my health. We are both too powerful to play games with one another. Speak plainly, or not at all."

Bayard leaned forward in his seat, leaning his elbows upon his knees. "My advisors tell me not to trust you. They are convinced that this is an elaborate ruse, meant to deceive us into lowering our guard," he said.

"It seems to me that I am the one who has taken all the risks," Josan said, "while you have ventured nothing."

"And so you came here, driven by a noble spirit, for what? To urge us not to attack your ships? Not to take revenge for our losses?"

Bayard's words were scornful, but Josan refused to let himself be drawn.

"Your country is no friend of mine," Josan said. "I have not forgotten that you sent spies to help overthrow Empress Nerissa. Twice."

"To place you on the throne—"

"To see Ikaria consumed by civil war," Josan pointed out. "If we wish to recount past sins, we will be here till dawn."

Bayard straightened upright, no longer confrontational. "Agreed," he said.

"I came because we have a common threat," Josan said. "I will not spend my men and my ships blindly, battling the wrong enemy, only to weaken ourselves so that we are ripe for attack by another. If you cared about your country, you would feel the same."

"I know my duty to my people," Bayard said.

"Then you know better than to act rashly."

"What do you propose?"

Josan took a deep breath. "Joint patrols, formed of equal numbers of ships from each of our navies," he said. "They will seek out these rogues posing as Ikarians and show that we are not to be taken by such tricks."

It was the best that he'd been able to come up with, and neither Chenzira nor Ysobel could think of a better plan.

"And once we find these pirates? If they are Ikarian?"

"If they are Ikarian, I will see them punished, and personally repay the owners of every ship that was lost," Josan said. "But if they are from Vidrun, as we have sworn to you, then you will be welcome to make cause with us as we strike back against them."

Bayard shook his head. "I do not want war with Vidrun."

"I do not want war with anyone," Josan said. "If you choose to forgive their sins against you, that is your right. But I will do as I must."

Or his successor would. Proconsul Zuberi and the newcomers had their own reasons to hate those who had driven their ancestors out of their homeland of Anamur, forcing them into exile in Ikaria. The newcomers had prospered in exile, but they remembered what their ancestors had lost, and Ikaria had spent much of Aitor II's reign in constant skirmishes with Vidrun. It would take little to reignite that conflict.

"They say that men see most clearly as they approach death," Bayard said. "Pettiness disappears when one is thinking of a legacy rather than one's own ambitions. Or so Telfor insists each time he advises me."

"I hope to be as wise when I reach his age," Josan said, refusing to admit that he was dying.

He held his breath, waiting for Bayard's answer. What he offered was the limit of what he could—he was confident that Admiral Septimus would agree to the joint patrols. Such was within his power even if another sat on the imperial throne.

At least until Septimus was replaced. Or condemned as traitor, for helping Lucius.

He pushed aside such worries and returned his attention to the man who would decide the fate of two countries.

"Agreed," King Bayard said. "I'll not ask my people to

fight a war based on mere rumors. Once I have the truth, I'll know who my true enemy is."

Josan repressed a sigh of relief. He wanted to express his gratitude but knew that such would be a mistake, serving only to reinforce the fact that Bayard held power over him. Instead he merely said, "Your wisdom serves your people well."

"You will, of course, remain as my guest until this matter is resolved."

Bayard was too polite to call him hostage, but both knew that was what he had meant. It was only to be expected. He had known from the start that the Seddonians would be loath to relinquish the advantage that his presence gave them.

"Of course," Josan said. "I know I will be treated as well here as I would be in my own palace."

He knew Bayard would take this for a polite lie, but Josan spoke the literal truth. He had as many enemies at home as he did here—and both were equally likely to take advantage of his helplessness.

Chapter 16

The temple of the triune gods stank of burning herbs that could not quite disguise the stench of their unwashed worshippers. Demetrios wrinkled his nose, wishing that he'd thought to bring a perfumed sachet. None of the other temples he'd visited had been so foul, but then neither the triune gods nor their followers were in fashion.

The official religion of the empire was the worship of the twin gods: Zakar, the giver of life, and his brother Ata, the giver of knowledge. The triune gods were a legacy of the former rulers, their only followers the ignorant poor or those too stubborn to accept that their gods were as powerless as they were.

He stood with Zuberi's supporters in a loose semicircle behind the altar. The head priest stood in front of the altar, flanked on either side by two junior priests, while Zuberi faced them, prepared to receive their blessing. The body of the temple was filled with worshippers come to witness Zuberi receive the blessing of their priests.

It was not the first such ritual that had been held in the weeks since Zuberi had, with feigned reluctance, allowed himself to be named emperor-in-waiting. The proconsul had received the blessing of each of Ikaria's major religions in turn, as they mourned their lost emperor and prayed for the health of their emperor-to-be.

Demetrios had attended each ceremony, and said his prayers, but they were not for Zuberi's health.

He was still furious at how easily Zuberi had outmaneuvered him, forcing him to pledge his allegiance or risk being the sole voice of dissent. But he was not defeated, merely biding his time.

Even as he'd informed Zuberi that he was willing to accept the role of proconsul and first minister in the new regime, he was already making his own preparations to assume higher rank. He'd cautiously begun assembling support from among those Zuberi had overlooked. While Zuberi had gathered the most powerful to his side, Demetrios had been forced to seek out their clients instead. Powerful men in their own right, they knew all the secrets of their patrons, while their loyalty could be bought far more cheaply. If his plan succeeded, when the time came Zuberi would not be the only minister losing his post.

The eldest priest began by offering a brief paean to Lucius, their lost emperor, the priest's voice quavering with sorrow as if he genuinely mourned for Lucius. The other priests had known better than to express their regrets in any but the most perfunctory of terms.

This ceremony was not about Lucius, nor the circumstances under which he'd given up his throne. Officially Lucius had disappeared, kidnapped by an unknown enemy. Most assumed that he was dead. As did Demetrios, who'd originally believed Zuberi's account that the emperor was missing, but then began to wonder if it was all an elaborate ruse, so that Zuberi could ascend the throne without seeming to have bloodied his hands.

It was likely that the emperor had been killed, his body disposed of quietly, perhaps buried in the catacombs under the palace compound, or simply dumped into the harbor after being mutilated so that he was unrecognizable.

In recent days, trading ships had brought rumors that Lucius had been sighted in the federation, but these were simply rumors. Likely Zuberi was also their source, as he sought to shift blame for the emperor's disappearance to the federation, and specifically upon Lady Ysobel, whose own absence was taken as a sign of her guilt.

It was possible that she shared the emperor's fate—an unmarked grave where she'd be mourned by no one.

After his brief remembrance of Lucius, the priest began listing Zuberi's many virtues and offering prayers for his health and longevity. Each of the triune gods was addressed separately, and those around Demetrios began to shift restlessly, though they kept silent out of respect for the emperor-in-waiting.

As the priests led Zuberi in a circle around their altar, Demetrios noted that he appeared as healthy as ever. If the stench of the temple bothered Zuberi, he gave no sign.

He wondered if all these prayers for Zuberi's health had power after all. By now Zuberi should have been on his deathbed, or, at the very least, shown signs that he was gravely ill. Demetrios had paid the poisoner for swift results, but so far his man had failed.

Pity. The man had done his job well before, ensuring that Prokopios never recovered from the stabbing that had nearly cost him his life. His brother's death had been a gradual decline that aroused the suspicions of no one. But this time he could not afford to wait for results; the official period of mourning was almost over. Zuberi was to be crowned within the week, and the senate would convene on the very next day to recognize their new emperor.

He could not let Zuberi be crowned. Even if Zuberi was emperor only for a day, his son Bakari would inherit, and Demetrios had no stomach for the murder of a child. No, Zuberi needed to die before the crown touched his brow.

Then, in all humility, Demetrios would offer to serve.

As the prayers drew to an end, Demetrios made up his mind. It was too risky to contact his agent within Zuberi's household, but neither could he wait on the chance that the man would be able to carry out his orders. He'd tried to be discreet—after last year's illness no one would be surprised if Zuberi succumbed to a malady of the stomach. But he'd run out of time—better to have the deed accomplished, even if it meant he fell under suspicion, rather than be too timid and risk Zuberi assuming the throne after all.

He knew a man skilled in knife work, who'd been begging for a chance to prove himself. Demetrios would give him that chance—and double his fee if Zuberi was dead before the next sunset.

So resolved, he was able to smile with genuine good humor as the priests pronounced the final blessing. As Zuberi made his way down the central aisle, the worshippers muttered his name with varying degrees of enthusiasm. Some stretched out their arms, reaching for the mere brush of his robes, and Zuberi took their acclaim in stride, as if he were already emperor.

Then an old woman brushed past the priests, and fell to her knees in front of Zuberi. "Emperor, give your blessing to this poor old woman," she cried.

She was the poorest of the poor, dressed in a shapeless robe whose hem dragged on the ground, with an equally filthy hood wrapped around her head, from which shockingly white hair protruded.

Demetrios felt his eyebrows raise.

"How dare she," murmured one of the men standing behind him.

Zuberi—who all knew detested the lower classes— merely smiled fondly and held out his hand. "All of my subjects will receive my blessing," he said.

The woman reached for his hand and kissed it. Demetrios felt his fingers curling into his own palms in disgust. As the old woman rose to her feet, she appeared to stumble, and Zuberi stretched out both arms, as if to ward her off.

She fell against him, and Zuberi toppled backwards. As the priests rushed to help him, the woman scrambled away on her hands and knees, wailing in dismay until she disappeared into the worshippers who pressed forward to see what had happened.

If she was smart, she'd flee, before Zuberi's escort

could find her and give her the whipping she'd so richly earned.

Demetrios glanced at the milling crowd, wondering why Zuberi had not yet reappeared.

"Stand back," one of the priests shouted. "Stand back!"

No doubt the press of the crowd was preventing Zuberi from getting back to his feet.

"This is better than a play," Telamon remarked, and Demetrios nodded in agreement.

There was a shriek, and then another, as the priests tried to restore order.

Something was wrong. Demetrios hurried forward, using sharp elbows to clear a path in a crowd that had not the wits to respect his rank. At last he reached the priests and looked over their shoulders—

To where Zuberi lay on the floor, both hands clutching his stomach as blood welled up between his fingers.

It appeared he wouldn't need that assassin after all.

Burrell shifted the bundle of books from one arm to another as he climbed the steep lane that led to the mansion. Who would have thought that a half dozen books would be so heavy, or have so many sharp edges? They poked him in the side as he walked but were too awkward to balance on his shoulder.

Some would have said that it was beneath the dignity of a marine captain to fetch books from the markets as if he were a mere servant, but there was little else for him to do. Lady Ysobel no longer needed a personal guard, but he was still technically her aide though his duties were greatly curtailed. Between her own trading house, and her father's servants, Ysobel had a host of people eager to do her bidding. She no longer needed him to make arrangements for her, nor were there plans to lay, nor enemies to deceive.

There was nothing to do but wait. Wait, and hope that the joint patrols would soon uncover proof that the so-called Ikarian attackers were simply mercenaries in disguise.

At least Ysobel had the affairs of her trading house to keep her busy. She spent much of each morning in the trader's guild hall, meeting with other master traders and negotiating agreements. From what he could gather her house was continuing to prosper; she'd just purchased a new ship to replace the lost *Dolphin*. King Bayard and his council might be reserving judgment, but her fellow traders were impressed by the woman who had delivered the emperor of Ikaria as if he were an exotic trade good.

The duties of a master trader might easily have filled her days, but she came back each afternoon to spend time with the emperor. Burrell did not understand why. She did not particularly like Lucius, but she was as attentive to him as if he were a valued member of her family.

Then again, she might merely be protecting her investment.

The strange wasting sickness that consumed the emperor had grown obvious to all in the days after his meeting with King Bayard. After consulting with her father, Lady Ysobel had arranged for the emperor to be moved into a hastily vacated suite of rooms on the ground floor, where it was easier for him to move about.

On good days, he was able to make his way into the courtyard to take the sun, or to the family's dining chamber to join them for meals.

On his bad days, he moved only from his bed to a couch, and then back again.

As the mansion came into view, Burrell noticed the two marines on duty were not even pretending vigilance; they were sitting on the ground tossing a pair of dice between them. The guards had been the war minister Quesnel's idea. Ostensibly a sign of respect for their visitor, they were in truth his jailers. Not that it mattered—Lucius was incapable of making an escape, and his watchers knew this.

When they caught sight of Burrell, the privates hastily came to their feet and saluted, but he ignored them. He was not their commander, and for that they should count themselves lucky.

He glanced into the courtyard but it was empty. So this was not a good day.

He turned and made his way down the corridor that led to Lucius's rooms. Captain Chenzira was leaving his own room, and he paused as he saw Burrell.

Chenzira's ship was part of the combined task force hunting the rogues, but Chenzira had refused to be parted from his emperor, turning his ship over to his first officer instead. Burrell understood such loyalty, though he knew Lady Ysobel did not. To her there was no higher duty than that of a captain to her ship, and, as a result, Chenzira now found himself the target of her scorn.

"Is he awake?" Burrell asked.

Chenzira hesitated, eyeing the parcel of books that Burrell carried. "He's awake, but in a foul mood. Hopefully those will cheer him up."

Unable to take part in physical activity, the emperor occupied his days with books, filling scrolls with his observations on what he had read. Burrell had been given an ever-increasing list of subjects that the emperor was interested in, and by now was well-known to those who dealt in rare books.

"I appreciate the warning," Burrell said.

The elderly functionary opened the door at his knock and bade him enter.

The emperor was reclining on a couch, a half-empty bowl of figs on the table beside him. For once there was no book in his hand; instead he played with the fringes of the blanket that covered his useless legs.

"Prince Josan, I've brought these for you," he said.

The name was one of the conceits they had devised to conceal Lucius's presence. Everyone knew that the emperor of Ikaria was the guest of House Flordelis, but officially the man in residence was Josan, a mere envoy. It seemed ridiculous to Burrell, but he had discovered that diplomats thrived on such transparent falsehoods.

Which made it all the more remarkable that Lady Ysobel had ever considered a career in the diplomatic service.

"Say my name or just prince, if you cannot bear to call me emperor," Lucius muttered. "I'll not be called by his name."

Burrell knew his confusion showed on his face; this

was the first time that Lucius had objected to the alias.
Perhaps the emperor was merely seeking to pick a quarrel
with him and could find no better cause.

"I've found these for you, as you asked," Burrell said.
"Four from your list, and two others that the bookseller
swore you'd find of interest."

He handed the books to the functionary, who untied
the package and handed it to the emperor. The first time
he'd tried to give anything directly to the emperor, the
functionary had thrust his body between them, as if fearing an attack. These rooms were a far cry from the emperor's own palace, but the functionary was determined
to preserve imperial protocol to the best of his ability.

Lucius accepted the books, his eyes flickering over
them. The first two, written in the Ikarian script, received
vague murmurs of approval, but the rest were tossed on
the floor. "I can't read these," he said, his tone petulant.

Burrell's jaw dropped open, as the functionary bent
down to pick up the rejected books. He'd never seen the
emperor treat a book in such a disrespectful fashion.

"Shall I return them?" Burrell asked.

"No," the emperor said with a shake of his head. "I
can't read them now, but later, perhaps. Unless he is
gone."

The emperor's words made no sense. Burrell had witnessed the emperor reading books in a half dozen different languages, including Taresian, yet the emperor had
stared at the latest offerings as if their scripts were completely foreign to him.

Perhaps it was merely his eyes that pained him, or an

ache in his head that made struggling to understand a foreign tongue too difficult at the present. Surely that must be what he had meant to say.

As soon as the emperor dismissed him, he sought out Lady Ysobel.

"I've just seen the emperor," he said.

"And how is he?"

"He was not himself."

"Which self?" she asked, then she shook her head. "Sorry, that was petty. What do you mean he was not himself?"

Burrell hesitated. The emperor's actions could be explained by the effects of his illness. All he had was his feeling that something was wrong, and he struggled to find the words to convey his unease.

"He threw the books on the floor," he finally said. "Ordered me not to call him Josan."

Ysobel nodded, unsurprised. "Was there anything else?"

"You expected this," he said. "What is it?"

She shook her head. "Better that you not know," she replied. "I wish I did not."

He wondered what secret she was concealing. Was the emperor's mind weakening, failing him just as his body was failing? Or was there something else?

Burrell had been under the impression that she trusted him.

Something of his dismay must have shown in his face, for she reached forward and put her hand on his arm. "It's not that I don't trust you," she said. "The secret is not mine to tell. And I will not break faith with a dying man."

"I would not ask you to. But if there is anything I can do—"

"Do what you have been," she said. "Forgive his ill temper, and be a friend to him if he asks. His servants believe the emperor's temper feeds his illness. When he is calm, he is much improved."

"I understand," Burrell said.

Ysobel pitied the emperor, but her advice was as much pragmatism as kindness. They needed Lucius alive. If it came to war between the federation and the empire, then the emperor's presence here was a useful bargaining lever.

But if the empire was innocent of the attacks, then the federation would have to move quickly to avoid being labeled as the aggressors. Only Lucius could testify that he had come to the federation of his own free will. Were he to die while in their custody, there was nothing to prevent the Ikarians from using this as the reason to launch the war they all hoped to avoid.

"I'll do my best," he said. And he prayed that the ships returned soon.

The bustling port at Sendat was the envy of every other civilized nation—more trade ships visited here in a week than visited Karystos in a month. But when Septimus looked at the crowded harbor, with its long piers interspersed with carefully tended warehouses, it was not their wealth that he envied but rather the sheer number of federation ships.

Merchant vessels for the most part, but that was no comfort. Any merchanter could be turned into a war vessel if hostilities broke out.

Though hopefully the news he brought would make that war less likely.

The rest of the flotilla was anchored outside the harbor, but Septimus's ship was allowed to enter and was given a berth along a pier adjacent to her federation escort. It took mere moments to clear customs, a feat of efficiency that he knew from personal experience was far more difficult than it looked. Then he was given the freedom of the city.

He'd watched as Commodore Grenville left to make his own report, so Septimus wasted no time in finding a runner who could guide him to his destination.

The mansion owned by the house of Flordelis was imposing, but Septimus wondered why Emperor Lucius had not chosen to reside at his embassy instead. Surely it would have made more sense—

Unless, of course, he was not free to choose where he would stay. If he was a prisoner . . . Well, Septimus was prepared for any eventuality. As were the ships of his task force, in case he should fail to make contact with them within the day.

He paid off his guide, then approached the open gates. Two federation marines were on duty, but they offered no challenge as a girl stepped forward to greet him.

"Admiral," she said, after surveying his uniform. "We've been expecting you."

He turned, realizing that the mansion's position on top

of a hill would give the upper stories a clear view of the harbor and any arriving ships.

"I am here to see—"

"Our guest," she said smoothly, cutting off whatever he was about to say.

"Your guest," he agreed. He'd thought her a servant, at first, but began to wonder if she was a Flordelis by birth. Her manner was far more poised than one would expect for a girl who had not yet reached maturity.

"Please, this way," she said.

He followed her through the gate and into a small courtyard, where an old man reclined on a couch, napping in the afternoon sunlight.

"Your pardon, but Lady Ysobel asked to be fetched as well," she said.

Septimus nodded, assuming that he would be taken to the emperor as soon as Lady Ysobel joined him.

The courtyard was smaller than he was accustomed to, and he paced in a circuit around the fountain.

"I'm awake," a voice said.

"I beg your pardon for disturbing you—" Septimus began. His next words died on his tongue as Emperor Lucius opened his eyes, and turned to his side to face him.

"Septimus," he said. "They told me you were coming."

Septimus swallowed, his mouth dry. He'd known that the emperor was ill even before he'd left Ikaria, and Chenzira's letter to him had confirmed as much. But this was far worse than he'd feared.

The emperor was barely thirty, but he had the frail, transparent look of an old man. Only his eyes were sharp.

"You have news for me?" Lucius prompted, as he pushed himself upright.

Septimus nodded. "You were right," he said. "We disguised three of our own as merchant ships, and when the mercenaries struck, we were ready for them."

Forming a task force out of two dozen ships from each country's navies ensured cooperation between the two, but the very size of the flotilla meant that the rogue ships would stay far away. It had been Commodore Grenville's suggestion that they form smaller groups of two or three ships, scattering them to draw the enemy out.

"Were you there? Did you witness this yourself?" Lucius asked.

"Not for the first capture," Septimus said. "But I was there for the second."

The enemy had fallen for two of their traps, and they'd managed to take most of the mercenaries alive—along with the worm-riddled ships they'd tried to pass off as part of the Ikarian navy. It had been sheer luck that he'd been there to witness the taking of the second ship and the interrogation of her crew.

Fortunately Commodore Grenville had been there as well, unwilling to let his counterpart out of his sight. If Septimus alone had made the capture, there might have been questions raised, but as it was, there could be no doubt.

He answered Lucius's questions as best he could, and when Lady Ysobel joined them, he repeated the story for her.

"Grenville has gone to report to Lord Quesnel, correct?" she asked.

"Yes. And to make arrangements for the senior prisoners to be transferred for interrogation."

"Good," Ysobel replied.

The mercenaries had been unforthcoming. They were Vidrunese by birth, but swore that they'd no allegiance to their homeland. Their officers portrayed themselves as lawless pirates, but pirates would not senselessly destroy both ships and cargo. Someone was paying these men for their crimes, and from the evidence aboard their ships, they'd been paid handsomely indeed.

"Commodore Grenville and his officers agreed," Septimus said. "Those were not your ships, and they were not crewed by your men. The quarrel they have is not with us."

"Well done," Lucius said.

Any satisfaction Septimus might have felt at this praise was overshadowed by the realization that his emperor was dying.

"If Commodore Grenville's story agrees with yours, and if the council sees reason, then the treaty between our peoples remains unbroken."

Lady Ysobel's caution was understandable. He'd judged Grenville to be an honest man, but honest men could be overwhelmed by the politicians.

"What happens next?" Lucius asked.

"The council will hear Grenville's report—" Lady Ysobel began.

"You will return home—" Septimus said, at the same time.

"No," Lucius said, raising his hand to cut both of them

off. "What do we do about Vidrun? We cannot allow this insult to pass unpunished."

Septimus looked at Lady Ysobel, then back at Lucius. "I think it best if we discuss this in private," he said.

Lucius shook his head. "I have no time to waste. Whatever you tell me, I will only have to repeat to our allies."

He did not like this. He did not trust Lady Ysobel, but Lucius was his emperor, and the order had been unmistakable.

"When your message reached us, I was already on patrol for a training exercise. Most of the patrol came with me, but two ships sailed back to Ikaria for . . . supplies, and have recently returned."

Lucius's lips quirked in a twist. "By supplies you mean our new weapons—"

"The Burning Terror, yes," he confirmed. At this rate they'd have no secrets left. They might as well invite Ysobel to join their war councils or sit in debate in the senate.

His flagship had already had sufficient ingredients to carry out a small attack, but once he'd heard that the emperor was in the federation, he'd sent orders that had stripped the arsenals bare. Every ounce that could be mustered was at his command.

He'd been prepared to use it to attack Sendat harbor, inflicting enough damage that the federation would be forced to yield Lucius to him or see their harbor destroyed.

He still might have to.

"And what do you suggest?" Lucius asked.

"That we return the insult. Our ships will sail east and attack the fortress at Anamur, burning it to the ground."

"And have you men enough to hold the island?" Lady Ysobel asked.

Septimus shook his head. "We go not to conquer but to punish. To show those of Vidrun the price they will have to pay if they go to war with us."

It would be a bluff, of course. The Burning Terror was a fearsome weapon—an unquenchable fire that devoured everything in its path. But it could not be used too often; it required a rare earth element that was nearly impossible to find, at any price.

"And what of us? Your pride was injured, but it was my people who lost ships, crews, and valuable cargo," Lady Ysobel pointed out. "We will not want to stand idle."

"You may send your ships to aid in the attack," Septimus said. "But you must arm yourselves."

The secret of how to prepare the Burning Terror was known only to Lucius, Septimus, and six of his senior captains. He knew the federation craved that knowledge, but he and his men had sworn to take the secrets with them to their graves.

"Where is Captain Chenzira?" Septimus asked. "*Green Dragon* is anchored outside the harbor, and we should make arrangements to send you home."

There were risks in sending the emperor back to Ikaria, where men like the proconsul were already scheming to take Lucius's place. But there were also risks in leaving the emperor here, at the mercy of his hosts.

But the emperor did not seem eager to leave. He waved

aside Septimus's offer, saying instead, "I have much to accomplish before I can return home, and I will start by speaking with King Bayard."

"I will make the arrangements," Lady Ysobel replied, and with that Septimus had to be satisfied.

Chapter 17

Lucius was bored. He was present—but as an observer in his own body. He could not take control, but neither could he escape into the oblivion that passed for sleep. The boundaries between the two of them had begun to blur. He could feel what the monk felt, see what the monk saw, hear what he heard. But at the moment he could not move a single muscle—not even twitch his eyes, which were staring at a scroll in rapt fascination.

The writing on the scroll was illegible, a grotesque series of angular lines that contrasted poorly with the flowing curves of courtly script. The monk, however, found this fascinating and had been reading the scroll all morning.

Struck by a thought, the monk unfurled the earlier section of the scroll, and if Lucius had had a voice, he would have groaned with frustration. But as it was he was merely a witness as the monk stared intently at a single line of writing.

For a moment the line swam in his vision, and he could nearly make sense of it. *A draught made from the berries of the endikot bush, plucked when they are neither green nor ripened red, will unchain a soul from the body, easing . . .*

And then he blinked, and the line was gibberish once more.

For a brief moment he'd drawn on the monk's skills. But it was not enough.

The monk resumed reading, and Lucius returned to his own contemplations. This was yet another reminder that the monk had skills he lacked. Were it not for the monk, he'd be forced to speak the common trade tongue, or to beg Lady Ysobel to serve as his translator. It was wholly beyond him to search for a cure—not that the monk was making much progress on his own.

They'd learned how to enchant a stone so that it always pointed in the direction of where it was made—far handier than a mere compass, which pointed to the north. And how to brew a tea that would render the drinker unable to resist the maker's sexual advances, but such seemed unnecessarily complicated. Far easier to ply the object of one's desire with unwatered wine, until the drinker's senses swam.

As for soul magic—there'd been precious little to discover. If he'd translated the line correctly, the berries were a clue, but merely untethering the soul would not be enough. How would the potion know which soul to unchain? What if it banished both of them?

Though he could not help remembering the drink that Brother Nikos had given him. He'd been told it was a tisane to help him sleep—but rather than a single evening of rest, he'd awoken five years later, the victim of Nikos's machinations.

Which argued that it had not been endikot berries after all, or that the effects of such berries were only temporary.

There's something missing, the monk's mind voice said, proving that their thoughts ran along similar lines. *And I don't know how much trust I put in this herbal. It hardly seems likely that a magician who spent two hundred lines describing how to cure toe rot would be capable of working soul magic.*

But you've found nothing else. Even to himself, the words sounded like an accusation, though he had not meant them as such. These days he was too weary to feel true anger.

Even the news that Zuberi had declared himself emperor-in-waiting had stirred mere concern rather than the righteous wrath he would have once felt. Though others had been suitably outraged, including Admiral Septimus, who'd urged Lucius to return to Ikaria and resume his rightful position.

But *Green Dragon* remained in port, even after Admiral Septimus had sailed with the task force to attack Anamur. News would arrive in Sendat faster than it would in Ikaria, though that was not the main reason he'd chosen to stay. Sea voyages had proven chancy for him in the best of health, and he had no wish to spend the remaining days of his life in a tiny cabin, heaving his guts.

I've not given up, the monk thought, but it seemed likely that he had. Reading books randomly chosen from market stalls was less about looking to reverse their decline than it was about filling the hours of the day. The monk studied because he knew nothing else to do.

If Lucius had been in ascendance, he could have found other ways to fill his time—it had been too long since he felt the pleasures of the flesh. Though whether his body would be able to fulfill his wishes was in doubt, so perhaps it was for the best that he was not in control rather than risk the humiliation of being unable to perform.

Finally the monk rolled up the scroll, then slowly rose to his feet, waving off the servants who tried to assist.

There were times when he was unable to stand on his own—when his legs dragged uselessly as his attendants pretended they were merely guiding him. Last week there'd been a day when none of his limbs obeyed him. Forced to endure the humiliation of allowing others to dress and feed him, he'd soon retreated to his bed, feigning sleep so he would not have to endure their pity.

But today was one of the good days, and the monk was able to walk unaided back to his bedchamber. After washing his ink-stained hands, he returned to the parlor, where he ate a solitary lunch before resuming his studies.

At the hour before sunset he made his way to the dining room. It was not strictly a dining room—Lord Delmar's private dining room was on the third floor, as part of his suite, and there was another large dining room that served the working members of House Flordelis, who were polite when they came across him but knew better than to socialize with their guest. This room had likely started life as an office, or someone's sitting room, and once he left it would resume its original function. But for the present it held a table where an intimate group of eight could dine, and couches where they could relax for conversation in the Ikarian fashion.

Lord Delmar had returned to Alcina a fortnight before, having neglected his duties there as long as he dared. But Lady Ysobel was still in residence, and when he entered he found her deep in conversation with Chenzira.

They broke off as soon as he entered—a sure sign that they had been discussing him. Or, perhaps, their latest plans to send him back to Ikaria, will he or nay.

"Good afternoon, Captain Chenzira, Lady Ysobel," the monk said. As his eyes swept the table, which had three place settings, he observed, "Your aide is not joining us?"

"He is fetching something for later," Ysobel said.

She poured a pale green wine into three glasses, watered it lightly, then let him choose which of the three to drink.

He took the center, and then Ysobel and Chenzira took their own glasses.

They'd little enough in common. Chenzira and Ysobel could discuss boats for hours, but while the monk would listen with interest to almost anything, he had nothing to contribute, and etiquette demanded that the highest-ranking member of the party at least participate in the conversation.

Politics was far too touchy a subject for mere casual discourse, and they'd long since run out of ways to describe the places they'd visited and sights they'd seen.

The monk had once tried to discuss his method of fixing a position at sea with Lady Ysobel, but she'd demurred, still considering herself bound to a vow of silence, even though such was no longer needed.

The few acquaintances they had in common resided under this roof, or back in Karystos, so there was no gossip to be had. And there was a limit to the number of times that they could discuss the weather, or compliment the dishes that the chef set before them. As he'd half expected, it was not long before conversation devolved into a two-sided discussion between Ysobel and Chenzira regarding Ysobel's newest ship. As a naval officer, Chenzira was accustomed to having crews assigned to him, so he was intrigued by the challenges Ysobel faced in having to compete with her fellow traders to hire skilled seamen.

Even the monk, with his endless quest for knowledge, found little to interest him in this discussion. Instead he allowed his mind to drift back to the scrolls he had read that day, while Lucius silently urged him to take another cup of wine.

After the meal they rose from their seats and moved to the couches, while servants brought cups of a warm tea spiced with cinnamon.

Captain Burrell entered, trailed by a diminutive older man whose shoes clomped on the ground.

The man was a laborer by his clothes, which were clean but not adorned. And as for his shoes—what Lucius had assumed were shoes were actually wooden pegs that thunked onto the tiles with each step.

At some point the man had lost both legs, but he seemed to have adapted to life without them. Lucius would have stared, but the monk politely averted his gaze.

"I know you have an interest in our local tales. This is

Brice, one of our best-known storytellers," Lady Ysobel
said, by way of explanation.

Brice stepped forward and bobbed his head.
"Gentlemen. Lady," he said.

It was an unusual form of entertainment, but better
than listening to another discussion on speed versus
cargo capacity, and he sensed the monk agreed.

"I'm sure it will prove diverting," the monk said, gesturing for Brice to take a seat.

Brice disdained the couches, instead pulling a straight-
backed chair from the table, and turning it so that it faced
his audience. At Burrell's signal servants brought Brice a
glass of well-watered wine, and a cup of tea for himself.

"Is there anything that you had in mind to hear?" Brice
asked.

He must know who Josan was—all of Sendat must
know that Flordelis sheltered a prince, if not an emperor—but Brice was obviously too shrewd to question
his betters. If Ysobel had not mentioned Lucius's title,
neither would he.

The monk shrugged. "A tale of the sea," he suggested.
"There are few of those in my homeland."

"I'll tell you the story of how I fell in love with a sea
maid, then lost my legs to her jealous husband," Brice began, launching into his story with enthusiasm.

That story was followed by one of a doomed voyage,
then a ribald tale of twin brothers who married twin sis-
ters and proceeded to swap mates every fortnight.

Brice was a good storyteller, but the monk's eyes were
repeatedly drawn to Lady Ysobel, who seemed uncom-
monly nervous. At least twice she'd leaned forward, as if

about to say something, then reclined back against her cushions.

When the tale of the licentious brothers ended, the monk set down his cup, the signal that he was ready to retire.

"Brice, if you'd be so kind, there's one more story I'd like to hear. I'd long forgotten it, but when I saw you earlier today you were telling a story that reminded me of it," Lady Ysobel said. She paused for a moment. "It's the one about the Taresian boy who takes revenge for his murdered father."

"The tale of Mikhal and Jahn?" Brice asked. "It's a grim tale for a pleasant night."

"Please," Lady Ysobel urged.

His curiosity piqued, the monk settled himself back against the cushions.

"Very well," Brice said. He emptied his wineglass, tipping it to catch the last drops, then wiped his mouth with the back of his hand.

"Mikhal lived in Tarsus, where his father Jahn was the henchman of the local lord. That's like a guard and an aide in one," Brice began. "But Jahn was too close to his master, and one day he saw the lord commit murder. Jahn would have held his tongue, out of love for his master, but the lord took no chances, and stabbed Jahn with the same blade that had just killed another.

"But he'd made a mistake. Jahn was dying, but not dead. Clutching his wound with both hands, he staggered home, where he was found by his young son Mikhal. The boy was barely nine, but at his father's command, he placed a piece of amber on his father's tongue. As Jahn breathed his last, the amber caught his soul."

The monk, who'd been listening with only half an ear, turned his head to stare at Brice. "It caught his soul?" he repeated.

"Aye," Brice said, with a vigorous nod. "Then young Mikhal strung the amber on a cord and wore it around his neck."

Brice described how Mikhal had fled, living in the woods until he was a man full-grown. Mikhal had numerous adventures in this time, none of which interested either Lucius or the monk.

"And then, on the tenth anniversary of his father's death, Mikhal returned to the town where the murderer held sway. He took the amber stone from its cord, and as he swallowed the stone, the spirit of Jahn possessed him."

Lucius felt light-headed, as did the monk, who had forgotten to breathe as soon as Brice had mentioned the amber stone.

The tale concluded with Jahn—wearing Mikhal's body like a cloak, to use Brice's phrase—challenging the lord to a duel, and defeating him. It was a typical Taresian tale, where even a seeming victory was marred by tragedy, for the cost of Jahn's revenge was Mikhal's very life, as Mikhal's spirit had perished. Jahn lived to a ripe old age in Mikhal's body, but he fathered no more sons.

The monk swallowed hastily against the bitter laughter that tried to well up inside him. After all this time, it had taken an illiterate fisherman to point out that he'd known the answer all along. Months before he'd come across a ballad that told of a man's spirit captured in a piece of amber. He'd even known that Brother Giles had studied the properties of amber and other so-called magical gems. But rather than seeking out these truths, he'd sailed the length of the Great Basin, facing one peril after another, all the while his body growing weaker. He'd come all this way—

To discover that the answer had been in Karystos all along.

If Brother Giles knew this tale, and had an amber luck stone as I breathed my last . . .

Then placed your soul in me, Lucius concluded.

They expected you to be cast out, the monk surmised. *Or perhaps they used endikot berries after all, but the effect was not permanent.*

"I'm sorry if my tale displeased you, sir," Brice said.

The monk blinked, then realized that his companions were staring at him. Lucius did not know how long they had been in private contemplation.

"It was a fine tale," the monk said. "All of them were. But I am tired and must rest."

The monk turned to Ysobel and caught her gaze. She met his gaze firmly, then gave a slight nod.

So the tale had been deliberate. Lucius wondered what she wanted to accomplish. Was she trying to help him find a cure? Or did she have a more sinister plan at work?

They had only her word that Brice was who he said he was, and that this was a true tale, not one invented expressly to deceive them.

The monk's mind voice was silent as he made his way back to their room and made his preparations for bed.

Only after the servants had been dismissed did the monk open his thoughts up to Lucius.

They knew I was dying. No, they let me die, the monk thought, his anger bleeding through their tenuous connection.

So they fed your soul to me? It sounded undignified.

Lucius had imagined a complicated spell, one requiring a blood sacrifice, perhaps, and skilled magicians the likes of which hadn't been seen in Ikaria for a dozen generations. It was lowering to think his body had been stolen with a simple stone, still wet with the last gasps of a dead man.

I don't see how this helps us, Lucius thought. If the story was true, all they'd learned was how to capture a soul in the moments before death and move it to another victim.

Even if they could trick this body into thinking that it was dying, what good would it do to capture their souls? Their new host—willing or otherwise—would undoubtedly awaken one day, and there would be three men fighting for supremacy, in a body that had none of the advantages that came with being emperor.

Nikos had intended to murder Lucius. To destroy his soul, if not his body. But for some reason he'd survived. Perhaps he was stronger than Mikhal had been. Or perhaps he was merely selfish. According to the story, Mikhal had willingly sacrificed himself for his father, while Lucius had not consented to what was done to him.

He wished they'd never heard the story of Mikhal and Jahn. Useless knowledge was worse than none at all.

Nothing had changed. He was still trapped in a failing body, with no hope for a cure.

The monk's mind voice was silent for so long that Lucius wondered if he'd fallen asleep with his eyes open.

Then, at last, he spoke.

There is a way. A way to set you free.

What do you mean?

If we brew the endikot tea—

No. He feared being trapped in a crippled body, but he also feared what would happen if his soul was unbound— what if it merely wandered the earth, rather than finding peace?

He could feel the monk's exasperation.

I drink the tea, the monk thought, in tones suitable for speaking with a child. *I place the amber in our mouth, and it captures my soul. Remove the stone, and this is once again your body, and yours alone.*

It could work. If he'd been in control, his heart would have sped up, his breath quickened, but there was no physical outlet for the desperate excitement that welled up within him.

We should do it as soon as we can. While we still have the strength, the monk thought.

No. The word slipped unbidden, before he'd had time to think it over.

He could feel the monk's relief, followed by shame.

It made him feel more kindly toward the monk. Only the most honorable of men could have proposed sacrificing himself as Josan had just done, and such virtue made Lucius uncomfortable. But it was easier to feel kinship

with someone who was selfish enough to want to live, regardless of the price.

As for his instinctive refusal—Lucius's first reaction
had been fear, which was only gradually subsiding. It was
not that he was afraid of losing Josan's presence, as much
as it was fear of trying the spell only to have it fail. But he
could not explain that to the monk.

I still need you, Lucius thought, and that was no more
or less than the truth. *If anything went wrong at Anamur,
we will need your skills to negotiate with King Bayard and
his councilors.*

It would be difficult enough to negotiate with Bayard
without having to explain why the emperor no longer
spoke fluent Decanese.

He sensed the monk's reluctant agreement. It seemed
strange that he'd be eager for his own death, but perhaps
having steeled himself for the sacrifice, he wanted to make
it as quickly as possible.

It might be a kindness to let him go. But Lucius needed
Josan's skills—as did the empire. Although it would not
be for much longer.

*I will gather what we need. When the time comes, I will
be ready.*

Chapter 18

Even in his sleep, Septimus could feel the change in weather, and when he awoke he already knew what his servant would tell him. They'd passed from fine weather into heavy seas, and their progress had slowed accordingly.

As was his custom while at sea, he was awake before dawn to dress and eat breakfast, so he could inspect the ship after the change of the watch. He was just finishing his tea when Captain Horacio entered, his fair hair plastered to his skull with rain.

"All is well?" Septimus asked.

"As well as can be expected in this weather," Horacio replied. Horacio hung his sodden cape on a hook, then poured a cup of tea before taking his seat.

"The federation reported one of their ships is off station," Horacio said. "She may not be lagging far, but visibility is too poor to tell."

"Which one?" Septimus asked. "Is it *Vachon*, again?"

Horacio nodded, then raised the cup to his lips and took a long sip. "She's too slow," he said. "Or up to mischief."

Horacio did not trust their temporary allies—the sign of a good flag captain. Septimus did not either, but he must act as if he did while preparing for any eventuality.

"I'll ask Commodore Grenville for his explanation. If she can't keep up, better that we sail with one fewer ship than wait for her," Septimus said.

Horacio nodded. "Our ships are all accounted for, at the moment. But if the storm strengthens—"

"Remind all ships of our course and where we will rendezvous if we become separated," Septimus said.

Even if this was a winter gale come early, they would not turn back unless they were at risk of foundering.

Though he wondered if they were indeed sailing the best course—the federation had helped plan this route, and offered up a deep-sea route previously unknown to imperial captains. But that did not mean it was the best route, merely better than one he could have found for himself.

It was difficult managing a flotilla of nearly thirty ships—harder still when half the ships only nominally recognized your authority. The ships had different capabilities, with the federation ships tending to be smaller and swifter, while the imperial ships were generally heavier, if slightly slower.

Federation ships sailed in a single line, forming staggered rows for battle. Imperial ships sailed in parallel columns and preferred a wedge formation for attack.

They did not even share a common signal language, nor was there interest in teaching the enemy the signals used in time of battle. Instead they'd agreed upon a dozen common signals for use during this voyage, and for the rest, messages were laboriously spelled out using the trading alphabet.

It was hardly efficient, but each navy was jealously guarding its own secrets. The federation likely still held the secret of the swiftest currents, choosing to share a lesser course instead. Similarly, Septimus would closely guard the empire's secrets, telling the federation captains only what they needed to know in order to complete their task.

Just in case these one-time allies should turn back into foes.

"Signal to Commodore Grenville to join me for final planning once the weather clears," Septimus said.

The rest of Horacio's report was routine, and after dismissing him, Septimus put on his oiled linen cape, pulling the hood over his head.

The rain was blowing nearly horizontally as he stepped out on deck, the bow crashing across the angled waves. Lines had been rigged to help sailors keep their footing on the slippery deck, and Septimus held on with one hand as he made his way to the wheelhouse.

Lieutenant Flavian looked up from the charts and drew himself to attention. "Admiral, the storm has slowed us a bit, but nothing yet to be worried about. We were able to take a midnight sighting and were on course at that time."

Their course was nearly due east, while the winds were currently shifting between south by southwest and southwest. Hardly ideal, but better than if they were coming from the east. Fair weather would be preferable, of course, or a storm from the west, but even this contrary wind was better than being becalmed.

He remembered the last time he had sailed to battle— the weather had been as fair as any he'd seen in all of his years on land and sea. Perfect sea weather the sailors had whispered, and they'd attributed their luck to the presence of Emperor Lucius in their midst.

It would be a handy thing to command the weather, but he would not want Lucius here. The emperor was a poor sailor even in the best of weather. For him, the current conditions would be agony.

If, that is, he survived them at all. No illness had been named, but the emperor's shocking decline could not be hidden. Likely poison that caused him to grow so thin, and for his hands and legs to tremble as if he were a graybeard. His mind was still as sharp as ever, but the body that housed it was failing.

Septimus had urged the emperor to return home, but understood why he had stayed. It was not just that news from Anamur would arrive in Sendat at least two weeks before it reached Ikaria. It was also a question of whether or not the emperor would be alive to hear that news.

The vessels that had stripped the arsenal bare had also revealed that Zuberi had named himself emperor-in-waiting. A prudent step, given that the emperor had left his realm without an heir, but Zuberi's patience would not last long. Sooner rather than later he would take the crown for himself. If Lucius returned to his realm, obviously weak and without allies, it would be a simple matter for Zuberi to welcome the emperor home, then see that the imperial physicians ensured the emperor's swift death.

Ironically, Lucius was probably safer in the hands of his former enemies than he would be in his own palace.

As for Septimus—he knew that he would share the emperor's fate. Even if he achieved victory at Anamur, the next emperor was unlikely to reward one who had shown such devotion to Lucius.

It was ironic. His own father, Septimus the Elder, had been executed because he had conspired with those who had hoped to depose Nerissa and put Lucius on the throne in her place. Septimus the Elder had known nothing of Lucius besides his bloodline. He'd talked not of the man who would be emperor but of the glories of the past, and of the days when the old blood ruled supreme, while the newcomers were kept in their place.

As for himself, Septimus despised those who reckoned a man's worth solely by his lineage. He had refused to take part in the rebellion, and for that reason his life had been spared.

If he'd realized the measure of Lucius's worth, he might have joined with his father and been executed along with the rest of Lucius's followers. As it was, it was only his indifference that had spared him to now serve the emperor.

If he survived this, he would ask Lucius about the rebellion, which in hindsight seemed out of character. The emperor he knew was not a man who asked others to make sacrifices. He was a man who risked himself, first. Empress Nerissa had never done anything that was not to her own advantage, and he was certain the same had been true of the old imperial line, for all that the other old bloods liked to talk about the glorious days when Constantin's descendants had ruled.

Lucius was different. He not only did great things, he inspired his men to believe that they could be great as well.

Septimus had never imagined himself as a war leader—he'd taken the post of admiral expecting to be a bureaucrat, much as he'd been when he'd been in charge of Karystos harbor. Lucius had changed how he saw himself—and how he saw his duty to the empire. As Septimus made his way back below, he vowed that he would not fail his emperor.

"All ships at anchor," Captain Horacio reported. "And the gig is bringing Commodore Grenville aboard."

"Very good," Septimus said. "Signal the lead captains to confirm that all is in readiness for tomorrow."

As previously agreed, they'd anchored for the night two hours west of Anamur, at a spot where they could neither see land nor be seen in turn. With luck, the attack tomorrow would come as a complete surprise.

The federation had long used such tactics, but until recently the imperial navy had been unable to reliably fix their position at sea without visible landmarks. Mounting a surprise attack against a fixed point onshore had required periodic forays to check one's position against land—and good luck that these navigation checks were not seen.

Since they planned to set sail just before dawn,

Commodore Grenville was coming aboard tonight. He'd asked permission to join Septimus aboard *Karzai* for the actual battle. Ostensibly it was so that the two commanders would speak with one voice, but he suspected that Grenville wanted a closer look at the mysterious Ikarian weapon known as the Burning Terror.

Septimus had agreed to his request. Grenville could look as long as he wished, but he would not be able to determine how the Burning Terror was made. He'd likely take away the impression that the weapons were crafted by sorcery—an impression that was widely shared in the Ikarian fleet.

Grenville had reportedly not seen the effects of the Burning Terror for himself, but his navy had not been so lucky. It was nearly a year ago that Septimus and Emperor Lucius had led the Ikarian fleet against a federation blockade, with devastating results. The federation forces had been utterly destroyed—and the federation itself had immediately sued for peace.

It was a lesson that he hoped Grenville remembered. And one that he planned to teach the Vidrunese tomorrow.

Ikaria needed her enemies to fear her. To understand that to attack the empire was to be destroyed. By showing overwhelming strength now, he hoped to avoid a conflict that would reveal this as a bluff.

He had limited supplies of the Burning Terror, and it might be months before the engineers were able to replenish them. Ikaria itself was already weakened from within, as the various factions competed to succeed Emperor Lucius. The empire was vulnerable, and if both Vidrun and the federation were to attack, the empire would not survive.

But their enemies did not know of this weakness. It was Septimus's task to project confidence in front of their allies and to win a victory tomorrow that would crush the Vidrunese utterly.

He went to the side to meet the gig that had brought Grenville over. Due to the commodore's missing leg, he could not climb the ropes, so instead a sling was lowered over the side.

Lieutenant Flavian swore under his breath at the sailors who were hauling the lines, promising dire retribution if they allowed their visitor to swing against the side of the ship, but Grenville was hoisted to the deck without injuring either his person or his dignity.

"Welcome aboard, commodore," Septimus said. "I am pleased that you will join me to witness our victory."

"Thank you, and I hope your confidence will be rewarded," Grenville replied. He continued to be cautious, making it clear that the responsibility for failure would be Septimus's alone.

Credit for any victory would of course be shared—but Septimus intended to make certain that all knew it was the Ikarian vessels that had struck the decisive blow.

Grenville was accompanied by his aide, an unsmiling woman who wore the uniform of a lieutenant as if she had been born in it. The lieutenant scrambled easily up the rope ladder with a satchel swung over her back, and after she climbed aboard, the sailors tossed up a leather sack that presumably held Grenville's luggage.

The lieutenant was directed to Horacio's quarters,

which would be Grenville's for this night, while Grenville himself accompanied Septimus to the large chamber that served him as a dining room, when it was not being used to plot war.

The steward was pouring out the wine when Captain Horacio joined them. Surprisingly, Horacio still wore his sea uniform rather than having changed for dinner to honor their guests.

"Admiral, my pardon for disturbing you, but the priest needs you to witness the sun's blessing upon our . . . mission," Horacio said.

His words were sheer nonsense, but Septimus nodded as gravely as if they had made perfect sense.

At that moment Lieutenant Flavian entered, trailed by Grenville's aide. "Lieutenant, if you would entertain our guests? I must see to the blessing," Septimus said.

Flavian blinked, then said, "It would be my honor, captain."

With a short bow, Septimus followed Horacio from the room. He waited till they were up on deck, out of earshot of their guests, before saying, "Priest? Blessing? What are you playing at?"

Horacio looked grim. "It was all I could think of," he said. "Maybe the commodore will think that our weapon is fueled by some ritual with the sun that you don't want him to see."

It was a clever thought, Septimus conceded, though he wished Horacio had thought to speak with him first about this rather than taking him by surprise.

"What is so urgent that you must invent children's tales to excuse my absence?" Septimus asked.

"Message from Captain Quintus. Appears he took more water in the hold than he thought. His stores of silver powder are soaked through."

"Damn him for an incompetent fool," Septimus swore. He began to pace back and forth on the deck, unable to keep still.

There was no excuse for such incompetence. Quintus had known how important the powder was. He should have kept it in his own cabin and slept in the cargo holds, if it came to that. And he should have discovered the damage when it happened, not when it was too late to do anything about it.

"Three ships for the attack should be enough," Horacio said. "We don't have to tell the federation why we are altering our plans."

"They'll know something is wrong," he said. "Grenville saw that we planned to use four."

Besides *Karzai*, four other ships were supplied with ballistae and both skilled engineers and the ingredients necessary to make the Burning Terror. Septimus had planned on using four vessels in the attack, holding one in reserve so that the emperor was not left wholly defenseless.

He could carry out the attack with three vessels, and it would probably succeed. But four would be better.

What would Lucius do if he were here? But even as the question formed, he already knew the answer.

"Tell Antilochus that he is to take Quintus's place," Septimus said. "As for Quintus, I will deal with him later."

He sent Horacio to change into his dress uniform, while in keeping with his excuse, Septimus waited on deck until the last rays of the sun had faded before rejoining his guests.

"All is as it should be," he replied. He accepted a glass of wine from his steward and raised it high. "To victory! And to the glory of Emperor Lucius and King Bayard."

His guests raised their own glasses. "To victory!" they echoed.

The island of Anamur had long lived in the shadow of its neighbors. Tribal warfare on the mainland had kept any from laying claim to it, but with the rise of the Vidrunese empire had come the first real threat. The Vidrunese were not sailors, but they did not need to be. They simply constructed a vast fleet of galleys to carry their soldiers, then launched an invasion. Hopelessly outnumbered, many of the nobility had fled to Ikaria, where their descendant Aitor would later rise to power as emperor.

Aitor had sought a reputation as a war leader and begun a series of conflicts with Vidrun—fought as proxy wars in the southern lands as both countries sought to extend their territories. His son had continued the tradition, seizing Kazagan, but able to advance no farther. It had been left to Empress Nerissa to codify the current stalemate, which her supporters had hailed as victory.

Not once had the empire tried to take the conflict directly to Anamur, where it had all started. This attack would go down in history, along with the irony that both the man who led the attack and the emperor who had ordered it were of the old blood.

The ships had set sail in the predawn mist, and as the

sun broke, they moved into position outside the main harbor at Anamur City, the capital of Anamur. From his position in front of the wheelhouse, Septimus observed the order of battle, Commodore Grenville at his side.

The harbor relied upon defensive fortifications. Two massive forts flanked the entrance to the harbor, and intelligence reported that there were usually two dozen galleys stationed within, including a handful that were crewed at all times. Galleys were not as fast as sailing ships, but they could be launched swiftly regardless of weather, and were well suited to defending shore positions. The Vidrunese had good reason to think this harbor impregnable.

After consulting Grenville, Septimus had made his own plans. Seven federation vessels formed the front line—their task was to intercept any galleys that made it out of the harbor. Just beyond the federation ships were the four imperial vessels that would strike the decisive blow, his own *Karzai* among them. The rest of the fleet formed a staggered wedge behind them, ready to lend assistance if it should be required.

At Septimus's signal, the four ships of the strike force dropped sea anchors, so they swung with their port sides facing the harbor, providing a stable platform for launching the attack.

"It is time," Septimus informed Grenville. "Would you care to witness the first blow?"

"Of course," Grenville said. He followed as Septimus led the way to the port side, the thud of his wooden leg against the deck providing an uneven cadence.

Septimus blinked at the scene before him. Captain

Horacio stood next to the brass kettle as a strange figure emptied the last wooden bucket of powder into the mix, then clapped his hands together three times, which was apparently the signal for the sailor to begin cautiously stirring the mix with a long wooden paddle. It took Septimus a moment to recognize the man as his engineer Antonio—who for some reason had chosen to wear a gold chain around his neck, a saffron-colored loincloth, and nothing else.

As Antonio saw their approach he deliberately turned his back on them, raising both hands to the sky as he proclaimed, "In the name of the All-Seeing Sun I command you, by the power of his rays we will smite down our enemies."

Apparently Horacio had told Antonio of his deception, and one or possibly both of them had decided to expand upon it.

Grenville was not a stupid man; he would suspect that he was being tricked. With luck he would decide that the religious trappings were meant to disguise the sorcery that gave the weapon its power.

After all, who would suspect that such a terrible thing could be assembled from a common recipe, much as a baker made bread?

"We are ready for your command," Captain Horacio said.

Good. He pulled out the long glass and saw the first signs of activity in the harbor.

"Raise the battle flag," Septimus said. As Horacio repeated his order, he turned to Antonio. "Now," he said.

Antonio gestured, and a sailor handed him a bundle of

rags, which were carefully dipped into the heated mixture, then pulled out. Gingerly the missile was loaded into a ballista. Grenville's eyes widened in disbelief as the sailors prepared to launch.

"When does it get set ablaze?" he asked.

"When the gods will," Septimus said, falling into the spirit of the deception. At Antonio's signal, the ballista was released as the first missile arched high into the air, landing on the roof of the northern fort.

In this stone-poor land, all buildings were of brick, including the massive fortifications. But their roofs were made of wood . . .

Septimus pulled out his long glass and stared at the fort, while beside him Grenville did the same.

He heard the sounds of more missiles being launched, and Horacio's reports that the other three ships had begun their own bombardments. He waited, his breath caught within his chest, until finally he saw the first flame blossom. The roof began to glow with first one, then two, then four separate flames burning. He swung the glass and saw that the southern fort had also caught fire.

He closed the glass with a snap. "Signal *Dauntless* and *Aitor's Pride* to switch to targets within the harbor," he ordered.

The Burning Terror could not be extinguished by water, nor by beating it out with blankets. It ignited upon contact and would burn until it had consumed all in its path. It was as terrifying on land as it had been when used at sea.

He turned and saw that Grenville's face was pale.

Septimus said nothing. There was nothing that needed to be said.

He left Grenville to his thoughts and returned to the wheelhouse, where Horacio kept him apprised of the battle's progress.

Though it was not a battle—it was far too one-sided to be called such. A handful of galleys managed to row out from the harbor and were swiftly destroyed, their crews leaping into the sea to avoid being burned to death. Most drowned in sight of shore, having never learned how to swim.

It took less than an hour for the forts to collapse, their brick walls no match for the inferno that destroyed the timber frames within. By then most of the buildings within reach of the ballistae had already been set ablaze. He'd given the order to cease fire, making it appear to be a deliberate choice, when in truth they were nearly out of missiles.

The destruction was even greater than he'd hoped, as a steady sea breeze spread the flames far beyond the reach of his weapons. By noon thick black smoke rose up over the island, obscuring what was left of what had once been a proud capital.

Four ships had achieved victory, while the rest had stood as witness. No one would forget what they had seen this day—especially not their allies.

It was just past noon when Grenville sought him out. The commodore's face was coated with soot, as if he'd spent the entire battle standing next to the engineers operating the twin ballistae.

"If you had five hundred men, you could take the city," Grenville said.

"And I'd need five thousand to hold it," Septimus replied.

Grenville nodded in agreement. "A terrible thing to destroy in hours what it took generations to build," he said.

It was a sentiment that Septimus agreed with, but he could hardly say so.

"If it makes the Vidrunese think twice about attacking us, then it will be worth it," Septimus replied.

"And what now? Will you stay to watch the city burn?"

Septimus shook his head. "We've done what we came here to do," he said. "We sail for home."

Chapter 19

Chancellor Telamon was dead—supposedly killed in the bath by his wife, who'd then taken poison. An improbable tale, but no one would publicly speculate on what must be obvious to all.

Zuberi's assassination at the temple of the triune gods had merely been the first in a wave of killings that were terrorizing the city. Some were clearly politically motivated, while others seemed to be using this opportunity to settle old scores. Petrelis, commander of the city watch, had doubled then trebled the patrols that protected the noble quarter, but it was of no use. A half dozen leading members of the court had been murdered in as many days, and there was no end in sight.

Even naming a new emperor might not be enough to stop the killings—it might merely give the assassins a single target to focus on.

In the days after Zuberi's death, Demetrios had subtly

advanced his own cause, while others had put forward the name of Telamon as emperor-in-waiting. He'd made his own plans to deal with Telamon, but once again another had struck before he could.

Was General Kiril behind this? He'd professed neutrality in public, but all knew that he'd been Zuberi's man. Or was it another, one who was hiding in the shadows, waiting for the other contenders to destroy each other so he could then step forward and assume the throne unchallenged?

Who had killed Zuberi? Was it a rival for the throne? Or was the answer more obvious? Could it be that Lucius still had his supporters, fanatics dedicated to restoring the old blood, men who refused to countenance anyone taking his place? If so, these men would not give up until they had proof that Lucius was indeed dead, and perhaps not even then.

Whoever was behind the killings, and whatever his ultimate goal, he had succeeded in sowing fear and confusion. Demetrios knew he was not the only one taking a hard look at those who had promised their support to him, wondering which one of his supposed allies was preparing to betray him. Without their support he could not declare himself as emperor-in-waiting, but if he trusted the wrong man, he would not live to wear the crown.

As it was, each time he left his mansion, it felt as if he were risking his life. He was not a timid man, but it had taken his full measure of courage—and an escort of a dozen guards—for him to make the journey to his office in the senate. Just so he could be seen as a devoted servant of the empire, intent on fulfilling his duties despite the chaos around him.

He spent the morning answering correspondence, making arrangements for the returning senators. The senate was set to convene within the fortnight—assuming there was an emperor to call it into session. Though if no emperor was yet named, as leader of the senate it would be fitting for Demetrios to welcome his fellow senators to their debates—and to let a carefully chosen delegation persuade him to declare himself as the next emperor.

Lost in contemplation of which senators could be trusted with such a delicate task, his head jerked up sharply as he heard General Kiril's voice from the antechamber.

"I must speak with him," he heard Kiril say.

Demetrios glanced around, ensuring that his two bodyguards were within arm's reach. "Stay alert," he told them.

Then he rose to his feet, so he was standing as Kiril entered the office.

"General, I did not expect to see you today," he said.

"My business is urgent," Kiril replied. He was in uniform, but must have left his sword at the entrance to the senate, as was custom.

That did not mean he was not dangerous. He had the potential to be either Demetrios's greatest supporter or his greatest threat, and so far he'd given no hint which side he would choose.

"Pray tell me what is on your mind," Demetrios said.

Kiril's eyes drifted to the two bodyguards. "We must speak alone," he said.

Demetrios hesitated.

"Come now, if I wanted to kill you, I'd not do it here, when so many could swear that I was the last to see you," Kiril said. He waited a heartbeat before adding, "I'd do it when you were alone and thought yourself safe."

Demetrios shivered at the casual tone of Kiril's words, which were far more effective than any shouted threat.

"Leave us," he told his men.

Kiril watched as the two men left, then closed the door behind them.

"Lucius is alive," Kiril said.

"Alive?"

"And he's just won a great victory against Vidrun, destroying their fortresses on Anamur in retaliation for their attacks against our ships, or so it is claimed."

Demetrios retreated two paces, groping behind him for his chair, then sinking into it. This was not possible.

"Who told you this?"

"There'd been rumors all along that he was in the federation, but this morning a navy ship returned bearing the news that Lucius had allied himself with the federation and led a combined fleet to victory."

Admiral Septimus. It had to be. Demetrios had thought little of it when Septimus and the bulk of the fleet had left on routine patrols. If he'd thought about it at all, he'd simply assumed that Septimus had chosen discretion over valor, hoping that his absence would convince Zuberi that he was not a threat to the next emperor.

But apparently the admiral had been following Lucius's orders all along. Which made Demetrios wonder just how many other men were quietly biding their time on Lucius's orders.

"Who knows of this?"

"Everyone," Kiril said. "If not now, then by nightfall. The captain of the ship gave all of his sailors leave, and they are telling this tale in every tavern and whorehouse in the city. By tomorrow we will hear that the gods rained fire down upon our enemies at Lucius's command."

Demetrios grimaced. The credulous among his supporters might hesitate to rebel against one who held the favor of the gods, while the more practical among them would see Lucius as a hero, a mighty war leader who had accomplished what his predecessors could not.

Demetrios knew his own flaws—he was respected for his political skills, but he did not inspire passion in his supporters. He had presented himself as the candidate of reason, the one who could best preserve the empire with minimal disruption to their privileged lives. His followers would have no stomach for bloody revolution.

He could have stood against the ghost of Lucius. Ignored the murmurs of those who swore that had Zuberi lived, he would have been a better choice for emperor. But Demetrios could not hope to stand against a popular emperor, one who had seemingly risked all to bring victory to his people.

"What will you do?" Demetrios asked.

"Prepare for the emperor's return," Kiril said. "I suggest you do the same."

* * *

Lucius had asked to be allowed to leave without fanfare or ceremony, so it was a small group that gathered at the dockside, their breaths steaming in the chill dawn air. Lady Ysobel, wrapped in a plain woolen cloak, was flanked by her aide, Captain Burrell, who wore a military cape that lacked any insignia.

Slightly apart from them stood Admiral Septimus, wearing a sea uniform whose brassware was tinged green from exposure to salt air.

Lucius's servants were already on board *Green Dragon,* as was Captain Chenzira, who was making ready to set sail.

Around them was the bustle of the port coming to life, but no one paid any special heed as two of the Flordelis servants helped the monk from the coach. Lucius knew he could take control, but instead he waited with growing impatience as the monk took several halting steps until he drew even with Lady Ysobel.

"Lucius," she said, inclining her head in a show of respect. "King Bayard has charged me to remind you of his friendship, and to offer you the hospitality of his kingdom, for as long as you wish to stay."

It was an offer that had been made before, but their answer was unchanged.

"Pray tell Bayard that I value his friendship, and his generosity, but it is time that I return to my own people," Josan said.

"Of course."

In truth, Bayard would be relieved to see his imperial

guest gone—a living emperor was a valuable hostage, even one who had been deposed. But a dead emperor was an embarrassment at best and a liability at worst.

"I hope your return voyage is pleasant, and your people welcome you as you deserve," Lady Ysobel said.

Lucius felt his face twist into a grimace. Her words were kindly meant, but he no longer knew what he deserved. "My thanks to you, and to your honored father for your hospitality," the monk said. "And I know you will not be offended when I say that I hope never to see you again."

Lady Ysobel gave a wry smile of her own.

She'd used him for her own gain—first as the figurehead of an uprising, then later attempting to hold him prisoner in order to control his empire. She'd proven a formidable foe—but once they began working toward a common goal she'd proven to be an equally formidable ally. He still did not like her, but he knew he could not have done what he did without her help.

And, though she might not know it, she had given him the key to unraveling the spell that bound him. At first he'd thought her help deliberate and waited for her to demand payment for her help. But she'd said nothing, even when the monk had prompted, which seemed out of character for a woman determined to wring the maximum advantage out of any situation.

He did not understand her. But he admired her strength of purpose.

"Captain Burrell," the monk said, and his voice was a shade warmer. "I will always remember your kindness."

The monk's feelings toward Burrell were less complicated than his toward Ysobel. Burrell was a simpler man—one driven by honor and duty rather than constantly scheming for advancement. The monk liked Burrell—and would have chosen him as a friend had circumstances permitted.

"Emperor," Burrell said, making a half bow in place of a salute. "I wish you a safe voyage."

The traditional farewell was to wish the traveler a safe voyage and long life, but in the face of Lucius's disability, wishes for a long life would seem pointlessly cruel.

"Admiral, if you would," the monk said.

Septimus extended his left arm, and the monk grasped it tightly. Slowly they made their way along the pier, to the wide gangplank that linked *Green Dragon* with the dock.

Septimus glanced around, and when he'd satisfied himself that they were out of earshot, he spoke.

"What course would you have me set?" Septimus asked.

"To Karystos, of course," the monk repeated.

He'd given the order yesterday, but perhaps Septimus had expected that it was merely a ruse, meant to fool his hosts.

Septimus pressed his lips together. "Are you certain that's wise? It's likely that Zuberi is already on the throne."

"It is home," the monk said.

Which was a lie. The monk could make himself a home anywhere there was knowledge to be found. Left to his own inclinations he would likely wander back to Xandropol, where he could find employment as a scribe and spend the rest of his days trying to master a fraction of the knowledge contained within the musty scrolls of the great library.

But the monk had resolved himself upon death. *He* would not see either Ikaria or Xandropol. The command to return home was not his, but rather Lucius's own selfish desire.

"The navy stands with you," Septimus promised. "No matter what comes."

"I know," the monk responded. "But it will not come to that. I will not ask you to attack our own people."

It was not nobility, merely pragmatism. In the islands of the federation, the backing of the navy would have secured his throne. In Ikaria, the navy was a trifle. Only the legions of the army could make—or break—an emperor.

"You're a better emperor than he'll ever be," Septimus declared.

The monk was silent.

Lucius was silent as well. He knew that the words were not meant for him. Septimus had given his loyalty to the man who had led the navy to victory against the federation. The man who had turned aside from a quest meant to save his life in order to spare his empire a pointless war.

Chenzira, Eight, and all those others who had risked their lives to find him, and to carry out his wishes, all swore allegiance to Emperor Lucius, but the man they venerated was not he. It was Josan, whose skills had given the imperial navy the edge they needed to succeed. Josan who had agreed to leave Xandropol, knowing that it meant their deaths.

Josan, who even now carried the ingredients of his

death within the folds of his robe and was resolved to make use of them.

Lucius had finally realized the bitter truth. The bloodline was his—but the true nobility came from the monk.

It was a shame that one of them had to die.

Septimus helped him up the gangplank. Captain Chenzira was waiting at the top, accompanied by Eight.

"Your orders?" Chenzira asked.

"Home," the monk said. "Take me to Karystos."

As Eight moved forward, the monk released Septimus's arm.

"Captain, you will keep station with me, while the other ships provide escort," Septimus said. "We want a swift passage, but a smooth one."

They'd already discussed this, as well. Septimus had wanted Lucius to join him on his ship, but Lucius had insisted that he preferred to travel with Chenzira, aboard the familiar *Green Dragon*. Septimus and the remaining members of the task force would ensure his safe arrival.

Two ships had already sailed ahead, bearing news of the victory at Anamur back to the empire. It remained to be seen how Zuberi would react to that news. Would he step aside? Or would he challenge Lucius?

He knew that his men were worried that the emperor would die at sea, but they did not know what Lucius knew.

It's time, Lucius thought. *Tell Chenzira to come to us after we're safely at sea.*

Chenzira?

Eight is not strong enough, and I trust no other, Lucius thought. *The stone must be destroyed.*

Of course.

After Septimus took his leave, Chenzira personally escorted the emperor to his cabin. Once they were settled, the monk said, "Captain, if you would be so kind, I would like to speak with you after we have set sail."

"As you wish."

After the captain left, the monk sent Eight to fetch hot water for tea. He knew the galley would curse such a request, since the coals would be banked as the ship was making ready to set sail, but Eight would rouse them.

Finally, the monk grumbled. *You nearly left it too late.*

If I could, I would wait till the great city was in view, Lucius thought. *But I dare not.*

He'd been waiting until he learned if Septimus's mission had been a success. But when the flotilla returned, it was to find the emperor lying insensible in his bed, apparently dying. It had been two days before they'd been able to rouse him.

The next time could prove fatal to them both.

The floor tilted beneath his feet as the sails caught the wind. Around him timbers creaked, and through the open porthole he could hear echoes of shouted orders over the sound of the waves.

Eight returned with the hot water, and the monk dismissed him, telling Eight that he would make his own tea. Here the monk's odd habit of performing menial tasks stood in their favor, for Eight did not question his emperor's whim.

Reaching inside his robe, the monk withdrew a pouch that held a perfectly round amber stone and a handful of dried berries that were neither green nor red.

He could sense the monk fretting, wondering if dried berries would be sufficient, but they'd had no means of acquiring fresh ones. With a mental shrug, the monk tossed the berries into the pot, then stirred them thrice. He let them steep for a quarter of an hour, then poured the brew into a plain clay cup.

The aroma was surprisingly pleasant, though endikot berries were known to be poisonous, harvested for use in dyes and inks rather than for food.

He could feel the monk gathering his courage.

Lucius, the monk began, and then his thoughts fell silent.

It seemed even a scholar could find no words for this.

The monk reached for the cup—

And at that moment Lucius struck. Using all of his carefully hoarded strength, he rose up and took control of his body.

He felt the monk's shock, but ignored him.

With hands that shook only slightly, Lucius lifted the cup and began to drink. The acid brew burned his lips, his tongue, and the length of his gullet. Still, he forced himself to keep swallowing until the last drop was gone. When finished, he wiped his lips with the sleeve of his robe, as if he were a peasant.

Then he picked up the amber luck stone, rubbing it between thumb and forefinger. He'd carried this stone since Karystos, part of the imperial gems that he'd taken to pay for his voyage. It was smooth to the touch—the same dark gold as the rarest honey, roughly the same size as an imperial gold piece.

Such a small thing to hold a man's soul. But if it were any larger, it would hardly fit in his mouth.

His fingers began to tingle, and then his toes, with a strange prickling sensation as if his limbs were being woken from sleep.

Perhaps the berry's reputation as a poison was well earned. It would be ironic if it killed them before he could complete the spell.

He could feel his strength ebbing, but he held on with every ounce of his will. Minutes passed, or perhaps hours, but finally there was a knock at the door.

"Enter," he called.

Chenzira came in, shutting the door behind him. "How may I serve you?"

"I've been poisoned," Lucius said.

Chenzira's eyes widened in shock. "Just now?"

"No. It was some time ago. Long before I left Ikaria," he said.

Chenzira's bewildered expression disappeared, as he realized that Lucius was talking about his illness. "What can I do?" he asked.

"Do you trust me?" Lucius asked.

"With my life," Chenzira vowed.

Such loyalty warmed his heart, even as it firmed his resolve, for he knew that he was not the one who had earned it.

"There is a spell," Lucius said, holding up the amber stone so that Chenzira could see it. "I will place this in my mouth, and it will absorb the poison. When I stop breathing, you must remove the stone and destroy it."

Chenzira nodded. He looked around the cabin, until

his gaze settled on the iron rod that was used to bar the porthole in bad weather. Swiftly he removed it from its fittings.

"When I stop breathing, not before," Lucius reminded him.

Chenzira swallowed hard, then nodded. "It will be as you command."

He was putting all his trust in Chenzira. Not to make the spell work, he could do that himself without any witnesses. But Lucius could not bear the idea of his soul being trapped forever in a stone, unable to join his ancestors. Hopefully smashing the stone would be enough to free him.

If not, he would have to hope that the gods would grant him mercy for his courage.

With one last deep breath, Lucius lay down on the bed. His hands were numb, and he nearly dropped the stone twice before it slid into his mouth.

He closed his eyes, and thought about his soul leaving. He could sense the monk's presence, but the monk was not strong enough to resume control.

You will be a better emperor than I, he thought.

And then he breathed his last.

Lady Ysobel watched the emperor's halting progress along the dock, until he climbed aboard *Green Dragon*.

Was it Lucius who had said farewell to her? Was it the monk? Or perhaps some blend of the two?

She'd wondered if Brice's tale would provide the

answers he needed to find a cure, but from his continuing decline, it appeared she'd been wrong.

Or perhaps it was simply that neither man was willing to sacrifice himself so that the other might live.

She shivered, and it had nothing to do with the chill air.

"What do you think will happen to him?" Burrell asked.

"If he's lucky, he'll die before he reaches Ikaria."

If Zuberi had claimed the throne, he would not lightly give up his prize. Especially not to an ailing emperor who had few political allies. Lucius would be imprisoned for his own safety, and then, if his malady did not kill him outright, the imperial physicians would.

"It seems a cruel fate," Burrell said.

"All politics are cruel."

She turned her back on *Green Dragon*. There was nothing more she could do. She'd offered the emperor sanctuary, but she understood why he had left. The federation was alien to him, while the *Green Dragon* was his ship, crewed by his people. It would be a good place to die.

When it came her time, she could ask no more.

She was too restless to return home, so waved off the carriage and made her way to the boardwalk that encircled the port. Burrell fell into step beside her, a familiar presence.

They did not need words between them. Each knew that the other had been unnerved by the contemplation of the emperor's probable fate. It was not often that one saw a man so clearly touched by the shadow of death.

Lucius, or whoever he was, had finally earned the

throne he had long coveted—but he would not live to reign over his people.

And what had she earned? She'd thought to use her political connections to secure the future of her trading house, but instead paid a heavy price for her ambition. Still she'd persevered, and none would deny that she'd been instrumental in averting a costly war with the empire. Bayard himself had expressed his gratitude toward her, in terms that made it clear she was in his favor, and his advisor Telfor had invited her for a private meeting, where he'd hinted that she could name her own reward.

She could have a seat on the king's council, or even the post of Deputy Minister of Trade—second-in-command to Lady Solange, and in line to succeed her should Ysobel prove herself worthy. She'd be more powerful than any born into House Flordelis in the past century—and she was barely thirty.

It was even conceivable that she might be elected queen, one day in the far-distant future. All it would take was sacrificing what remained of her soul.

Her thoughts turned over and over, but the familiar sights and smells of the port failed to soothe her restlessness. She skirted precariously stacked crates, stepped neatly around coiled lines, and nearly lost her balance crossing a swath of discarded fish scales.

Finally, they reached the southernmost point of the harbor. From here they could walk no farther, so instead she climbed the stairs until they stood atop the wall.

The harbor lay spread out before her, each ship within reminding her that there was far more to life than could be found in council chambers or grand palaces.

"What now?" Burrell asked. "Where will you go?"

"Somewhere I've never been," she said.

He blinked at her, and she realized he'd been asking if she wanted to return to the mansion.

"Will you go home first?" he asked.

"Yes," she said. But not in the way that he meant. House Flordelis was no longer her home—it was merely a place where she could take refuge when she needed.

"I'm off to Alcina tomorrow," she said. "I've changes in mind for the new ship, and I want to oversee them personally."

Disappointment flashed across his face, but then his features smoothed. "A good choice. Your house needs you, and I've always thought you were happiest at sea."

If Ysobel returned to life as a trader, then she would have no need for an aide who happened to be a marine captain. Once they parted, it was doubtful their paths would cross again.

She let him help her down from the wall, and by unspoken accord they turned their steps in the direction of the mansion.

"*Western Star* will be refitted for an extended voyage," she said. "I plan to take her out of the basin, up north along the coast of Tarsus, and from there, I'll see what is to be found."

Few ships sailed out past the western edge of the Great Basin, and fewer ships had ever ventured north of Tarsus, where there were no maps, only mere rumors to guide a captain. It would be the adventure of a lifetime—and the opportunity to be the first to discover new trade goods and new markets.

"Come with me," she said, turning to face him.

"I could wish for nothing more, but—"

"You will be my price," she said. "King Bayard has promised me whatever I want if I'll stay—and I'm sure Lord Quesnel will be equally willing to give me what I want to make sure that I leave."

Quesnel was minister of war, and no friend to Ysobel. Her success had angered him, and he'd be happy to see her gone.

And if not, Bayard owed her a favor or two.

Burrell paused, his mouth open.

She was seized with a sudden doubt. What if he didn't want this? Had she presumed too much? He'd been in the marines since he was a young man.

"It is your choice," she said, a trifle stiffly.

"I've never been a trader," he said. "Nor a sailor."

Her lips curved in a smile as happiness rose up inside her. "You know the sea," she said. "The rest can be learned."

Burrell grinned back, appearing five years younger.

She could never have asked him to share her old life. But this new life would be one worth sharing.

"There's just one condition," he said.

She began to ask what it was, just as he cupped her face with both hands. Bending down, he brushed his lips with hers.

She gasped, and what had started as a chaste kiss quickly grew fierce, as Burrell finally showed her just how much he wanted her.

When they broke apart, they were both flushed and

panting. But there were stars in his eyes, and she was sure that she looked equally infatuated.

A passing apprentice clapped to show his appreciation, until he wilted under their combined stares.

"Well, then," she said. "That's settled."

Chapter 20

Josan gasped desperately, struggling for air. Pain consumed him as his muscles tensed, arching his body off the bed—then just as suddenly he collapsed upon it, boneless. He could hear the sound of a hammer, mingled with Chenzira's desperate curses.

As his frantic breaths slowed, Josan opened his eyes.

Chenzira's gaze met his—eyes wild, holding an iron bar suspended over his head with one hand. With a ringing crash, Chenzira brought the bar down against the table.

The spell. Josan's memories came rushing back to him.

"Enough," he said, then coughed.

The bar clanged to the floor as Chenzira came over to help him sit upright.

Josan's senses swam, but as he blinked the dizziness passed. He swallowed a few times to clear the foulness from his mouth.

"Did it work? Are you well?" Chenzira asked.

Josan hesitated, not knowing how to answer the question. *Lucius,* he called out. *Lucius!*

But there was no answer. He closed his eyes and tried again, summoning all of the focus he had learned in years of patient study, but there was nothing. Not even the vague echo that he had come to associate with those times when Lucius was unable to communicate with him.

He pushed Chenzira aside and stood. The amber stone had been pounded into fine crumbs—Josan brushed a few into his palm, but there was no sense of magic, no feeling of connection. If Lucius's soul had been in that stone, it was there no longer.

"Emperor, are you well?" Chenzira asked.

Josan nodded, not trusting himself to speak. He'd steeled himself for death, hoping merely that his passing would be swift. Coming back to life in this fashion was as painful as any birth.

He let the stone fragments fall on the floor as he held his hands in front of him, turning them over, then bringing them together, reveling in the sensation as flesh met flesh.

He could *feel.* For the first time in months, the sensations were not dulled. It was only now that he realized how much Lucius's presence had affected him. His body was still weak, but it was his, from the chill of his bare feet against the rough wooden deck to the ache of his head.

It was as if he'd awoken from a long illness, or a dream.

But why had Lucius done it? Josan had been willing to

die. He had never expected that Lucius would take his place.

Was it a sudden whim? Or a secret that Lucius had held for days, until it came time to act?

He had not thought Lucius had the strength within him to sacrifice himself. And yet he had. Lucius had given his life for the sake of his empire. In the end, Lucius had proven his nobility—he was what he'd always wished to be, the equal of any of his illustrious ancestors. Ikaria was poorer for his loss, though no one would know to mourn him, except Josan.

"I could not have done this without your help. Thank you," Josan said.

Chenzira eyed him critically. "Not to be difficult, but you don't look any different."

"It's what's inside that matters," Josan told him. "My body will recover now that the curse is gone."

Chenzira's eyes widened at the mention of magic. "You said it was poison."

So he had. "It was both," Josan explained. "But it is over."

"Are you certain?"

"Yes."

He knew that Lucius's soul was gone, but he could not say where that certainty came from, merely that he felt it within the very bones that were now his. No longer would he struggle for survival in a body that was at war with it-self. That part of his life was over.

It was up to him to decide what came next.

*   *   *

The sun was high in a cloudless sky as *Green Dragon* sailed past the moles into Karystos harbor. Josan looked up at the terraced hills, his eyes traveling from the markets, to the nobles' quarter, to the copper roof of the collegium, which was barely visible behind its neighbors. And, finally, the great palace, dominating the scene effortlessly from its perch upon the great hill.

Admiral Septimus peered through his long glass, then twisted it shut with a snap. "They're waiting for us," Septimus said, faint disapproval coloring his words.

Yesterday they'd anchored off of Eluktiri, and at Josan's command, Septimus had sent a ship ahead to Karystos. He had no intention of sneaking into the city as a thief. All would know that the true emperor had returned. After some grumbling, Septimus had obeyed— then insisted on joining the emperor aboard *Green Dragon* for their arrival.

Josan had agreed, knowing that their fate was shared. Whether Septimus stood beside him or was aboard another ship would not matter. The rest of the navy might be spared, but whatever happened to the emperor would happen to Septimus and Chenzira as well.

The breeze ruffled his hair, and Josan took a deep breath, then another, savoring the feeling of being alive and whole.

Ever since he'd awoken to find a frantic Chenzira smashing the stone to powder, Josan had been a changed man. He no longer had to fight for each breath, to struggle merely to perform the simple tasks that others took for granted. His appetite had returned, and his sleep was untroubled by dreams.

He was not the man he had been, when years of tending a lighthouse had gifted this body with both physical strength and endurance. But each day he grew stronger, and given time, he knew he would recover fully.

He heard Chenzira's shouts, as the topmost sails were furled and the ship prepared to drop anchor.

"There's still time to change your mind," Septimus said.

Josan did not have to do this. Chenzira would have sailed him anywhere he wished to go. He could have shaved his head and disappeared, become a scribe writing letters for those too ignorant to write their own, or a clerk in some foreign city.

Or even resumed his life as a monk, joining the brethren in Tarsus or some other place where they'd never heard of Brother Josan. Nor of Brother Nikos.

It was possible. Some would say it was the wisest choice. And his supporters would have understood.

But Lucius would not.

In the end, Lucius had finally understood duty, and that the power he'd inherited was not a privilege but a responsibility.

Lucius had sacrificed himself for his empire, and so that Josan might live. Josan could do no less.

Eight approached, carrying the casket that held the lizard crown.

"Admiral, if you would?" Josan asked.

Septimus flushed at the honor, then carefully he lifted the crown and set it on Josan's head. The familiar warmth greeted him, and for a moment he thought he heard lizards chattering.

The crown still recognized him. He knew that Lucius would have taken this as an omen.

Chenzira guided the ship to the imperial pier, which was reserved for the emperor's own ship. It was vacant, which could be taken as a sign of respect—or merely that they wished to make it easy for him to surrender. As they approached, Josan saw that the wharves were crowded with people, their voices rising and falling in excited utterances. All around the harbor, imperial flags flew, adorned with purple streamers, likely left over from Zuberi's coronation.

At the very end of the pier a canopy had been erected, and he saw a small group of people standing there, though he could not make out their faces.

It made no sense. He thought he'd be met by Zuberi's men, or perhaps a squad of General Kiril's troops, ready to take the former emperor into custody. But this crowd was more than mere casual spectators—all of Karystos would know what happened here today.

It was not like Zuberi to make this kind of mistake. But perhaps he'd had no choice—word of the victory at Anamur would have reached Karystos a week ago by his reckoning, and such news could not be kept quiet.

Zuberi might have had better luck suppressing the news that today was the day of the emperor's return, but he could not control rumors, and any preparations he made for Lucius's arrival would serve as warning to Lucius's allies.

If he had any supporters left besides the men who currently stood by him.

A handful of men approached, but even with their help,

it seemed to take an eternity for the ship to be made fast and the gangplank to be lowered in place.

To his surprise, once they'd tied off the ship, the men retreated back down the short pier. He waited for a heartbeat, but no group of soldiers took their place.

It seemed Zuberi was waiting for Lucius to come to them. So be it.

"It is time," Josan said.

He led the way down the gangplank, flanked on either side by Septimus and Chenzira. He recognized Senator Demetrios standing beneath the canopy, accompanied by General Kiril, Petrelis, and a handful of other senators and dignitaries. Oddly, several key figures were missing, including Chancellor Telamon.

And there was no sign of Zuberi, but armed men wearing the uniforms of the city guard formed a solid line that held back the crowds on either side, likely by Zuberi's command.

He heard the crowd chanting, "Long live the emperor," and wondered who it was that they hailed.

As Josan's foot touched the pier, he summoned his will, and a rainbow appeared, arching from the harbor up over Karystos, coming to rest at the spires of the palace.

The crowd gasped, then cheered. It was not a subtle display, but he knew that Lucius would have loved it.

The magic had been Lucius's final gift to him—tied to the very blood that flowed through these veins, regardless of whose spirit commanded it.

He pasted a confident smile on his face as he drew near those who awaited him.

General Kiril was the first to step forward, followed a

heartbeat later by Demetrios. Kiril looked much the same as he remembered, but Demetrios was pale, with a half-healed scar across his neck that even a high-necked robe could not wholly conceal.

"Where is my proconsul?" Josan asked. He would not grant Zuberi the title of emperor.

"Dead. Assassinated," Kiril said bluntly.

Josan blinked. That possibility hadn't even occurred to him. He looked quickly at Demetrios, then scanned the rest of his welcomers, to see who had taken Zuberi's place, but none wore a crown, nor even the thin gold circlet that proclaimed the wearer as the emperor-in-waiting.

"But I know he would have wished to be the first to greet you upon your victorious return," Kiril added.

These were not the words of a man preparing to arrest his former ruler. Kiril had risen to his post because of his alliance with the emperor—and his ability to sense the shifting winds of power.

But it could not be this easy, could it?

And yet, even as he wondered, Kiril dropped to his knees, followed by Demetrios, and the rest of the greeting party.

Demetrios bowed his head, saying, "Emperor Lucius, your loyal subjects welcome you home."

He wondered if anyone else perceived the irony in those words.

Apparently Zuberi's assassination had meant that there had not been enough time to name a new emperor, or perhaps that no suitable candidate had been able to muster the necessary support. Merely because Demetrios knelt to him now did not mean that he had given up his ambitions.

The same could be said for the rest of the court. Those present were at least as much of a danger as those who had not been chosen to greet him.

The support of the navy, and the resounding victory at Anamur—a victory that for all their striving Empress Nerissa and her ancestors had never been able to achieve—had apparently secured his throne. For the moment.

If he wished to remain as emperor, to rule Ikaria and not merely pose as a figurehead for others, it would take everything that he had. Every bit of energy, every scrap of cunning, every bit of wisdom that he could muster. It could be no half effort—he could no longer play at being a scholar and leave the governance of his realm to others.

The scholar must give way to the emperor, as Lucius had given way to Josan. In the end, each had sacrificed what he valued most, so that the best part of the other would survive.

Just as no one would know to mourn Lucius, there was no one who would realize that today was the day that Josan the monk finally perished.

"Rise, my loyal friends," he said. "It is good to be home."

About the Author

PATRICIA BRAY grew up in a family where the ability to tell a good story was prized above all others. She soon realized that books were magical creations that let the author share stories with people he'd never met, and vowed that someday, she, too, would have this magic power.

A corporate I/T project manager by day, she wishes to note that any resemblance between her villains and former coworkers is entirely coincidental. When not at her home in upstate New York, she can be found on the SF convention circuit, or taking bike trips in exotic locations. Readers can find out more about Patricia and her latest projects by visiting her website at www.patriciabray.com.